FALSE FLAG

ALSO IN THE RED RAIN SERIES

Red Rain
Project 74
Crook Q
Prisoner 120518
Andromeda
Aurelius
Fox Hunt
Catalyst
Blue Fire
First Light
Operation Thunderbird
Laodicea
Jonah
Queen Sacrifice
Green Dragon
False Flag

FALSE FLAG

RED RAIN #9

RACHEL NEWHOUSE

rachelnewhouse.com

To Miss Anita, Jasmine, & Zoey

How's that for justice?

AUGUST 2076

1: PHILADELPHIA

I killed my uncle.

The world froze while I struggled to swallow that fact. The conference room was utterly silent. Jael, the only other person in the room, stood as still as a mannequin as she stared at the dark projector. There was no ticking of clocks, no whirring of vents; even the factory on the floors beneath us had grown quiet. Outside the windows, the city of Beijing seemed motionless, like it was merely a picture in a frame.

I stared at the laptop on the table in front of me. The livestream had long since shut off, but I could still see the horrid images reflected on the black screen. Police surrounding our outpost in Boston, the blue-red lights glaring off the windows. Stanyard, my boyfriend, being dragged from the building in handcuffs. Guards beating Lev, one of my Jewish followers, and tossing him into the back of a van.

And my uncle, lying dead on the sidewalk.

Time abruptly restarted, off-kilter and out of focus. *Why is this happening?* Reality lay shattered in front of me like a broken mirror. I tried to shift through the pieces, struggling to see any meaning in the tragedy, but the only truth I could find was that this was all my fault.

I forced myself to rehearse the events. I was—*am*—Philadelphia Smyrna, known to the world as Blue Fire, the figurehead of a revolution. My rebellion had been an accident; I'd only wanted to destroy Red Rain, the chemical superweapon my father had created, and keep it out of the hands of the government. With help from my mentor Nic, I'd burned their factory to the ground. A video of my act of defiance had leaked onto the internet, and Jael, a powerful tech mogul with control over the algorithm, had used my name to build a revolution.

I looked up at her where she stood across the table. The bangles on her wrists rattled as she agitatedly tapped her thigh. Jael was the true leader of the resistance. She'd been working anonymously in the background for months, manipulating the algorithm to push my content past the censors. She'd targeted the unassimilated, the oppressed, the discontent—anyone who was tired of submitting to a government that allowed no religion, no national borders, no individuality whatsoever.

And the people had responded.

In mere months, revolution had gone from fiction to impending reality. Millions of people all over the globe had pledged their allegiance to the "thunderbird." In Beijing, I was a household name; even some legions of the Chinese military had vowed to defect. I was both a celebrity and a public enemy, and in a few weeks, Jael and I would use that influence to end the United.

On September 17th, Operation Blue Fire would launch. At my signal, everyone who followed the thunderbird would fight the system. They would walk out of school, quit their government jobs, abandon their military outposts. Guards would destroy weapons, secretaries would burn files, and teenagers would post Bibles and other illegal documents on social media. On September 17th, the people would say *no*—together.

"If we all stand up together, they can't make us all sit down," my former ally Jayde would have said.

It was working. The world was in an uproar, and the government was losing control. Even Asia, my nemesis in the Council, couldn't deter my followers, no matter how high she raised the bounty on my life. All the tides were turning in our favor, to the point where I believed—no, *knew*—that God had to be behind it all.

I'd believed it. Until this morning.

"I have a message for all United citizens…"

I turned towards the back wall of the conference room, where the projector had generated a 3D rendering of the news. On live TV, Asia had raided my headquarters in Boston, where all my important American allies were hiding. I was forced to watch, unable to do anything but scream his name, as they hurled Stanyard into the back of a van. They arrested everyone— except my uncle.

"Be advised that associating with Smyrna will be considered an act of terrorism…"

My uncle was military. That meant he was worse than a rebel; he was a traitor. And the government had no mercy for traitors.

"And the punishment for terrorism…"

My emotions exploded in raw, unprocessed tears. I covered my face and sobbed, the only penance I could give for the uncle I'd barely known. Uncle Bart—or "Tower," as I'd called him—was the only extended family I had left. Now he was gone. Just like Mom, Nic, and my father. Just like everyone else who was dead or in prison or had their memories wiped because of me.

"Oh Philadelphia, don't you know it's too late to go home?"

"Philadelphia…" Jael's steady voice tried and failed to reach me through the waves of panicked thoughts.

"I killed him!" I shouted. Not out of accusation, but as a declaration—hinging on the desperate belief that if I confessed my sins, maybe, just maybe, the pain would go away.

"These things happen in war," she deferred, the answer practiced, thoughtless.

"In the war *I* started!" Jael may be controlling the algorithm, but I was the one who had endangered these people's lives by antagonizing Asia. I thought God had called me to some glorious purpose in China, and I'd tried to make it happen on my own terms, ignoring Nic's and Stanyard's advice time and again. I'd deluded myself into thinking I could save a planet when I should have just shut up and gone home months ago.

"God didn't choose you for anything, Phil."

I rubbed my eyes with the heel of my hand, trying to shove the tears back in. "You were right. I should have gone back to Boston. This is all my fault—"

"Enough!"

I jumped. Jael was shouting—and she sounded very, very upset.

Her heels clicked and her giant earrings swayed as she strode towards me, making her look like twice the woman. "I will not tolerate that attitude from you."

I instinctively scooted my chair back. "What—"

She cut me off with a slash of her finger. "You did nothing to cause this."

Nothing? I did everything. "But I—"

"Don't interrupt me!" she snapped, then sighed. She leaned her knuckles on the table. "Philadelphia." Her voice softened, if only marginally. "You need to stop this. You cannot keep blaming yourself."

Who else is there to blame?

The question must have made it onto my face, because Jael arched her eyebrow. "Did you not just tell me that I'm in charge?"

I nodded. I had, in fact, said that, a mere twenty minutes ago—right before Asia came on the news.

"And did you not say that you trust my judgment?"

That's exactly what I'd said. I recalled the oath of allegiance I'd sworn as I'd submitted to Jael's authority and put "Blue Fire" in her hands.

"If you tell me I'm done, I'm done. You have my word that I will not go behind your back, and I will not try to undermine you. I trust your judgment, so whatever you tell me to do, I'll do it."

I was not in control. After weeks of fighting and trying to protect my reputation, I'd surrendered. God had given Jael authority in my life, and I trusted her. I still did.

Jael let the silence grow pregnant before she continued. "I told you when we met that I wanted you to fight a war, not lead one. You were only following orders. I'm the one who gave those orders, which means the blame is mine."

She stood back from the table. "I'm the one who put you on air. I'm the one who let you visit that group home. I'm the one who didn't set up more safeguards for our friends in Boston." Her eyes glimmered with shame. "I am the leader of this operation. This situation is entirely my responsibility—not yours."

My stomach twisted, but I held back the words and waited.

Jael let out her breath, releasing a thousand regrets with it. "It's okay to grieve. It's okay to have questions. You can be mad at everyone, including me. But you cannot—you *will not*—blame yourself."

It wasn't a suggestion. I looked up into her face as she came to stand beside me and gripped the back of my chair. "Blaming yourself is a childish luxury you don't have anymore. You work for me now, and your only job is to listen and obey. And I'm giving you new orders."

I straightened. She tipped her chin back and announced, gently and deliberately, "Your orders are to trust. Be honest. And do not give place to guilt."

I struggled to repeat the words as they ricocheted around in my chest.

Trust. Be honest. And do not give place to guilt.

Jael almost smiled. "Do you understand, soldier?"

I nodded reflectively, but I didn't understand, not at all. I stared at her, wishing her words would put a period on my anxiety. They didn't put a period on anything. Instead, my pulse raced faster and my guilt screamed louder as it swirled with nothing to land on. *But what's going to happen to Stanyard? What about Lev? They'll kill him when they find out he's Jewish! What am I going to do—*

I stopped when I realized that wasn't the question I should be asking. I had no idea what was going to happen, and I absolutely didn't trust myself. But there was one thing I was confident of.

You are not in charge anymore.

I closed my eyes and inhaled through my nose. Then I looked up at Jael and whispered, "What do you want me to do now?"

She drummed her acrylic nails on the back of my chair. "I don't know," she said slowly, her thick Hausa accent filling the gaps between words. "Right now, my first concern is getting you out of this building. Too many people know you're here."

As if in answer, the conference door whooshed open. Lanzhou Tang rushed in, his cousin Bowen a step behind him. The Tangs owned the factory and were old friends of Nic's parents, the Von Nieuwenhuyses. Mr. Von had granted Lanzhou's father an exclusive contract to produce a patented part for space stations, and the Tangs had profited handsomely. They'd used that wealth to buy security for the underground church that met in their cafeteria—and for me. For the past month, I'd been living in their home and using Bowen's many connections to build the revolution in Beijing.

I shakily stood up as they approached. If anyone was in danger for assisting me, it was the Tangs. Even though I wore a disguise when out in public, using wigs and colored contacts to switch between my multiple identities, thousands of people had seen me at the Tangs' nightly prayer services. *If any one of those people calls the police...*

"Lanzhou," I started, my voice croaking with fear, "I'm so sorry. I—"

He wasn't listening. He bypassed propriety and gave me what I needed most: a hug. He pulled me to himself and gripped my shoulders with his strong hands—just like my father would have, if he were here.

I accepted the mercy and sniffled into his shoulder, feeling love and forgiveness radiating from his posture. It was no wonder he was a pastor.

"We saw the news. What happened?" he asked, directing the question over my head at Jael.

"I put her on air to stall Asia," she said, snatching the blame before I could even think about claiming any of it. "I was hoping to distract them while I found out where they're holding these executions."

I flinched when I remembered the dozens of people who were scheduled to die this afternoon if we didn't intervene. My friends in Boston weren't the only people Asia was holding hostage; she'd also raided one of the underground hospitals I'd visited in Beijing. She'd arrested all the residents—most of whom were disabled or terminally ill—and ordered their public executions.

Their crime? Associating with the thunderbird.

I pulled back from Lanzhou and turned to Jael. "Can you do anything?"

Her face held neither hope nor despair. "I'll do what I can."

"Let me call my contact at the police station, see what he knows," Bowen offered, barely suppressing the shake in his voice.

Jael nodded curtly. "Get on it. Your job," she pointed at Lanzhou, "is to get her out of sight until I can sort this out. I want her off the premises. Too many people have seen her at this factory."

Lanzhou started to answer, but Bowen spoke first. "With all due respect, I think we should put her back on air."

"What?" Lanzhou snapped.

"I think she should go back on air," Bowen repeated, eyes on me, "and expose Asia."

That was the *last* thing I should do. "Didn't you see what just happened?" I pointed at the dark projector. "I'm only making it worse. She just *shot* someone because of me."

"And she's going to do it again if you don't stop her," Bowen whispered.

My throat dried.

Lanzhou put himself between us. "Absolutely not. We are not putting her on air. She's going off the grid until this calms down."

"This isn't going to 'calm down,' and you know that." The tremor left Bowen's voice as he met his cousin's gaze. "Are we going to stay quiet while Mong murders another dozen people? Phil needs to go on there and demand an explanation for these executions."

"Jael will handle it," Lanzhou returned with a confidence I wished I felt. "But I am not putting Philadelphia through that. Not now."

"He's right," Jael cut in. "Asia is expecting us to retaliate. She wants more conflict. I'm not going to give it to her."

"And in the meantime, she's out there burning Phil at the stake. Have you looked at social media?" Bowen spun to face Jael. "The internet is eating her alive. There's rumors that the operation is a hoax, and I've already heard of several people who are bailing. If we don't fix this now, the entire operation will collapse."

I sucked in my breath. That's just what Asia wanted: for the revolution to crumble, and all the blame to fall on Blue Fire.

"We'll do damage control later," Jael said with a sharp glance at me.

"No, we need to strike now, before Asia writes the narrative. We have to fight fire with fire." He turned back to me, as if I had any authority.

Lanzhou blocked his view. "Enough—"

The trill of my tablet cut him off.

I looked at the device where it lay on the table. All three of us stopped and stared as it rang once, twice, three times, then silenced.

Jael moved towards it. "Who...?"

I had no idea. I'd borrowed that tablet from the Tangs, and very few people knew how to contact me on it. Most of those people were now in prison.

I thought of Stanyard's constant messages and winced. Stanyard had always been there for me, texting even when I didn't want to text back and answering the minute I called. Now, for the first time ever, I'd be the one staring at a blank screen as my messages sat unread.

Tears stung my vision, but I blinked them away. *Later*, I coached myself.

I stepped forward and picked up the device. I swiped on the screen and read the notification—and my heart failed.

It was a friend request from a user I'd never seen before, followed by a simple, cruel message:

HELLO SWEETIE. IT'S ASIA. READY TO TALK?

2: PHILADELPHIA

Lanzhou read over my shoulder and muttered a prayer. Jael stepped up beside us and spat something much less holy.

Asia called again. "Do *not* answer that!" Jael ordered.

I let the call ring out. I stared at the vibrating device in my hands as the whole room seemed to twitch and stutter. *She found me. Asia found me!*

My device silenced, and an emptiness settled in my soul. Where there should have been panic and adrenaline, I found only despair.

It's all over.

Bowen picked up the slack. "How did she get that number?" he demanded.

As if she were eavesdropping, Asia sent a text and answered his question.

WHEN WERE YOU GOING TO TELL ME ABOUT YOU AND STANYARD? I'M SO HAPPY FOR YOU. HE'S SUCH A SWEET BOY.

I felt nauseous as the weight of the world shoved its way up my throat. Of course, Asia had Stanyard in custody. All she had to do was take his phone and see who "Aurelius" had been talking to recently.

Jael muttered to herself and grabbed her own device, swiping furious commands onto the screen. Asia sent another message and twisted the knife deeper.

DO YOU WANT TO TALK TO HIM?

I imagined her leering over Stanyard as he struggled, cuffed to a chair in an interrogation room or shoved to the corner in a dark cell. I knew she wasn't actually in the same room as him; she was here in Beijing while her guards did the dirty work in Boston. But that didn't stop the horrid images from flashing across my vision.

Please don't hurt him, I wanted to beg, but the words didn't make it to my lips, much less to my fingers. I dropped my tablet on the table and gripped the edge.

Lanzhou laid a warm hand on my shoulder. "Can she track the device to here?" he asked. His calm voice was the only thing in the room that wasn't wobbling.

Jael swore again. "Is that one of the tablets I gave you?"

"Yes, ma'am."

"Then no," she declared, sliding her phone in her pocket. "I specifically programmed that device to be untraceable for this very reason. It routes all its traffic through an evolving proxy chain. She'll know it's a hacked device registered to a dummy file, but she won't be able to pinpoint an exact location. All she has is Philadelphia's username and chat history with Stanyard." She glared at me. "Did you tell him about the Tangs?"

I shook my head so hard my neck hurt. "Not in a text." Stanyard had been explicit that I not send him any sensitive information over chat.

"Then we're safe," Bowen said, his pitch warbling like he lost his confidence halfway through the sentence.

"*You* are. I've spent a decade making the connectivity of your home and factory as ironclad as possible." Jael adjusted her turban like a queen straightening her crown, and the army general resumed command. "However, I doubt our other associates took such precautions."

I moaned when I realized she was right. I wasn't the only person Stanyard had been talking to. Hundreds of people had accessed the servers on base—servers that contained detailed plans for Operation Blue Fire.

Lanzhou squeezed my shoulder.

Jael pointed at Bowen. "I need you and your men to start making calls. Call all of our partners and find out if any of them have been in contact with Boston." She fired the commands rapidly like an automatic rifle. "I need a list of everyone whose name might be on those servers, and I need it five minutes ago."

Bowen turned and ran out of the room without a word.

My mind started compiling a list of victims. "Data!" I gasped.

Data had become the unofficial leader of the resistance in Boston after Jayde betrayed me. Data knew more about the demonstrations planned for operation day than I did. If his information was compromised, the resistance of the entire eastern seaboard was in danger.

Jael didn't need to be told. "Call him."

Lanzhou stepped back. Grabbing my device, I minimized the chat with Asia and dialed Data. It rang once, twice, and I began to panic—then he picked up.

"Blue Fire," he panted, sounding like he was running. The line crackled with chaotic background noise.

"Where are you?" I demanded, raising my voice to be heard.

"At the exact moment, running to catch the subway."

As if reinforcing his statement, a garbled voice over the intercom announced the arrival of a train.

"We got away—we weren't on base when it happened," Data answered the implied question.

Lanzhou muttered thanks.

"We?" I asked, and dared to hope.

"Your father's with me."

"Oh, praise God," I gasped, and meant it with every fiber of my being. "Dad, are you okay?"

"I'm fine, Philadelphia," my father called in the background. He sounded rattled but unhurt. I knew he must be terrified. My father had recently been revived after being cryogenically frozen, and he only had a month's worth of fresh memories. He had no idea what was going on. Did he even realize his brother-in-law was dead?

Jael stepped up beside me. "What of the others?"

"I've made contact with Andes, the Vons..." Data rattled off some other callsigns I knew but didn't have a face for. "I can't get ahold of the Dasses. There was no one at their apartment, and they've gone off the grid."

Stanyard's family. I bit my lip. Stanyard had left his parents and sister Mira behind in Boston. I could only hope their radio silence meant they'd escaped and gone dark—not that they'd been captured.

Please, God, protect them. Save this family.

"We're scattering," Data continued. There was a rush of noise on his end of the line, then silence, as if he'd stepped onto an abandoned subway car. "I've told everyone I can get ahold of to disconnect their servers and relocate."

I started to relax, but Jael did the exact opposite. She drummed her fingers on her arm restlessly. "It may not be enough. What about your program?"

I stiffened. Data had coded a program that allowed us to hijack the government's broadcasting system. With a few clicks, we could commandeer any TV channel—and on operation day, we were going to use it to make my stream mandatory viewing on every registered device on the planet. Without his program, there would *be* no operation.

"All of the code was hosted on my server. I disabled remote access, so they can't get to it from Stanyard's computer. He might have some notes, but nothing they can exploit." There was a pause as Data reconsidered his statement. "I'll do some reconfiguring to be safe."

"And how much information about operation day was on that server?" Jael demanded.

Data hesitated. "I don't know."

Jael was not satisfied with ignorance. "Find out. As soon as you're in a safe place, I want you to search your history and give me as much information as possible. I need to know what demonstration sites are potentially compromised."

Asia grew tired of being left out of the conversation. She sent another message, the notification superimposing over Data's call.

I DON'T WANT TO HURT STANYARD. I KNOW
HOW MUCH HE MEANS TO YOU.

I gripped the tablet.

The others continued to chatter. "Do we need to reschedule the operation?" Lanzhou whispered, almost as if he were afraid to suggest it.

"We can't just 'reschedule,'" Data mocked. "We'll never get back this momentum if we stop now."

"But if Mong sends the army to the demonstration sites—"

"Calm down," Jael admonished them both. "These people knew the risks. We'll do our best to warn them..."

BESIDES

Asia let that one word hang for several seconds before she finished her sentence.

WE BOTH KNOW SUCH JUVENILE THREATS
DON'T WORK ON YOU. YOU PROVED THAT WHEN
YOU ABANDONED NIC.

An involuntary gasp of pain retched out of me before I could stop it. Asia was Nic's ex-girlfriend, and she'd taken great delight in torturing him to blackmail me. She'd arrested him, convicted him for his involvement in Red Rain, and publicly humiliated him with a fake trial. All the while, she'd constantly reminded me that she could make it all go away if I turned myself in.

I didn't—if only because Nic ordered me not to.

"No matter what happens to me, no matter what you hear, I need you to promise that you won't come for me. Do you understand?"

When I didn't show up, Asia had sentenced Nic and shipped him off to a remote prison. I had no idea where he was—and if Asia had her way, I'd never see him again.

Of all the people I'd lost to Asia's cruelty, Nic was the one who hurt the most.

Jael moved in my peripheral. "Philadelphia? What is it?"

Asia texted again before I could answer.

SO LET'S UP THE ANTE, SHALL WE? YOU HAVE UNTIL 3PM TO TURN YOURSELF IN BEFORE I EXECUTE YOUR FRIENDS FROM THE HOSPITAL.

I blindly held the tablet out to Jael as everything heaved— my breath, my stomach, the room around me. I knew that threat was coming. I knew surrender was always an option. I knew I could end the bloodshed at any moment.

But I wouldn't.

"What's wrong?" Data barked into the sudden silence.

"Is my daughter okay?" Dad murmured in the background, and my heart lurched.

Jael ignored both questions and took the tablet. "I've got calls to make. Contact me as soon as you're in a safe place." She punched the button to end the call before anyone could argue.

I vaguely registered the ping of an incoming message through the daze. I looked down at the screen and saw the text beneath Jael's fingers.

THAT'S 38 LIVES, IF I COUNTED CORRECTLY. PERHAPS THAT MATH IS MORE AGREEABLE TO YOU.

"Oh God," I groaned, and could come up with no words to finish the prayer. I pinched my eyes shut and braced myself on the back of a chair.

"Philadelphia," Jael called, sounding like she was on the other side of a glass wall. "You know you can't."

Lanzhou moved beside me. "Don't ask her to make that decision," he grunted, voice husky.

"She's not making that decision. I am."

Jael's fingernails brushed my chin. I forced myself to look at her, even though I was sure that if I opened my eyes, I would throw up.

She held my gaze, all the fear and grief locked behind a shield of authority. "I will handle this. This is not your decision to make. Do you understand?"

I nodded, even though every muscle movement felt like a lie.

"Remember your orders," she commanded, voice as intense as her gaze.

Trust. Be honest. And do not give place to guilt.

I closed my eyes again, unable to keep the room upright. I trusted her, I really did. She was in charge, and this was her decision.

I could only hope *I* had made the right decision by trusting her.

3: PHILADELPHIA

We failed.

Jael was unable to stop the executions. It didn't take long for her to figure out where everyone was being held, but the information did us no good. Asia knew we were coming and increased security, closing all the vulnerabilities Jael could exploit. Jael spent the afternoon frantically making calls, pulling on favors, and offering bribes, but to no avail. Asia had taken every precaution to ensure there was nothing we could do.

Everyone was going to die.

Jael forbade me from watching the demonstration on TV. Instead, I sat in the conference room and stared at the clock as it mercilessly ticked on towards 3pm. The artificial *tick, tock* synced with my labored pulse, filling the empty room with the roar of a hurricane.

2:51

I gripped the table with both hands, afraid that if I didn't hold onto something, I would run. Every nerve in my body screamed at me to *get up*, to find a device and text Asia, to beg Jael to change her mind. The shrieking choir of a thousand accusations rang in my ears, telling me this was wrong, that my life wasn't worth it, that I was the one who deserved to die.

2:52

I didn't know how to answer the voices. The only thing I could do was try to drown them out.

I can't I can't I can't!

I shrieked when Lanzhou touched my shoulder. I hadn't even heard him come in. He stood next to me, watching the clock, silent.

2:53

He closed his eyes and began to speak in Mandarin. I couldn't understand the words, but I could tell by the pitch that he was praying.

I slid down to the floor and did the same. "God, please, save them!"

2:54

"You're the only one who can do this. You're the only one who can stop Asia. Intervene! They're innocent people!"

2:55

I hyperventilated. Every word I thought of felt too stiff, too theological, too unfeeling. My prayers were inadequate. *I* was inadequate.

2:56

I settled for the only plea I had left. "God, don't let this happen. Why is this happening?"

Desperation—no, *rage* seized me. There was no reason this should be happening. I served a God of miracles. I'd seen a dead man raised to life. If that were possible, then why shouldn't this be possible? He could intervene. He could disable guns, scramble communications, take out the power. Something, *anything*.

2:57

"This isn't right! Those people belong to God, and they are protected! You can't have them!"

2:58

Lanzhou's prayer rose to a shout. I broke off and muttered in tongues, pounding the floor with both fists.

2:59

"God, move, *now!*"

3:00

A bell clanged in the factory below, signaling the turn of the hour. I thought I heard a wail from the other room. Then, silence.

Lanzhou opened his phone. The air left him in one long sigh. "It's done."

I wept, collapsed on the floor and screamed into the cold laminate. Not because I wanted to cry, but because I had no idea what else to do. It was over. I had made my choice, and Jael had made hers. Now thirty-eight bodies had been added to my record.

And I wasn't even supposed to feel guilty about them.

"Why, God, why?" I moaned, even though the words had no substance. There was no why. I knew that. There was absolutely no reason for all this horrid, senseless bloodshed.

Senseless bloodshed that could have been prevented.

Why didn't You do anything, God? I winced as pain gripped my chest. The question made me feel cold and isolated, like I'd cut the line on the only thing holding my soul together. Still, it lingered. It floated there, bobbing on my consciousness like pieces of shipwreck in a dark sea.

Why didn't God save them? He'd saved Nic. Nic had *died*, stopped breathing for almost thirty minutes, and he'd come back to life at the touch of a hand, a single prayer. If God could do that, why didn't He prevent this?

Why didn't You answer our prayers?

If the Holy Spirit responded, I couldn't hear Him. All I heard was cavernous silence as I continued to shiver and weep for the mistakes I couldn't undo.

There was rustling as Lanzhou sat on the floor next to me. His hand found my back, and he started to pray again. This time, it was in English.

"Father," he said, the word gentle and intimate. "Bring Your peace. This is Your daughter, and she needs You."

My sobs hitched in my throat. He was praying for *me?* I didn't need prayer; the families of all those people who had just been slaughtered needed prayer. I didn't deserve—

Lanzhou pressed down on me, as if sensing my objections. "She needs Your comfort, and she needs Your compassion. Show her Your mercy. You are the God who weeps with those who weep, and that's the Lord she needs right now."

Let Me help you.

I felt it. That incomprehensible swirling in my soul that told me the Spirit was moving, the loving conviction that warned me I was avoiding what I needed most.

Don't resist Me.

I gave in. I went limp on the floor and wept, letting the Spirit roll over me in heavy waves. Lanzhou continued to pray. His hand held me steady like an anchor as the competing emotions caught me in their whirlpool. I felt anger and disbelief and confidence and hope all at once—and then, nothing.

My tears evaporated. The emotions faded, leaving me weak both inside and out. Grief still filled my throat, and my mind was black and empty, but I sensed through it all a solid feeling that I could only describe as *peace.* It wasn't warm. It wasn't happy. But it was stable, almost like it was a rock I could hold.

"You may not feel any better," Lanzhou warned as I pushed myself up. "But that doesn't mean He's not there—or that you didn't make the right decision."

I wiped my cheeks and looked into his eyes. "Did I make the right decision?"

"By obeying Jael?" he said, avoiding the dozens of other qualifiers that could have muddled the question. "Yes, you did."

I gave the statement time to soak into my broken soul. "Thank you. For everything."

He smiled, the crow's feet winking around his narrow eyes. "You're part of my congregation now. That means I'm going to take care of you." He studied me, and his expression sobered. "Philadelphia. You can't help anyone if you blame yourself."

I flinched. "I know, I—"

He didn't let me finish. "You're a leader now, and you can't save someone else if you don't let God save you first."

I frowned and listened.

"You are just as valuable to the Lord as all those people who lost their lives today. He cares about your hurts and fears, even if you think you brought this on yourself. He wants to help you, and you're not helping anyone if you cut yourself off from His love."

I swallowed. Is that what I'd been doing? Telling God He couldn't love me—that He didn't know *how* to love me?

"Guilt is not just about finding someone to blame. When you feed guilt, you're denying yourself of the forgiveness God wants to give you. You're telling Him that the cross isn't good enough—that you've found a better way to deal with your problems."

My neck and cheeks burned as everything came back into focus. Suddenly, I understood why guilt and shame were so easy, so familiar—almost comfortable, in a way. It was easy to feel guilty because that meant I was still in control. I didn't have to trust anyone else with my problems *or* the solutions. I didn't have to deal with big, scary questions like *"Why didn't God save those people?"* when I could blame everything on myself.

Lanzhou gave me a minute to process before continuing. "Trust isn't about blindly following orders and ignoring your feelings. It's about letting the Holy Spirit help you manage those feelings—and then asking for wisdom about what to do next."

I knew he was right. Even Jael had given me permission to grieve. My emotions were not a problem—but I still had to surrender them, same as everything else.

I closed my eyes and took a deep breath, inhaling the truth with it.

God, I'm scared. I'm confused, and I'm worried that I didn't make the right decision by staying quiet, and... I do feel guilty. I know I'm not supposed to blame myself, but I do.

The air slowly came back into my lungs, like someone had unlatched a window. I sat up straight and tipped my face towards the ceiling.

I'm giving this back to You. This war is in Your hands. Show me what You want me to do.

The door opened. I looked over to see Jael approach. I struggled to stand. Lanzhou jumped up and helped me the rest of the way.

Jael stopped in front of us. "I'm sorry," she declared, although whether she was apologizing to me or to the people we had lost, I couldn't tell.

I just nodded, not trusting my voice.

Jael also seemed to realize there was nothing more to be said and moved on. "I hate to ask you to do this, but I need you to record a video." She tapped my tablet, which she had tucked under her arm. "Bowen is right—the media is propagandizing this, and we cannot let them write the narrative. I need you to go on air and condemn the executions. I'll give you a script."

The thought of going on air made me want to hurl, but I nodded. "Whatever you need me to do."

She indulged in a small smile. "I want you to keep this in case Asia or any of our friends try to contact you." She held my tablet out.

I instinctively took it. "Shouldn't we block Asia and change my username?"

Her dangling earrings thwacked against her neck as she shook her head. "I want to keep that line of communication open. Just… in case."

In case we need to bargain? I unlocked the tablet and opened the messenger.

"I deleted all the texts she's been sending for the last six hours," Jael explained. "You don't need to read those."

I clicked on the chat with Asia and saw it was blank, except for the message she'd sent just a few minutes ago:

YOU KNOW IT DOESN'T HAVE TO BE THIS WAY. I DON'T ENJOY THIS ANY MORE THAN YOU DO. MEET ME AT THE NOLAN ESTATE, AND WE CAN END THIS TONIGHT. I PROMISE NO ONE WILL KNOW WE TALKED.

The Nolan estate? I stared at the screen, imagining the gorgeous mansion on the other side of Beijing—the mansion I owned.

Thames Nolan had been an associate of Asia's and was one of the many people who had used me and my family for political gain. He was also, in a cruel irony, my "adopted" father. He'd created a false identity for me—"Andromeda Nolan"—intending to convert me into the daughter he never had. He didn't live to see it happen, but I'd had no choice but to adopt the forged file. Since my birth identity, "Philadelphia Smyrna," was on the United's most wanted, I'd begrudgingly assumed the name of Nolan—and the massive inheritance that came with it.

When we first met, Asia had wanted nothing more than for me to become a Nolan in word and deed. She'd pampered me, introducing me to all her high society friends, and told me over and over that I "deserved this" and "belonged with them." I knew why, now: She'd wanted me to kill her father.

I flipped my right hand over and studied my palm. You couldn't tell underneath the healed skin, but I knew there was a network of wires woven through my fingertips—the remnants of a bomb. When I'd first come to Beijing with Jayde, I'd been intending to assassinate General Secretary Mong, the supreme leader of the United. Asia had invited me to a prestigious party and introduced me to her father. Had he shaken my hand, the chip in my palm would have sent him into cardiac arrest and killed him.

I'd reconsidered at the last minute and greeted the General with a bow instead. He'd been amused by my perceived humility and extended his favor, even going so far as to accept my impromptu invitation to dinner. Jayde, on the other hand, had been furious. He'd betrayed me, kidnapped me, and tried to kill me, and I was sure he would finish the job if he ever found me again.

Asia, of course, knew all of that. She'd wanted the assassination to succeed so she could take her father's throne, and when that plan failed, she'd hunted me across the province. Surely, she was smart enough to realize that I'd since gotten my chip removed; the leftover wires in my hand were harmless. I wouldn't kill her father.

That left us with two options. We could continue to trade blows until the only option was war.

Or I could turn myself in, so she could quietly kill me and clean up this mess before it got further out of hand.

I knew which one she would prefer. Asia hated an unnecessary mess.

The tablet pinged again. Clearly, Asia insisted on having the last word.

THINK ABOUT IT. WHEN YOU'RE READY TO TALK, YOU KNOW WHERE TO FIND ME.

I shivered. Such a sinister word: "when."

Jael glanced at the notification but didn't seem perturbed by the contents. "Get changed and meet me in the recording studio. You're on in—"

She was interrupted by the whoosh of the door. Bowen jogged towards us. "I reached out to every contact I have and traced down every name I thought might be on the Boston servers," he panted.

"And?" Jael prodded.

He paused to take a gulp of air. "Some of them have already gone dark."

I sucked in my breath.

Jael glanced at me. "Tell me in my office. We'll meet in thirty minutes after Philadelphia and I are done recording."

Bowen focused on me for the first time, his eyes flickering with a sorrow he daren't express in words. "We need to get you out of here."

Lanzhou joined the conversation. "I agree. We need to get her to a safe place—too many people have seen her here."

"Unfortunately, now that Asia is hunting down all our associates, this factory *is* the safest place. This is one of the few buildings where I can completely control the internet traffic, and there are a lot more places to hide here than at your house." Jael propped one hand on her hip. "However, you're right. There are too many people here. We need to clear the building."

"But…" Bowen objected.

Jael ignored him, fixing her gaze on Lanzhou. "I know you trust your employees, but Asia is offering a sum that would test any man's loyalty."

I swallowed. The Tangs had managed to hide a church in their basement for decades. Would someone betray them now just for the money?

I looked up at Lanzhou as his expression furrowed, calculating. "If there were to be an equipment failure…" He gestured. "I could shut the line down for a few days, send everyone home on paid leave."

Funding everyone's salaries while his enterprise ground to a halt for who-knows-how-long sounded devastatingly expensive. "I'll pay you back," I blurted.

He smiled gently. "We can afford it."

So can I. The Nolans were stupidly wealthy, definitely more so than the Tangs.

"Make it so," Jael ordered before I could argue. "I want the dock gates locked at all times. No one steps foot on these grounds without your or my approval. And cancel the church services."

My gut pinched. Of course, it was the right thing to do. It wasn't safe for anyone to meet here, especially while I was still on the property. But that didn't stop me from feeling a crushing load of shame. For the first time in a decade, people would not be worshipping God in this building tonight—and I was the reason.

I closed my eyes and pushed the thoughts away before they could take root. *Do not give place to guilt.*

Lanzhou took a breath like he was about to say something more, then stopped. There was a beat of awkward silence while he tried and failed to start his sentence twice. Finally, he turned to Jael. "Have you considered canceling Operation Blue Fire?"

I stiffened. *Cancel the operation? We can't give up!*

I could tell by the arch of Jael's eyebrows that the notion wasn't on the table, but Bowen spoke before she could. "No! It would kill the resistance. We've already lost so many people because of what happened today. If we show any weakness now, we're finished. The United wins."

I winced. It terrified me to admit it, but I knew he was right. If Operation Blue Fire failed, the United would crush the unassimilated, and people would be too afraid to try again. The revolution was hanging by a thread as it was. If I—if *we* failed, we wouldn't get another chance. Not for this generation.

And I wasn't willing to give my generation up without a fight. *For such a time as this.*

"We'll be worse off if the government slaughters hundreds of thousands of innocent people because we told them where to look." Lanzhou's voice was even, but his fists were clenched. "We don't know how much information was on that server. Asia may know exactly where most of the demonstrations are planned. If the government stakes them out, the revolution will be over before it starts."

I looked to Jael in a panic, begging her to deny it. "It's a possibility," she admitted without emotion.

"Then we have to prepare for that," Bowen returned. "We can relocate some of the demonstrations, arm the people, send Phil's military to counteract."

He said it so casually—"Phil's military"—like they were chess pieces I played with in my free time. But I did have a military. Several troops of the Chinese army had pledged to defect to me on operation day. General Jin was my primary contact; he alone commanded five thousand soldiers.

Along with lots and lots of heavy artillery.

Lanzhou paused, the silence harsh and sinister. "What are you suggesting, cousin?"

"I'm suggesting that we defend ourselves. We can store weapons here, use this as a command center—"

Lanzhou cut him off with a flick of his arm. "Absolutely not. This is a *factory*, not a military base. We've worked for decades to make this a safe place where people can worship God, and I'm not sacrificing our position with the police to turn this into an armory. I'm not endangering my employees or my congregation like that."

Bowen bristled. "It's my congregation, too. And they're ready to fight—"

"Then you should consider what 'your congregation' needs from their pastor." Lanzhou raised his voice only slightly, but it was enough. "You have a family, a company, *and* a church to lead, Bowen. You need to remember that."

"I know what my role is," Bowen returned, low and cold. "That's why I'm going to do everything I can to protect them *and* this building."

He swiveled to glare at me. "And you should too."

Before anyone could object, he turned and stormed out of the room, leaving his words echoing in the silence.

4: NIC

I knew something was wrong when the dreams started.

Correction: I knew something was wrong when Asia called to threaten me. She hadn't visited since I'd been banished to Russia, a weird act of mercy, so I knew my luck was over when she summoned me to the visiting room. She radioed in with a freaky hologram and tried to sweettalk me into revealing Philadelphia's location, vacillating between "I'll give you a full pardon" and "I'll kill everything you love." When she finally let me get a word in edgewise, I advised her to save the oxygen.

She left in a huff, blathering about how I was going to regret this. Even though I never would have admitted it to her face, I knew she was right. Phil was running out of time, and I was about to have so many regrets.

If Asia was coming to me, that meant she was desperate. And desperate people were deadly, especially when they were oversaturated with wealth and power like Asia was.

Unfortunately, she hadn't given me any details on the next phase of her evil plan, so I was forced to ask around. I asked my bunkmates, Vance and Ryan; I asked the minions who worked under me at the lab; I asked every guard who would give me the time of day. I even bothered Warden Ivanova on her lunch break, falsely assuming she had at least some contact with the outside world.

No one knew anything. Absolutely no one had any recent information about "Blue Fire" or the revolution. Probably because we were all stuck 20,000 feet in the air in a prison factory on a snow-capped mountain in Russia.

I finally asked the omnipresent Voice in my head. In retrospect, I probably should have asked Him first. But we'd only been on speaking terms for about a month, and I was still forming the habit.

"Look, we need to talk," I hissed into the darkness of my cell. I kept my voice down to avoid waking Vance and Ryan; they had an annoying habit of commandeering (or providing theological commentary on) my conversations with the Lord. "It's about Philadelphia."

I've been waiting all day for you to ask, He responded amicably.

"I'm sure You have," I grunted. "She's in danger."

Yes, she is, He admitted without fear.

"I need to help her—no." I backpedaled before He could correct my grammar. "I want to help her."

I know you do.

I rubbed my mustache. "You told me to help her."

Yes, I did.

I remembered the exact moment the Lord had so indelicately reminded me that my life was not my own. I'd been running across Beijing with Phil, intent on going back to Mars and forgetting the rebellion existed, when the Lord made it clear that was unacceptable. He said He wanted Philadelphia to stay in Beijing, embrace her heritage as Andromeda Nolan, and challenge Asia on even playing ground. Phil would finish what I'd failed to do ten years ago—and I was going to help her.

I had no doubts that all this oddly specific information came from the Lord, because He revealed it in the most obtuse, heavy-handed way possible: He gave me an open vision.

I was prepared to ignore it, just like I'd been ignoring my dreams for the last ten years, ever since I dumped Asia and she put my parents under the knife. I was perfectly content to disobey the Lord and accept the consequences—until I saw that Philadelphia was in danger of losing her own faith.

I knew I was going to hell. But I had no intention of bringing a plus one.

I'd tentatively said yes to God—and then everything went to hell anyway. Everything that could go wrong had gone wrong, and now I was stuck in a prison thousands of miles away doing the exact opposite of what the vision said.

I sighed and studied the unidentified stains on the concrete ceiling. I wasn't stupid. I knew there had to be a reason for this Russian detour. But it would be nice to have some clearer instructions. "*How* am I supposed to help her?" I prodded.

You're helping her right now.

I rolled my eyes; it was low-hanging fruit. "Granted, but You were very specific that You wanted her to be a Nolan and fight Asia, and I was supposed to stay in Beijing with her. Last I checked, she's hiding underground, Asia has the upper hand, and I am nowhere near Beijing."

You've only been here a month. Have more patience.

I rubbed my temples. So that's where this prayer was going—the same place my prayers always dead-ended. "Look, I didn't call so we could have a repeat of this conversation."

Then why are we talking?

I grimaced, convicted. He sat in forgiving silence. I waited until I had scraped together some humility before confessing, "We're talking because… I'm worried about Phil."

He listened.

"Asia is running out of patience. If she finally snaps, she'll either kill Phil or kill everyone she loves, and I'm not sure which is worse."

That was a lie. Having been on the receiving end of the latter, I knew which was worse.

He let my dishonesty slide. *What do you want Me to do about it?*

"Bust me out of jail" would have been the most precise answer, but I knew I wouldn't get away with it, so I broadened the parameters. "I know You have plans for Phil, and I know she doesn't see them. She has no idea what she's doing or who to trust. She needs wisdom. I… need wisdom."

What are you asking? He nudged, ever the teacher.

"What is Asia planning? What do You want Phil to do—what do You want *me* to do?" I sat up and stared into the dark room. "Tell me what I need to know."

He didn't answer directly—which was highly unusual for us. But He did send the dreams.

Only one problem: The dreams didn't answer any of my questions.

It wasn't that they were bad dreams. Usually when I lost control of a situation, I had visceral nightmares; my gift of prophecy was twisted into a cruel joke as I imagined a future I could not change.

Not tonight. My dreams were benign; had I been in a better mood, I might have even dared to call them good dreams. Philadelphia was there, doing exactly what my vision had predicted she would: changing the world. I saw her standing in the courtyard of a white-stone mansion, receiving party guests with perfect grace. I saw her presiding over a board meeting, with several faces I knew gathered around the table: Bowen, Warden Ivanova, my father.

And again and again, I saw her speaking to the Council in Beijing, confronting them with prophetic speeches that I forgot as soon as I woke up.

It was exactly as I had envisioned it a month ago, except Philadelphia was perhaps a little older. Her dark brown hair had grown back in, and she had a wedding ring on her finger—no doubt given to her by that brooding Pizza Boy.

I woke up then. I came into cold, musty reality with a groan and a crick in literally every joint of my body—probably because I'd clenched every muscle thinking about Stanyard laying his lips on my daughter.

I sat up and rubbed my face. "You're not helping," I grunted, unsure whether I was talking to myself or the Lord.

He didn't respond, not that He had a chance to. *"¡Buenos dias!"* Ryan crowed at an indecent volume. His head popped over the edge of the bunk like a possessed jack-in-the-box. "Rise and shine! You're going to be late for work!"

"You're not my boss anymore," I mumbled, and contemplated going back to bed. Ryan had been my supervisor in the factory for all of two weeks. I'd since gotten reassigned to the lab, where I was the boss over a motley crew of scientists, but Ryan had been unwilling to let his superiority go.

"Maybe, but I still told the warden I'd keep an eye on you. Up, up, up!" He grabbed my blanket and yanked it from me. The force was too sudden for his barely-five-foot frame, and he tumbled off the ladder with a yelp.

Vance caught him. "The fact that you have been given a position of management does not mean standard working hours do not apply to you," he accused. "In fact, because you are in authority, I imagine Warden Ivanova is expecting a higher level of adherence…"

Thank you for the early morning sermon, I thought but wasn't stupid enough to say. Even though we were, against my will, friends, Vance's hulking frame, scarred knuckles, and penchant for dissecting my every sentence made me think twice about using sarcasm in his presence.

He's right, you know, the Voice in my head joined the conversation.

I slapped the thin mattress. "Of course, he's right. They're always right!"

"Hi God!" Ryan called. He jumped up and waved; I could barely see his hand over the edge of the bedframe.

Tell him I said hi.

I pinched the bridge of my nose. "God says hi back."

Ryan whooped like he'd won a ticket out of jail.

And tell Vance I agree with him.

"I'm not telling Vance anything," I snapped.

"Excuse me?"

I gave you this factory to steward. So, steward it.

I groaned in defeat. God had, in fact, given me this factory; Vance, Ryan, and I were running the place. When I'd first arrived, the prison, while a fascinating piece of ice-crusted architecture, had been in shambles. The assembly line was grossly inefficient, and the place was bleeding resources. The only thing Warden Ivanova had under control was the discipline.

I would have been content to let the place burn, but the Lord had other plans. He told me to use my three PhDs to fix it. Warden Ivanova, much to my surprise, actually took my advice, and within two weeks we'd completely restructured the factory. Production had doubled and profits even more so. The influx of wealth had brought the warden the approval of her superiors, and she'd returned the favor by promoting us. Ryan now supervised the production floor, Vance managed administration, and I'd been given charge of the lab, where we developed the products to be assembled in the factory.

It'd be a very nice arrangement, if I weren't a convicted felon and completely cut off from the one person I cared about on this planet.

You have a job to do, the Voice in my head came like a cattle prod.

"You still haven't answered my question," I shot back.

I answered your question. I told you what you need to know.

"If the Lord has given you a message for me, it's imperative that you relay it," Vance interrupted, crossing his arms over his concrete slab of a chest.

"There's no message," I groaned, and the statement applied to both of us. Apparently, the Lord thought I didn't need any additional information.

I knew what that meant. And I didn't like it.

I swung my legs over the edge of the bunk and jumped down. Satisfied I was awake, the boys had mercy and left the room. I took my time digging through the clothes on the floor to find an unsoiled lab coat. My promotion had earned me the privilege of not wearing prison orange, so I donned a button up and pair of slacks and checked my reflection in the mirror. My goatee was overgrown and my hair was somewhere between "hippie" and "electrocuted," but I couldn't be bothered.

I stumbled down to the cafeteria, soldiered through Vance and Ryan's invigorating table talk, and then took the scenic route to the lab. The lab was in one of the subbasements of the prison, a good ten floors down from the cafeteria, but I decided to walk instead of taking the elevator. I strolled along the railing, giving the coffee time to make it to my bloodstream and admiring the marvel of the factory.

It was a genius, if not ostentatious, design. It was built like a silo with a hollow center. The assembly line was staggered across the circular levels, while supplies and workers were ferried up the middle on a spider web of pullies and elevators. The building had so many floors that you couldn't see the top from the bottom. The place rang with enterprise, the sounds of productivity echoing in the cavernous space like an eerie choir.

I leaned over the railing and admired the ingenuity. It would be a delightful view—if it weren't also a prison.

"Von Nieuwenhuyse!"

I jumped and almost dropped my coffee cup over the edge. "It's too early for that many syllables," I groaned, and turned around.

Warden Ivanova strode towards me, her usual entourage of guards in tow. "You're needed in Storage Bay 5," she barked.

"Why? I just marked all the bins with a label maker yesterday."

She halted and glared up at me. "I don't have time for your emasculated sense of humor, Nic. Get down there."

I tried and failed not to be offended. Normally, Warden Ivanova could match me wit for wit. The fact that she'd lost her sense of humor meant something was very wrong.

I switched gears. "What happened?"

"Another powercell exploded."

"Again?" It was the third time this week.

Of the many products manufactured in the factory, powercells were the most profitable. We produced a whole range of sizes for different applications—from cells as big as oil drums for interstellar transits to miniature batteries designed for electric pistols and household appliances. The assembly line had just finished a special order of the latter. All had gone stupendously well, thanks to my engineering—until the powercells reached the quality testing phase. Then, suddenly, the batteries started exploding like popcorn kernels.

At first, Warden Ivanova automatically assumed it was sabotage and went on an interrogation spree. When she failed to find anything suspicious, she set up additional security on the assembly line. The next explosion was clearly an accident—and that's when she called me in. I ran a diagnostic and found several of the testing chambers were out of alignment. I corrected the issue and deemed it safe to continue production.

Apparently, I was wrong.

"It's not the testing equipment," I assured her, and hoped she wasn't about to exact all her frustration on me.

"I know it's not," she intoned. "This cell exploded by itself. In a storage bin. On the other side of the factory."

She held it out to me—or rather, what was left of it. The only thing that remained was a charred stub, like someone had chewed off the cap to a pen.

I took it and held it up to the light. "Well, that's not normal."

"This batch had passed testing. I saw the report myself. So, either you miscalibrated my testing machines, *or...*"

I looked up. "I take it I'd better supply the 'or' if I don't want to get sent to bed without dinner."

She sighed. "You want my personal opinion? I think it's by design." She pointed at the fragment in my hand. "This is a proprietary model we haven't manufactured before. They claim their patent has passed federal inspection, but I don't trust the government."

"I can get behind that mantra."

She snorted. "I want you to get the lab on it. Figure out why these powercells are going nuclear. I need a full report ASAP. A shipment of these have already left the warehouse, and my buyer is not patient."

"What about the other assignment you gave me that's due tomorrow?" I returned. It was an honest question, not that you could tell by my tone of voice.

Her expression froze over like the ice on the windowsills. "I think this is more important."

I cleared my throat and adopted a more appropriate attitude. "Yes, ma'am." Just because I was management didn't mean I was above the warden's discipline, and I was not in the mood to give her any free stress relief today.

She accepted the penance with a nod, then stormed off, her guards following like a line of ducklings.

I studied the powercell fragment in my hand. I had to admit, it didn't look natural. I'd overloaded a few powercells in my day, but I'd never seen anything like this. Normally, an overloaded powercell would melt, swell, or catch fire, just like any battery. This fragment looked like it had spontaneously exploded. To make matters even stranger, the edges of the inner component were rough and pitted, almost as if it had been eaten away by acid.

I ran my finger over the sharp edge. Powercell casings weren't made of weak material, for obvious reasons. They were specifically designed to contain caustic chemicals. What could have deteriorated it?

My mind began running through the periodic table, searching for possible candidates, when I abruptly realized the Holy Spirit was hovering over my shoulder.

"All right, all right," I consented without looking back. "I'll use one of my three PhDs to fix it."

He smiled, satisfied.

I slid the fragment in the pocket of my lab coat and started down the hall. "I can take a hint," I said. "But there had better be a *very* good reason for this side quest."

5: PHILADELPHIA

"As much as I hate to admit it, Asia did us a favor."

I stared at the graph on the computer in Jael's office and tried to rationalize any other explanation for the analytics, but I couldn't. The numbers didn't lie. In some twisted and sick irony, the executions had saved the revolution.

The first forty-eight hours after the fall of Boston were a nightmare. Jael and her team scrambled to warn everyone who could be traced from Stanyard's computer; I went on air and begged my allies to save themselves. It was a losing battle. Asia mobilized the army, and within twelve hours she had raided a dozen other outposts on the East Coast. Hundreds of my supporters were arrested. Some vanished as Asia locked them away where we couldn't find them, just like she had with Nic. The rest were systematically executed, one right after another.

Everything crumbled like a house of cards. The media slaughtered me and the revolution. The Council, at the encouragement of Asia, voted unanimously to increase the punishment for associating with the thunderbird. Under the guise of restoring order, Asia instituted curfew and flooded the streets of Beijing with soldiers, and the people bought the lie. Views on my videos plummeted while Chinese civilians praised Asia's decisive action. For two terrifying and agonizingly long days, it looked like Asia would win.

And then, suddenly, the tides reversed.

I put out a video condemning the executions, just like Jael had instructed. The script she gave me was unorthodox; I barely talked about Asia and her politics at all. Instead, I spent most of my airtime honoring the victims. I put faces to the statistics as I went into heartbreaking detail about the mothers, fathers, nurses, and disabled children the United had murdered. I let the whole world know who was really suffering in this war.

And the world listened.

The video trended, more so than any of my other content. Within twenty-four hours, that stream and its reposts had amassed more views than all my previous videos combined. It broke past the censors and dominated the home page of every social media site—even on networks Jael *couldn't* control. It defied the algorithm, to the point where even Jael called it a miracle.

Suddenly, I was writing the narrative. Public opinion shifted sharply as the Chinese questioned Asia's ethics. The people were enraged, and my followers seized the opportunity. They joined me online and exposed the United's other sins, reminding everyone who the real enemy was. Jael let the cycle run its course for a few days, then put me on air to call people to rejoin the fight.

They answered. Most of the groups who had committed to Operation Blue Fire publicly pledged to demonstrate as scheduled, no matter the risks. Dozens of new mass demonstrations were planned. Even the military continued to cast their lot in with me as several more regiments joined General Jin in vowing to defect.

The world was ripe for revolution. It was just like when my father had tried to launch the original Operation Blue Fire four years ago, before my mother died. The United had made an error when they instituted the unassimilated containment camps, and the people had been willing to fight. Now, Asia had made the same mistake. She had gone too far and upset the balance, and her retaliation was adding fuel to the fire. The more she threatened, the more people she executed, the more my popularity grew. She was turning her own people against her and sending them running to me.

Jael was right; Asia did us a favor. And that worried me.

"We're going to let it rest for another twelve hours," Jael was saying, having already moved on to another tab. "I want to give your supporters a chance to raise their own voices and second your latest video. Then I'll have you go on, thank them, and give people additional instructions."

I watched her neon-colored nails clack on the keyboard. "Okay," I mumbled, only half-listening.

She stopped typing. "What's wrong?"

I shifted my eyes to her face. "Nothing," I said, and it was the truth. The fact that Asia was losing was a good thing—wasn't it?

She propped her chin on her fingers. "Philadelphia. I thought your orders were to be *honest* with me."

I flinched and looked away. "I don't... know. I'm not sure what's wrong," I admitted, which was at least slightly more accurate.

She reached down and found my hand. "Just try. What are you thinking?"

I stared out the window at the hazy green river flowing past the docks, giving myself a minute to think. "I just... This doesn't make sense. Why would Asia let us gain this much ground? Surely, she realizes what she's doing." I turned back to Jael.

"It may not be her decision." The swiftness of her response told me she'd been considering the same questions. "Just because she's the public face doesn't mean this is her policy."

That was a possibility, but I didn't believe that—and I could tell Jael didn't, either. We all knew Asia was in charge in every way that mattered.

"She may also be desperate. Violent people tend to escalate with more violence when they're losing control," Jael suggested.

I didn't believe that either. Yes, I was sure Asia was furious with me for scorning her blackmail and death threats. But this wouldn't be the first time her plans had been complicated, and she'd always found a way to compensate. She'd proven again and again that she was willing to play the long game to avoid an unnecessary mess. All this chaos and media attention was not her style—which meant she must have another plan.

Nic would know. Nic knew Asia better than even Jael did, and he was a shrewd politician in his own right. If he were here, he'd be able to decipher Asia's actions—and tell me exactly what I needed to do to stop her.

But he's not here. I looked down at the table as pain filled my chest. Now more than ever, I realized Nic was exactly the person I needed in my life. I could only wonder if he missed me half as much as I missed him.

Jael squeezed my hand. "Take a break. We'll record after dinner."

I nodded. I stood up and let myself out of the office, then waited until the door had shut behind me before taking a breath.

The unnatural silence in the hall settled like a layer of dust. The factory was dead; only a few office staff still worked out of the building, just enough to keep up appearances. The eerie quiet wrapped itself around me like a draft and reminded me that I was very much alone.

I hadn't been allowed to leave the factory for a week. All I could do was wander the halls and pray. It was almost like being back on the science station on Mars—except it was nearly impossible to get lost in the factory, and a security team was watching my every move.

I smiled at the guard who stood by the elevator nearest Jael's office. He gave me a respectful nod.

I turned away and continued down the hall. Pulling out my tablet, I opened a streaming service and searched for a repost of my latest video. There were dozens, some of which were nearly twenty-four hours old—a sure sign the censors were failing. I clicked on the top result and watched the views and likes climb in real time.

What was Asia doing? The government never allowed my videos to trend like this. Asia must be letting it happen. That was the only explanation I could accept—because the other possibility was one I was too afraid to consider.

The other explanation was that we really *were* winning. The government was failing. The algorithm was caving in on itself. Asia was losing control, and in her desperation, she was hastening her own demise. The revolution was succeeding—because God wanted it to succeed.

Is this God?

A week ago, I would have said yes, without hesitation. But now, the thought made me sick, like it was food I couldn't swallow. We were winning—why did that make me uneasy?

Was it because we were morbidly profiting off of people's deaths? That wasn't anything new; martyrs had been winning wars for thousands of years. Besides, Jael had been using my life's story as propaganda for months now. If that truly bothered me, I wouldn't continue to be the thunderbird.

And even if I did disagree with Jael's methods, I would still firmly believe that God could turn anything for good. It was in His rulebook to redeem what the enemy meant for evil. For the past six months, my entire life had been a string of redemptions as God had used death and imprisonment and loss to bring hope and freedom and love.

So why was this time any different? For the last six months, I'd looked at my circumstances and sworn it was God. Why couldn't I do that now?

The answer came to me, cold and formless, like a stranger looming just out of sight behind the fog.

Maybe I was scared because the last time I claimed to have heard God, I was wrong.

I stopped in the middle of the hallway as the ugly memories caught up to me. God had given Nic, of all people, a vision about my future, and I thought I knew what it meant. I thought I knew exactly what God wanted me to do and how He wanted me to do it. I'd stubbornly insisted on staying in Beijing, even though everyone who cared about me—including Jael—wanted me to go back to Boston. And now hundreds of people were dead because of that choice.

I couldn't make the same mistake again. I couldn't lead a war thinking it was God if it wasn't.

I looked at the ceiling. "Is that you, God?" I whispered.

I was more than a little terrified when a real voice answered me.

"Nah, don't be silly. It's just me!"

Before I could turn towards the sound, a hand struck out of the shadows in the side hall and grabbed my arm.

6: PHILADELPHIA

I shrieked. The guard at the elevator reacted, drawing his weapon. My assailant shushed me sharply. "Shh! You're going to get us in trouble!"

I relaxed when I recognized the voice. I stopped struggling and squinted at him. "John? Err, Dowe?"

He grinned. "You had it right the first time. It's John."

I took his word for it. It was impossible to tell which one it was with his face creepily half-shrouded in shadow. John and Dowe weren't twins; they weren't even related, according to rumor. But they looked so cannily alike that my best guess as to their origins was "failed cloning experiment." They were ancient but didn't act like it; they were also supposedly Jael's best secret agents, but they didn't act like that either. They were loud and shameless and had a terrifying habit of appearing in places they shouldn't have been, almost as if they had teleported there. But despite the fact that everything about their behavior defied both logic and physics, they were some of the best friends I had.

Except, maybe, when they were leaping out of the shadows like murderers.

"Don't scare me like that," I grunted, pulling my arm from his grasp.

"Sorry, but I need you for a *covert* mission." He leaned around the corner and scanned the hall shiftily.

"Well, if you're going for subtlety, scaring me out of my wits was probably not the best option." I glanced at the guard. He rolled his eyes and holstered his weapon.

John started walking, gesturing for me to follow. "Come on—and keep a low profile. Jael *cannot* find out about this."

I hesitated. Not telling Jael sounded like a terrible idea, even coming from John and Dowe. "Where are we going?" I whispered, not sure why I was playing into the secrecy.

"The conference room," he hissed back. He tiptoed across the hall—to the conference room, which was all of three yards away.

I looked at the guard. He shrugged. "You're on your own with that one."

I indulged in a chuckle and followed John. I supposed there was only so much trouble we could get into in the conference room.

After making a scene of checking both ways—even though the guard was definitely the only other person in the hall—John opened the door and waved me through. I walked in and halted. "What happened in here?"

"Glitter happened!" John crowed, and that was an accurate description. The conference room was a mess—in the most glorious, colorful way possible. The entire table was coated with craft supplies, from construction paper to scalloped scissors to jars of glitter, several of which had already contaminated the room. There was glitter on the chairs, the windows, the whiteboard. The whole room sparkled like it had been blessed by a fairy.

"How'd you manage to get glitter on the windowsill?" I pointed.

John scratched his head nervously. "I, uhh, tried to get Tommy to help me with a collage…"

"What?" I exclaimed, but a petulant meow answered my question. I looked down to see my cat rubbing innocently around my ankles.

Tommy was a yellow-eyed stray Nic and I had picked up while running across Beijing a month ago. Well, *I'd* picked him up; Nic had tried his hardest to get rid of him. In any case, it was, perhaps, a bit selfish to think of the animal as "mine." If anything, he was more attached to John, who was supposed to be keeping him at the Tangs. Lanzhou had expressly forbidden me from bringing my cat to the factory—something about cat hair and delicate equipment.

I picked Tommy up. He was *covered* in glitter; his gray fur sparkled like a disco ball. I held him at arm's length, even though I knew it was too late; I wasn't getting out of this room unscathed. "You're right," I murmured. "Jael probably shouldn't find out about this."

"Don't worry, we'll clean up the evidence," John said.

"You'll probably have to burn the whole room down," I remarked. There was no way that stuff was coming out of the seat cushions.

Tommy mewed and flicked his tail, sending glitter showering through the air.

I laughed and gave up arguing. "So, what is this 'mission,' exactly?"

"The mission is for you to have fun!" someone whisper-shouted. I looked up to see Dowe sitting at the end of the table, waving a marker-stained hand at me. Next to him sat Sienna.

I sucked in my breath. Sienna was one of the residents of the hospital I had visited a few days ago. She'd managed to escape with us; we'd used the fire exit in her room, and my security got her to safety. She'd been staying at the factory since then because, like me, she was a wanted criminal—although her only crime was failing to meet the United's standard of physical and mental perfection.

She was also, I abruptly realized with a stab in my heart, one of the only residents of the group home left alive.

"Hey, what's that face? You're failing the mission already," John chided. "Come on, let's make a paper chain or something."

He guided me towards the table. I followed and took the chair next to Sienna, settling Tommy in my lap. "Hey," I greeted her softly.

She didn't acknowledge me, but I wasn't offended. Sienna was severely autistic and non-verbal. She rarely even looked in my direction. *"The important thing,"* Jael had said, *"is to treat her like you would anyone else—even if you don't get the response you're expecting."*

I leaned over to see what she was working on. She was coloring, gripping the crayon with fierce intent. I couldn't quite tell what the image was supposed to be, but it was elaborate. She had used every color in the box, filling in all the white on the paper with precision.

"It's beautiful," I said, and it was. I watched her work, trying to find something more to say. I couldn't come up with anything—so, I grabbed a clean piece of paper and started coloring with her.

As was usually the case with John and Dowe, their chaotic methods proved weirdly effective, and the "mission" was a success. I did have fun—and Sienna did too. This was the calmest I'd ever seen her, and she repeatedly engaged with Dowe. She laughed and clapped and responded to his questions, using her body to fill in the gaps where words failed her. I watched in silence and let a little joy into my soul. Not everyone from the group home had been lost.

Thank you, Jesus.

"What is the meaning of this?"

I jumped and dropped my glue stick. Jael stood in the open doorway, hands on her hips. "John Dowe!" she screeched.

Dowe scrambled up, overturning his chair. "I can explain, I swear!" He ran towards her, hands clasped in penance.

She sidestepped. *"Don't* touch me. Where in the world did you get all these craft supplies?"

He looked puzzled. "The craft store?"

I snickered before I could stop myself.

She shot me a glare. "Never mind. I'll court martial *all* of you later."

She sounded serious, and Dowe panicked accordingly. John groaned and flopped back in his chair like his mom had just told him to clean his room. "Ugh! I don't wanna go back to jail!"

"At least she can't send us back to Rott," Dowe reasoned.

"Watch me," Jael muttered. She yelped as Tommy wrapped himself around her ankles, rubbing a visible amount of glitter into her pantyhose. She gingerly pushed him away; he pranced right back over and sat on her foot.

She made a heroic effort to plaster a smile on her face and turned to me. "You have a visitor."

Who...?

I stood up as Seoul waltzed into the room. She looked like a video game character come to life with her cocky blue hair and junkyard-rat outfit of overalls and loaded toolbelts. Her omnipresent goggles dangled around her neck as she winked at me. "'Sup, girlfriend," she greeted with a casualness only she could afford. She was the tech who had safely removed the bomb in my hand; I'd let her get away with anything.

"Hey, Seoul," Dowe crooned. He tried and failed to lean nonchalantly on the table. He slipped, crashing to the floor.

She blithely ignored him and looked over at John. "Hey, baby."

John beamed and wiggled his fingers.

Dowe blistered red all the way up to the roots of his hair. "It's like I'm not even here."

I put myself between them. "What are you doing here?"

"Getting paid for a job well done," she smirked.

I stiffened. "Did you...?"

For an answer, she reached into her messenger bag and withdrew a small metal box. She pressed her thumb to the lock, and it released with a beep. She held the case out to me.

I gingerly took it and opened the lid. Tucked on a bed of foam and shielded by a sheet of glass were three miniature computer chips, no bigger than a square centimeter each. A dozen fine wires sprayed from the circuitry like spider legs.

"Three brand-new memory augmenters," Seoul whispered, giving the treasure the reverence it deserved.

I closed the lid and grasped the box to my chest as warm tears splattered my cheeks. These chips were my ticket to bringing my father back from the dead—and maybe, just maybe, saving Nic's parents.

My dad was the victim of cryogenic freezing. Paul and Roseanne Von Nieuwenhuyse were the victims of something arguably worse: neurosurgery. It was a barbaric corrective procedure that involved severing neural pathways to selectively rewrite the criminal's psyche. It was so grossly ineffective that even the United had restricted it.

That was exactly why Asia had subjected Nic's parents to the procedure after he'd failed to give her Red Rain. She'd killed them in every way that mattered, stripping them of their memories, their personalities, and their ability to function as independent adults.

The Vons weren't the only people I knew who had survived neurosurgery. John and Dowe were also recovering victims. When I'd first met Seoul, she'd bragged about the chips she'd implanted in their brains that had given them (some of) their memories back. According to her, John and Dowe were functioning on prototype knockoffs because they were "cheapskates," which was why they could only retain a couple terabytes of information, most of it useless.

The chips I held in my hand were not prototypes. With enough programming and therapy, they could enable my father and the Vons to access their lost memories.

It might not work. My dad's brain could be damaged beyond repair. For the Vons, they'd undergone surgery almost a decade ago; time may have rewritten their neural pathways beyond retrieving.

But for my family, both literal and honorary, I was willing to try—even if it cost the entire Nolan fortune.

I looked up at Seoul. "How much do I owe?"

"A lot," she intoned. "But I'll accept part of my payment in the form of a private flight out of the country and a couple of hulks to help me move my shop gear."

I frowned. Her weary smile didn't make it to her eyes as she said, "No offense, but Beijing is not a safe place for your friends right now."

"Of course." I sighed and turned to Jael.

She nodded. "I can make the arrangements."

Seoul popped her chewing gum. "Well, guess we're even. It was nice doing business with you, Blue Fire. Good luck with the implants—call me if you have any problems."

I gripped the box as an idea raced through my mind. "Since you're already leaving town... How would you like to extend your employment? I need some work done in America. For an additional fee, of course."

She lifted both eyebrows.

I held the box out. "I need someone to install these. And I heard you're something of an expert on these devices."

Her face split in a grin that bordered on maniacal. "You heard correctly. But you do know that the surgery is almost as much as the device."

I shrugged. "You get what you pay for."

She started to reply, but then the eagerness faded from her expression. "Unfortunately, a mechanic is only as good as her tools, and I won't have my full lab in America."

Jael spoke up. "I'm sure I can find—"

I raised my hand. "I know someone with facilities. Find Andes, tell him Blue Fire sent you. He'll give you everything you need. And if he doesn't, call me, and *I'll* tell him to give you everything you need."

Seoul barked a laugh. "I like this plan."

I paused and reconsidered what I'd just told her to do. "I'll warn you, though—don't expect a warm welcome. He's been running the scene in Boston for longer than I've been alive. He probably won't be thrilled that I've outsourced."

I thought of Andes's bulging muscles and tattooed skin and wondered if I'd just sent a petite, blue-haired David to face down a Scottish Goliath.

Seoul fingered the sadistic array of tools she had in her belt, perhaps involuntarily. "Sounds like my kind of challenge."

Jael took over. "Follow me, we'll get the paperwork done."

"We'll miss you!" John crowed from the table. "Right, Sienna?"

She grunted and scribbled on her paper.

I stared at her as the Holy Spirit whispered in my ear.

Seoul blew John a kiss. "I'll miss you, too."

Dowe squinted. "Is that a plural you, or singular…?"

I spoke before Seoul could retort. "Actually, you're both going with her."

"We are?" John and Dowe exclaimed together.

"No way." Seoul put both palms forward. "I'll take John but not Dowe."

"You'll take whoever I tell you to. I'm paying you, not the other way around," I reminded her.

Seoul gaped. Jael propped her chin on her hand and looked mildly impressed.

I turned to face the boys. "John and Dowe, I have a mission for you. I need you to go back to Boston and take care of some business for me."

Dowe scrunched his nose so hard it was in danger of folding back into his face. "That sounds vaguely like a non-job to get us to go away."

"It's not. I need you to take Sienna with you." I watched her as she continued to color. "Find a family that will take care of her and keep her off the grid."

There was sudden silence in the room except for Sienna's scratching on the paper. Abruptly, she stopped, the crayon dangling from her fingers. Then she glanced up at me.

I smiled.

Dowe laid a hand on my arm. "We'd be honored."

Seoul blew a strand of hair out of her face. "Fine, I promise not to kill Dowe on the way."

"Charmed," he grunted.

I looked to Jael for approval. She winked.

"Just one question…" John called.

I glanced back at him.

He folded his hands under his chin and did his best to look cute. "Can I keep your cat?"

7: PHILADELPHIA

One hour and thirty-seven minutes. That was how long it took to walk a lap around each level of the factory, from the third floor to the basement, and that was information I wish I didn't know.

It was a crime that I should be so bored while the world was waging a war in my name. Even though the public saw me as the leader of the resistance, the reality was that "Blue Fire" did very little. Jael handled all the coordination and planning. While I was very grateful that she was managing the difficult decisions, it meant I spent the better part of the day alone. I would record for an hour, and then maybe kill another hour or two in strategy meetings where I mainly listened to everyone else make decisions. For the rest of the day, I would wander the halls, bored and very, very lonely.

The factory had gotten even quieter with John, Dowe, and Sienna gone. I didn't even have my cat to keep me company; I'd made the difficult decision that Tommy would, in fact, be safer with John. The group had returned to Boston and made contact with Andes, but that was the last news I'd received.

Meanwhile, Bowen, the one person who was always happy to involve me in whatever he was doing, was hardly on the property anymore. Lanzhou made an effort to talk to me when we passed, but I knew he was busy keeping his family business from collapsing, so I tried not to harass him. Everyone else in the building had jobs to do.

And, with Stanyard gone, there was no one to talk to online.

My dad called a few times. They were bittersweet conversations as I patiently answered questions he should have known the answer to: *"How old are you? When's your birthday? What do you remember about your mother?"* But I knew he was trying, so we made the most of each moment.

I was finally able to tell him the good news about Seoul and the memory implant. I forced myself to be realistic; the device would take a lot of programing, just like any algorithm, before it would start recalling the correct memories for each word. It could take weeks of visual therapy before the implant would think of me and not the city when someone said "Philadelphia"— and that was if his memories were salvageable at all.

"It will take several months of therapy to start working," I said. "But I'll help you, I promise. Ephesus will too."

My older brother Ephesus was currently hiding in a remote mining base on Mars with his wife Cea—who also happened to be Nic's sister. We hadn't had time to celebrate our complicated family tree. The mine was so deep in the wilderness that it was difficult to get a call through; it took over a week for me to reach him and break the news of our uncle's death. But Ephesus and Cea wouldn't have to hide for much longer.

After operation day, the unassimilated wouldn't have to live in the shadows anymore.

Dad turned to face the camera, and for the first time since he'd woken up, his eyes gleamed with the tiniest sliver of hope. "We'll do it together. As a family."

Even though we both wanted to talk more, Dad could only handle about ten minutes at a time before he got tired of fighting the implants in his brain—and that was on a good day. Andes constantly had him in and out of surgery as they tweaked the wiring and tried to resurrect my father's science degrees. I could tell Dad was overwhelmed at best, so I pretended I had things to do and hung up whenever he grew anxious.

I only wished I weren't lying when I said I was busy.

I was on my third or fourth lap for the day when something finally broke the monotony. I had just stepped off the elevator into the basement cafeteria, where the church services used to be held, when I heard Bowen's voice. I followed the sound to the back hallway and found him and a military officer I didn't recognize unloading crates from the service elevator.

"Phil!" Bowen welcomed me with a grin.

The soldier paused to give me a long, respectful look—which was how strangers usually greeted me—and then threw a salute.

I acknowledged it with a smile. "What are you doing? And I can I help?" I asked, even though I doubted the latter. Even Bowen was struggling under the weight of the crates.

He dropped the last one in the hallway with a grunt. "Well, I need to catalog these, and then some are getting sent to other churches…"

I nodded; Bowen was well-connected and knew at least a dozen other underground pastors in the province. "What are they? Bibles?"

His lips twitched. "Not… exactly."

The soldier keyed a passcode into the crate on top of the stack. "General Jin sends his regards."

Then he threw the lid back, revealing a row of shiny electric pistols.

I gasped.

"One of your wealthy allies provided the funding," the soldier explained, even though I hadn't asked. "General Jin is redistributing them across the city."

"But—what are they for?" I demanded, even though I knew exactly what guns were for.

"Operation day," Bowen answered. He picked one up and slid his hand down the polished barrel.

"Just what kind of demonstration are you planning?" I struggled to hear my own voice through the panic screaming in my ears.

"The demonstration this city needs." Bowen glanced back at me. "Phil. You know it's too late for peaceful negotiations. The government is going to do everything they can to retaliate on operation day—unless the people defend themselves."

I knew he was right—was he? I knew shots would be fired on operation day; it was unavoidable. But that didn't mean I was going to *fund* the violence, sending weapons to innocent civilians.

This isn't right. This isn't what Operation Blue Fire is supposed to be!

I gripped the straps of my backpack, afraid that if I didn't hold on to something, the floor would cave out from beneath me. "Bowen, I—"

"What is going on here?"

I whirled to see Lanzhou storming down the hall, Jael a step behind him. "Bowen!" he shouted. "Put the gun down!"

He obliged. "Cousin, it's not what you think—"

Lanzhou didn't give him a chance to finish. He shoved him aside and glared into the open crate, his face washing white and then red. "No, it's *exactly* what I think. You went behind my back! And who are you?" Lanzhou shifted his glare from Bowen to the officer.

The soldier looked up from his device long enough to point at the name patch on his fatigues. "General Jin's regiment."

"You need to get out of here before someone sees you. Bowen." Lanzhou took a deep breath and made a heroic effort to remain calm, but every muscle in his body was tense. "You need to get these out of here. If someone reports this—"

"Who's going to report it? Everyone in this building is loyal to Blue Fire." Bowen also tried to talk peaceably, with about as much success.

"It doesn't matter! Our bargain with the police explicitly states we won't possess weapons except our own security. If they find out you're storing guns here, we'll lose the church."

"We'll lose the church if the operation fails," Bowen argued. "If the revolution doesn't succeed, a couple of prayer services won't make a difference."

"They'll make all the difference," Lanzhou whispered.

Jael stepped between them. "Enough. Lanzhou's right. I need to keep this building secure, and if that means bribing the police, so be it. Put these back on the truck." She flicked a jeweled finger at the officer.

He pocketed his device. "It's too late."

"Excuse me?" she snarled.

Before he could offer any clarification, my tablet pinged.

I froze. I think, instinctively, I knew who it was and what was about to happen.

The soldier smiled.

My device beeped again. Everyone stared at me as I scrambled with my backpack and pulled out my tablet.

It was Asia.

THERE YOU ARE

The panic returned—and this time, there was nowhere to run.

IT'S OVER, SWEETHEART

"What have you done?" Jael screeched.

"I thought you were with General Jin!" Bowen echoed.

The soldier ignored them both. "If you're going to ask why I did it," he locked eyes with me, "your ransom will pay for my children's retirement."

I stumbled back as Jael's warning flashed through my mind.

"I know you trust your employees, but Asia is offering a sum that would test any man's loyalty."

"You fool!" Jael shrieked, although it was hard to tell who she was yelling at.

The soldier reached for his weapon, but Lanzhou reacted first. He snatched a gun from the crate and flicked it on, planting himself in front of me.

The soldier eyed him. "You don't want to fire that."

Lanzhou aimed the weapon at his face. "Bowen, take the girls and get out of here."

"But—"

The soldier spoke over him. "Don't even try. Asia has two dozen soldiers surrounding the property right now." He looked past Lanzhou to address me. "If you come quietly, she'll let the others go."

Asia sent another text and seconded his statement.

YOU HAVE FIVE MINUTES TO COME OUTSIDE BEFORE I BURN THE PLACE DOWN. DON'T KEEP ME WAITING.

"Don't listen to him, Philadelphia," Lanzhou said. His voice was deceptively steady even though his chest was heaving. "Bowen, now. You know what to do."

Bowen started to back away. "Lanzhou—"

"Now," he ordered. "Keep Philadelphia safe. Don't come back for me."

I whimpered, remembering the last time this scene had played out—and how it ended.

"Don't ever come back."

Bowen lurched into motion. He snatched two more guns, tossing one at Jael, and took off running. "This way, hurry!"

Jael grabbed my arm and hauled me down the corridor. I struggled to shove my tablet in my backpack as I stumbled after her. The soldier seemed unconcerned by our retreat. "It was a pleasure meeting you, Blue Fire."

I cast one last glance back at Lanzhou, but he didn't turn to look at me.

We raced around the corner and across the abandoned cafeteria to the elevator. "Where are we going?" Jael demanded.

"There's another way out—we planned for this." Bowen called the elevator and waved us in ahead of him. Then he reached up and yanked on the fire alarm mounted on the wall. I flinched as a siren blared, thundering in the empty hall.

He stepped in and keyed a code into the panel, punching the buttons for multiple floors like he was dialing a phone. The doors hissed shut and the elevator moaned as it descended. "This leads to a tunnel that runs under the canal." The warning light in the ceiling drowned his face in bloody red as he explained. "We built it in case the church ever got ambushed. It will dump us out six blocks away—should be far enough."

"It better be." Jael held me close to her, her nails digging into my shoulder.

I braced myself against the wall as the elevator lurched. *God, please, protect Lanzhou!* I begged, even though I knew it was a useless prayer. Lanzhou wasn't getting out of this, not unless he was willing to shoot—

As if in answer, a scream ripped from somewhere above us, seeming to vibrate in the metal shaft. I heard several shouts, a large crash—and then an explosion.

This time, Jael screamed. Bowen cursed. The entire elevator shook. I stumbled into the corner, but before I could find my balance, another explosion rocked the air. Then another. Debris pummeled the roof of the elevator. The car groaned and shifted to one side—then plummeted.

I couldn't even scream as the floor dropped out. Air rushed around me like a surging river—and then the elevator hit the bottom, and so did I. We'd only fallen a few feet, but the world still briefly washed black as I slammed into the ground, elbows first. I moaned and hacked, trying to get air.

Jael and Bowen were shouting, but I couldn't make out the words around the ringing in my ears. Dust rained from the dented ceiling. Bowen crawled to the panel and pulled the emergency lever. The doors thudded as the hydraulics released. He dragged himself up, grunting in pain, and shoved the doors open.

Jael kicked off her broken heels and staggered to her feet. She reached down and pulled me upright, murmuring something in my ear. The only part I understood was "Phil." I nodded and followed her out of the elevator.

The tunnel beyond was cold and nearly dark except for a row of dim lights running down the middle of the ceiling. The sound of the river grinding on the concrete was terrifying; it felt like we might be crushed at any moment.

"What happened?" I managed.

Bowen didn't hear me. "This way!" He coughed and stumbled around the corner. A large object covered by a tarp was hidden in the shadows. Bowen yanked the tarp off, revealing an old SUV. The door squeaked as he opened the driver's side and rooted under the seat for the key. "Let's go!"

Jael shoved me towards the car. She helped me into the backseat, then claimed shotgun. Bowen got behind the wheel and turned the key. The engine sputtered, then ignited. He flicked the headlights on and gunned the engine. The tires crunched on gravel and trash as he raced towards the end of the tunnel.

Jael tried to catch her breath. "Did she bomb us?"

"I-I don't know," Bowen stuttered.

"But it hasn't even been five minutes!" I cried. I shrugged my backpack off and struggled to pull out my tablet with sweaty hands. There was no signal.

Blurry light appeared ahead. Bowen slowed as he neared the end. He pulled carefully out of the tunnel and onto a dock behind an abandoned warehouse. There were no police cars in sight.

I scrambled across the seat to look out the window. Several blocks behind us was the factory.

It was gone.

The building was completely collapsed. Chunks of concrete spilled into the canal like a crumbled cookie. Smoke billowed into the sky as flashing lights swarmed the yard.

"Lanzhou!" I screamed, the sound inhuman. I slammed my fist into the window and wailed.

He's gone he's gone he's gone, oh God!

Bowen yelled something in Mandarin and slammed on the brakes.

"Keep driving!" Jael ordered. "We have to get away from here!"

Bowen obeyed, but the car swerved as he struggled to hold onto the wheel. "This is all my fault!"

I sagged against the seat and sobbed. *No, it's mine. It's mine!*

"Drive!"

The engine revved. I became vaguely aware of the sounds of traffic as Bowen drove out of the lot and merged onto the road.

"This way!" Jael pointed. "I know a safe place."

"No, we have to go by the house!" he insisted. "I have to warn the family—they'll be coming for them."

"Under no circumstances! We have to get Phil out of the city!"

He wasn't listening. He took a sudden left, to the complaints of several other drivers. I grabbed the upholstery to keep from being thrown to the floor.

Jael reached for the wheel. "Bowen!"

He gunned it.

I braced myself against her seat as we violently passed the car in front of us. I scanned the road, watching for police, and that's when I saw it—more smoke, this time a few blocks ahead.

"Look—"

I didn't finish. Bowen let out a sound of pure anguish and cranked the wheel. I smashed my shoulder into the window as he raced the last few blocks. We spun around the corner and came within sight of the Tangs' courtyard home.

We were too late.

The place was in flames. The cruel red-orange light illuminated the historic woodwork like some twisted silkscreen show. A police barricade blocked the road as officers herded a family member into the back of a van. I couldn't tell who it was from this distance, but it didn't matter.

Asia had already won.

"Turn off!" Jael shrieked.

Bowen surprisingly obeyed her. He swerved into the alley at the last minute, taking us out of sight. He threw his door open almost before the car was in park and took off down the road.

"Bowen, don't do this!" I begged, pounding the window. "Please!"

"Bowen!" Jael called. "Stop!"

He didn't. He disappeared around the corner, and I heard a shout in a megaphone.

I slapped my hands over my ears. *Please no please no please!*

Jael cursed. She hiked up her skirt and slid across the console, taking the wheel. She slammed the door shut and stepped on the gas. The car pitched over potholes as she navigated around dumpsters and abandoned bikes back to the main road. She slowed long enough to defer attention before pulling out.

I sobbed as the world continued to quiver. Jael swore over and over, slapping the wheel with her bloody hand. I covered my face and tried to block out the shaking, the screaming, the smell of smoke and the sound of concrete falling. *They're gone, they're all gone!*

I'm not sure how long we kept driving. Minutes, maybe hours. It seemed like an eternity before Jael spoke.

"Well." There were a million regrets crammed in the word. "I guess you're coming home with me."

My tablet beeped. I swiped on the screen and squinted at the notification through the tears.

It was, of course, Asia.

OH, WHAT A BIG, UGLY, UNNECESSARY MESS

8: NIC

It took me several days to figure out what was wrong with the powercells, a fact neither I nor Warden Ivanova was happy with.

The issue was, of course, that the design wasn't faulty on paper. If it had been, they would have figured it out during production. As it was, I had to use one and half of my three PhDs to break the design down to the molecular level and find the flaw.

The powercells were composed of four layers: a solid conductive core, a protective inner casing, and a liquid cooling barrier, all housed in a metal shell. A fairly standard design, and none of the components were inherently explosive. I replicated all the elements in the lab and combined them in a dozen ways, but I produced nothing except toxic fumes.

While the lab aired out, I reviewed the logs from the testing stations and tried to calculate the common denominator. As usual, math was forthcoming with the truth: All the powercells that exploded had been subjected to temperatures higher than 250 degrees Fahrenheit.

That explained why only some of the powercells detonated and why the idiot designer may not have caught it. The average consumer wasn't heating their batteries to extreme temperatures. If used in a low-wattage device like a toaster or hair dryer, the powercells would have operated as intended. But when they were exposed to high temperatures for a prolonged amount of time or subjected to repeated bursts of energy, the coolant couldn't keep up, and that's when the magic happened.

After running several tests, I discovered that the elements in the solid core reacted at high heat and melted to form a new, highly corrosive chemical. That chemical could eat through the inner casing, causing the boiling-hot coolant and corroded inner core to mix.

And that combination was *highly* explosive. The hotter the battery, the faster the reaction and the bigger the impact. It was lucky I was running my experiments in a nuclear-grade testing chamber, or we would have lost the entire lab and I would have gone to meet Jesus for the second time in so many months.

I wanted to believe the whole thing was a fantastic accident. If the batteries were being marketed for toasters, government regulations would have only required them to be tested at household levels of energy. It was completely feasible that the original designers had simply been lazy and not subjected their powercells to extreme temperatures.

But I didn't have that much faith in humanity, and neither did Warden Ivanova.

"I hate it when I'm right," she grunted as she glared at the report I'd presented on her desk.

"Me too." I tapped the tablet screen. "How many have already gone out?"

"A couple hundred thousand."

I blinked. "Oh, so only enough to light about a quarter of the world on fire, that's not too bad."

"I notified the buyer and all the requisite governing authorities, but it's up to them to do anything about it."

"Do you know what they purchased the batteries for? If it's electric toothbrushes, that might buy us some time while the government slogs through their paperwork."

She shook her head. "No idea. It was a distribution company. Could be a shell for all I know."

It is a shell, the Voice in my head informed me.

I sighed and looked at the ceiling. "This was not the apocalypse I wanted to be responsible for. There are so many better ways to end the world."

"I stopped the last shipment. Should I be worried about the ones in storage?"

"If they haven't been through high-wattage testing, then no." I thought of the errant powercell that had almost burned Storage Bay 5 to the ground. That particular batch had been tested at energy levels just barely high enough to trigger the chain reaction, hence the delayed explosion. Everything in storage had been there for at least three days at this point, so in theory, we were safe. But I wasn't about to be proven wrong again. "But maybe let's err on the side of caution."

She nodded. "I was thinking of taking them out back, trying to start an avalanche. Wanna come?"

Before I could pull out my calendar to pick a date, a knock came at the door. A guard poked his head in. "There's someone here to see you, warden."

She glanced at her computer screen. "I don't remember giving anyone permission to dock."

"They didn't need permission."

Warden Ivanova swore gloriously and elaborately in Russian. I resisted the urge to echo her; I was trying to break the habit, and it wouldn't have sounded nearly as tenacious in English.

There was only one entity who could barge in unannounced: the government.

"As if this day couldn't get any more pleasant," Warden Ivanova groaned. "Fine. Send them in."

I backed away. "I'll give you your privacy."

But before I could make myself scarce, the door banged open again, and an officer needlessly decorated with the United's insignia crawled in. I could tell by the greenish look on his face that he'd just stepped off the elevator and wasn't handling the sudden altitude well. "Warden... Ivan...ova?" he slurred.

"What do you want?" she barked at a decibel that would have put the fear of God in anyone.

He staggered back and nearly fell on his rear. "I have a... delivery for Dr. Von Nie-when-house."

He nearly vomited after attempting my last name, which was what I usually did when I heard it. "It's Von Nieuwenhuyse, and he's not here right now, would you like to leave a message?"

He took a gulp of air and struggled to contain his stomach. "I'm supposed to tell you, 'Asia sends her warmest regards, and she hopes you like the gift.'"

It was my turn to contemplate throwing up as my day went from bad to hellish.

Warden Ivanova glared at me. "I thought you two broke up?"

"It's complicated. And whatever it is, I don't want it." I shooed the soldier away. "Return to sender, and tell her 'no thank you.'"

He grimaced. "I can't return *him*."

"Him?" the warden snarled.

The guard turned and gestured at someone in the hallway. I had two seconds to calculate the worst possible scenario before that scenario walked through the door.

Bowen.

He jerked. "Nic! You're alive!" He darted towards me, as if he were somehow going to attempt a hug with cuffed hands.

I took a step back. What little serenity I had collapsed like shattered glass as I put two and two together and reached my worst nightmare.

"Phil," I said, and that was all I needed to say.

Bowen hesitated, looking like a kicked dog with his bruised face and guilty eyes. "She escaped. I think."

"I'm going to need a better answer than 'I think,'" I snapped, even though I knew I was directing my rage at an unworthy source. But the most deserving object was several thousand miles away in her cushy Beijing office, and Bowen was, regrettably for more reasons than one, within arm's reach.

"I'm going to need a lot of answers," the warden inserted. "Who are you, and who's Phil?"

Bowen ignored her. "She's with Jael, that's all I know."

"Who's Jael?" the warden asked.

"Great, and where are they?" I demanded.

"They were in the car. I'm assuming they got away."

"Got away from *what?*" I shrieked. The room trembled. It took a minute for me to realize I was the one shaking.

Bowen swallowed. "Asia found the factory."

I braced myself against the warden's desk, but it did nothing to keep the world upright.

"What factory? What's going on? Can they not hear me?" The warden turned to her guard, who shrugged.

"It's all gone." Bowen's whisper barely reached me through the waves of terror. "They arrested the whole family. My aunt, uncle, everyone."

"What about Lanzhou?" I hissed.

He didn't respond, and I had my answer. I forced myself to look up.

Tears blurred his bloodshot eyes. "Lanzhou's dead."

The room went silent. There wasn't a single sound except in my head, where everything was screaming, screaming.

"Nic," the warden called. "What's going on?"

I gripped the edge of the desk. "Leave us."

"Excuse me? You can't—"

I looked up at her. "Please."

She hesitated, her expression cycling between friend and foe.

After a heavy pause, she chose friend. "Ten minutes," she said, and herded the others out the door.

I waited until their voices had faded before sinking into her vacated chair. "From the beginning," I demanded.

Bowen obeyed, explaining everything that had happened since I'd been sent to Russia. The more he talked, the more my fears became reality. Everything I'd prayed wouldn't happen to Philadelphia had happened, and worse. Not only had she gotten caught in a shootout and nearly killed—*twice*—but she'd lost Lanzhou, Stanyard, her uncle, and everyone that mattered. She was stranded in Beijing with a woman I barely knew, leading an army of disillusioned rebels who were prepared to start a war in her name.

And there was no one left to save her.

"I'm sure she and Jael made it out alive," Bowen repeated for the third time, as if that mattered at this point.

I shoved the chair back and stormed to the door.

"Nic?" Bowen called after me. "Nic! Wait!"

I ignored him. I strode out into the hall and nearly collided with the warden, who was, unsurprisingly, waiting around the corner. "Nic! What's going on?"

"Don't talk to me," I snapped, and shoved her out of the way.

The Voice in my head was the next to attempt conversation. *Slow down.*

"I said, don't talk to me!" I shouted. I punched the button to call the elevator and descended to the lowest floor, where the lab was.

The clatter of flasks and the chatter of people assaulted me as soon as the doors opened. Half a dozen scientists busied themselves around the testing equipment, yakking about molecules and boiling points.

One of them spotted me and scampered over. "Doctor! I have the simulation results you asked for." He held out a tablet.

I grabbed it and threw it on the ground, shattering the screen. "Get out."

"But sir—"

"Are you deaf? I said get out! All of you!"

Thankfully, I'd yelled loudly enough for the entire room to hear me, so I didn't have to repeat myself. They rushed to the elevator like a gaggle of scared chickens. I kicked the broken tablet aside and stomped over to a worktable.

The Voice followed me into the room. *What are you doing down here?*

"I don't know, does it matter?" I returned, because it sure didn't to me. I grabbed a random tube and popped the cap, swirling the contents. "Maybe I'll create a world-ending superweapon, I haven't decided yet."

Incidentally, that's what I'd done the last time I was this angry. Because if the world wanted to play with fire, then at least I would have the last laugh.

That's not why you created Red Rain.

He sounded far away, like He was hovering by the door. I glared over my shoulder, half-expecting to see Him there. But of course, the lab was empty.

"Oh no, that's *exactly* why I created Red Rain—because I want this entire stupid planet to burn."

I didn't use the word "stupid," but the word I did choose felt weak, inadequate.

No, you don't. The Voice came from the other side of the room this time.

I whipped around. "You really want to argue about this?" I snapped, as if He weren't in my head anyway. "Well, then let me state it for the record: I hate this planet and everyone on it, and if You hadn't interrupted, I would have gotten some epic revenge. That's all there is to it. I'm sorry if that's not the deep, introspective answer You were hoping for." I replaced the cap and tossed the tube back on the table.

If all you wanted was revenge, He returned coolly from where He was leaning against the whiteboard, *you would have done it ten years ago. As you said, there are so many better ways to end the world.*

He was right, and I hated that. I could have gone to war against Earth any time I wanted; I had more than enough bombs and computer viruses to have a fighting chance. Red Rain was a ludicrous plan, always had been. What's more, I'd realized about two years in that I wasn't smart enough to complete the formula.

And yet, I'd persisted. I'd hired a hundred scientists and wasted all my money constructing Wing 74. I'd even kidnapped Ephesus and forged his death to protect my secret, all in pursuit of a project I knew was science fiction.

You knew it would never work, the Voice prodded.

"Well, forgive me for trying," I spat, and then grimaced at the irony.

You didn't create Red Rain because you wanted revenge, He continued. *And that's not why you're down here now.*

"You're right, I have no idea why I'm down here. But it seemed like a better option than murder." I turned my back to Him and rooted through the implements on the table, just to hear them clatter against the tray.

You shouldn't be alone, He admonished. *Go find Ryan.*

Ryan, with his screeching voice and unfounded optimism, was the last person I wanted to be around. "I'm busy," I snapped, and then proceeded to make a good show of it.

The command repeated, more a premonition than an audible sentence. *Go find Ryan.*

I resorted to ignoring Him. I grabbed two of the nearest test tubes and combined the contents without reading the labels, savoring the brief rush of adrenaline. Much to my disappointment, nothing exciting happened, not even a fizzle.

Stop before you hurt yourself.

Hurting myself sounded like a wonderful idea. I grabbed another flask and contemplated the warning label.

Nic. He was close, too close, sucking the oxygen out of the room.

I clenched my hand around the tube. "Leave me alone!"

Put the glass down, He ordered.

I obeyed, literally. I slammed the flask down and then swiped my arm across the table, sweeping the entire contents onto the floor. The shatter of glass and crash of metal was terrific, and for a very brief moment, it drowned out the hurricane in my head.

I did it again. I walked to the next table and flipped a tray of instruments onto the floor. Then a burner, then a microscope, then a laptop. I stomped on the screen until the glass cracked. That wasn't nearly satisfying enough, so I turned to the storage cabinet and emptied the contents shelf by shelf. Flask after flask hit the floor until the linoleum was covered in a sea of sparkling glass.

I swiped my hand across the shelf and came up empty. There was nothing left in the cabinet. I hesitated, panting, long enough for that hated silence to return.

I had to find something else to fill the void. I spun around and scanned the room. There were plenty of things to destroy—but once I finished ransacking the lab, what then? I would have to find another distraction, and I knew, deep down, that it would never be enough.

And maybe that was the real reason why I had created Red Rain.

He appeared again, right beside me. *Deeper.*

I sank to the floor, glass crunching under my knees. "I created Red Rain… because I couldn't stand the silence."

It was the perfect excuse—the exhausting schedule, the constant deadlines, the endless pursuit of a project that could never be completed. Red Rain left no time for grief—or other people.

Deeper.

I stared at my bloody hands, as if I could find the truth in the wounds. "I created Red Rain… because I wanted to be alone."

There was always a reason to distrust people when you were a criminal. I'd spent years training my sister to fear me and my employees to hate me. Because if everyone hated me, they would never want to know me.

It had worked beautifully. Until Philadelphia.

She was the first person who wasn't scared. She'd brazenly ignored my warning signs, throwing back the curtains and asking the questions I refused to ask. *"Why did you abandon Red Rain? Why don't you go to church anymore? Why don't you visit your parents?"*

Why don't you visit your parents? He echoed.

I shuddered. I could feel it seeping into the room, like floodwaters soaking through the floorboards—the terrifying answer I had avoided for ten long years and could avoid no longer.

The same reason I created Red Rain.

And why is that?

I gripped the edge of the shelf behind me, wondering, briefly, if this is what it felt like to drown.

Tell Me.

It wasn't a suggestion, and I couldn't disobey. *Because I didn't want to feel.*

Feel what?

Everything.

The betrayal, the heartache, the shame at the realization that I'd actually *loved* Asia. The guilt, the self-loathing, the knowledge that I'd brought it all on myself. The disappointment, the anger, the grief over a dozen things that should be but never would—including myself.

And through it all the disgusting, maddening realization that the one time—*the one time!*—I'd let down my guard and allowed an innocent teenage girl into my life, my mistakes had caught up to me and brought us both down to the grave.

I'd let Philadelphia change my mind. And now I was going to lose her.

Just like my father.

Nic. He was closer than a breath. *Why did you create Red Rain?*

I finally answered the question. "I created Red Rain... so I wouldn't have to admit that I missed my dad."

Everything shattered. All the lies, anger, and rebellion I'd used to build my fortress crumbled, stripped of their power. I sagged against the cabinet as all the emotions, guilt, and fear—so much fear—rushed in with nothing to stop them. There was nowhere to run, nowhere to hide.

So, I didn't. I just sat there and let it all crash down on me like brick after brick until everything was broken. By the time the silence returned, there was nothing left to resist it.

And then, for the first time in ten years, I put my face in my hands and allowed myself to grieve.

9: PHILADELPHIA

It took them over thirty-six hours to pronounce Lanzhou dead.

Jael drove me to her apartment across town. It was a modest high-rise on the edge of an industrial park, where the maze of warehouses afforded some privacy from prying neighbors. She claimed she owned the building and everyone in it, so I'd be safe—for now.

She set me up in the guest bedroom of her top-floor penthouse, then left me alone with my grief while she did damage control. Not that there was much she could do; it was the same tragic song and dance. Bowen, Mr. Tang, and the rest of the family were arrested and vanished off the grid while the media vilified the "traitorous oligarchs" who were funding the rebellion at the expense of their impoverished workers. The overblown story couldn't be further from the truth, but it didn't matter. Asia would use any excuse to mock me.

I spent the day pacing the empty apartment and repeatedly refreshing Lanzhou's file. I knew he was gone; there was no way anyone survived those explosions. But I had to see it for myself. So, I held back my grief and kept the tears from falling until they finally excavated enough of the rubble to retrieve his body and make it official.

It was a mercy the Tangs had shut down the line and put most of the staff on leave; the building had been nearly empty, and only half a dozen people lost their lives in the collapse, a relatively small body count for me. The damage also took out most of the evidence that I had ever been on the property, and Jael was able to secure their cloud servers remotely. Asia wouldn't be able to trace the Tangs to any more of our allies. It was, all told, a minor inconvenience for the revolution—and Asia knew it.

"You got lucky this time," she texted the next day. *"Really, it's my own fault. I should have investigated the Tangs sooner. After all, they've been friends with the Vons for years."*

That's when I cried. I thought of a sane Mr. Von, a younger Nic not yet scarred by Asia's cruelty, and a faithful Lanzhou who should have inherited his father's empire—all the people who couldn't be resurrected. I huddled on the couch in Jael's living room and wept into my knees, mourning the man who had been brave enough to help me and kind enough to pastor me.

That's how Jael found me when she came home after dark. The cushion sank as she sat down beside me.

I sniffed and unfolded myself. "It's official."

"I saw."

Wiping my eyes with the back of my hand, I picked up my tablet and stared at the headshot on Lanzhou's file. "What now?" I whispered, afraid of the answer.

She straightened, drawing herself together with a long breath. "We keep fighting. You'll stay here—"

"Until Asia finds me, and we play this scene all over again."

I hadn't meant to cut her off. The exclamation ripped out of me like a knife yanked from a wound, angry and bleeding.

She didn't deny it. "I know the risks."

So did I, and for the first time in several weeks, I was questioning if it was worth the cost.

"Freedom always comes with a price," she declared, reading the tension. "The world falls when people are no longer willing to pay."

I knew that. I knew this was the right thing to do. But that was neither the question nor the answer.

She touched my knee. "What are you thinking?"

I struggled to sift the fear out of the chaos. "What if... what if I'm alone?"

"What do you mean?" she prodded, but slowly, as if she knew where this conversation would end.

I stared out the balcony windows at the black night and finally conjured the words. "What if, when this is all over, I'm the only one left?"

It was a real possibility—so real that, in some morbid way, I'd subconsciously started preparing myself. Nic was gone. Stanyard was gone. My dad would never be the same, memory device or not. Ephesus was so far away that he might as well be gone—and now Lanzhou was dead. Jael was all I had left.

What if I lose her, too?

I knew leading the revolution was the right thing to do. It wasn't a choice, not really. I had to do it, and I would. But with every ally that fell, I lost a piece of the reason I started this war in the first place. I burned down that factory on Rott because I was determined to fight for the people I loved. I would jump off speeding trains, release deadly viruses, and stare down loaded guns, all for a chance to save my family.

What if, when this was all over, my family was the one thing I *didn't* save?

"You might be."

I looked up. Jael sat rigidly, as if posed for a stoic portrait, staring at some unknown point on the blank wall. "You might be alone."

She sighed, then reached up and unclipped her giant earrings. "Have you ever heard of the United Republic of Nasarawa?"

"Um... no," I said, and wondered if I should feel stupid.

She smirked. "I'm not surprised. They did their best to censor us. It's a fancy name for what was left of Nigeria at the end of the 50s. We were independent from the United for almost three years."

I gave that statement the wide-eyed respect it deserved. "No wonder they censored that." The history textbooks they'd used in school had invariably claimed that the entire free world joined the United unanimously and peacefully. Any dissidence came from evil villains who were swiftly arraigned by the government's global justice.

She set her earrings on the coffee table, then started yanking the bangles off her wrists. "They didn't want to engage in nuclear warfare because we controlled the oil fields, and that was a resource too precious to lose. So, they put us under siege and played the long game: Poison."

I swallowed, my throat closing at the word.

Her voice was stiff like a scabbed wound as she relayed the story. "It was a slow genocide. You think you've seen evil; I can't even bring myself to repeat some of the atrocities they committed to try and force us to surrender. They were contaminating water sources, releasing biological weapons, and using chemical warfare that's been outlawed since the first World War."

I shuddered. It didn't take much imagination to picture the pure wickedness.

"I think most of the Western world would have ceded from the United had they found out." Jael twirled a bangle in her hand before stacking it with the others. "The union was still relatively young and fragile. They couldn't afford to tarnish their reputation of perfection. So, their best defense was to silence us."

"What do you mean?"

She slid her phone out of her pocket and stared at the screen contemplatively. "We went for a whole year without electricity and even longer without internet. They released drones that created a dampening field over the entire country. Even our radios didn't work."

I tried to imagine waging a war without any communication; there wouldn't be a "Blue Fire" if it weren't for Jael's control over the algorithm. "How did you fight back?"

"By raising our voice every way we knew how. I forged credentials and snuck across enemy lines to break into an abandoned cell phone tower. I wanted to hack through the dampening field so we could get a signal out."

I studied her as her story pieced together, almost as if she suddenly became a whole person before my eyes. "That's how you got started."

She nodded and smiled at the memory, but the joy quickly faded from her face. "My hope was that if I could release even one video on social media, the United would have to pull back to save face. It might have been enough to turn the war."

She hesitated, and I sensed the guilt in the silence. "It didn't work, did it?"

She didn't answer. Instead, she removed her necklaces one by one, arranging them on the coffee table in a row. She seemed to shrink, like she was shedding a layer of her armor with each piece of jewelry.

"I couldn't get a signal out," she confessed finally, "but I managed to hack into the internal communications for the United army and intercepted their battle plans. They were going to split the front line: Half of their forces would attack our capital, while the other half would bomb the villages on the border. The hope was that our limited defenses would be divided, and we'd lose both fronts."

I gripped the edge of the couch. "What did you do?"

"I had no way to contact anyone. I knew I could make it to our primary military base in time, but they'd have to pick one front or the other. Either we protected the capital, or we saved the villages."

"What did you decide?" I braced myself, knowing, instinctively, that there was no right answer to that question.

"There was no choice." The declaration was bland, final. "All our remaining resources and important personnel were in the capital. If the capital fell, we fell. So, I didn't tell anyone that I knew about the plan to attack the villages." She avoided my eyes. "I didn't want anyone else to have to make that decision."

The silence stretched between us as the weight of her decision took the air out of the room. I felt sick—even as I wondered if I would have made the same choice.

"I'm sorry," I whispered, all the useless condolences dying on my lips.

"They called me a war hero," she said without pride. "We sent all our resources to the capital and caught the United off guard. We held our independence for another six months."

I dreaded the period at the end of this story, but I had to know. "What happened to the villages?"

"Not one survivor. The United razed every single town." She closed her eyes. "Including mine."

The room blurred as everything I thought I knew about Jael came crashing down. All her friends and family were gone—and she let them die.

Oh God, have mercy.

"I won't lie to you, Philadelphia." Tears clogged Jael's voice, tangling with her thick accent and making the words almost unintelligible. "I wish I could say that I'll protect your family, but no one can promise that. When this is all over, you may be alone."

I started to cry, but for who or what, I didn't know.

"But I know you, of all people, have the strength to face that reality."

I sucked in my breath. "What?"

She finally turned to look at me. "When you destroyed that factory on Rott, did you expect to make it out alive?"

I struggled to recall the person I'd been in that moment. I couldn't remember making a conscious decision to die; I couldn't remember thinking about myself at all.

"All you cared about was destroying Red Rain," she finished the thought for me.

I nodded. Anything to keep that vile weapon out of the hands of the government.

"You wouldn't have survived. Even if they didn't execute you, you wouldn't have made it off the island. And the government certainly wouldn't have spared your family. If anything, your crimes would have put them in more danger."

I wanted to deny it, but I couldn't. I knew when I decided to stand up against the United that I was sacrificing myself—and my family.

"You didn't do it for them," Jael insisted. "If your only priority had been to keep your father safe, you would have stayed quiet and let Thames adopt you."

It was true. I'd had so many chances to sit down, shut up, and save myself, just like my father had. But I didn't. I couldn't.

"There was no choice," I repeated her words.

"There wasn't. And that's why I chose you."

I looked up and met her gaze, even though I was terrified of what I would find.

She didn't smile, but her voice betrayed all the admiration her actions did not. "When I saw that video, I knew I'd found someone who would make the right decision even when it cost them everything. Someone who would save the world even if they couldn't save themselves."

Someone like you.

I twisted my fingers in my lap. Was that who I was now? Was that the person God wanted me to be?

She grasped my hands with both of hers. "I'm not asking you to hide your grief, Philadelphia. Your emotions are what makes you human. If you were just a mindless killing machine who only wanted revenge on your enemies, you would be no better than the United."

I held my breath as her words slowly warped and reformed my reality into something clearer, brighter.

"I don't want you to stop crying. I don't want you to stop asking questions. Even when it comes time to put your feelings aside and follow orders, still ask questions. That sensitivity is what makes you the hero and not the villain. Heroes are leaders who give second chances and save life when they can."

Abruptly, I remembered when Stanyard had said the exact same thing.

"You don't kill people, Phil. You save them," he'd declared, gripping my shoulders. *"You give them second chances when they don't deserve them—like me."*

"This war will change you, Philadelphia. There's no way to prevent that." Jael's voice hitched again. "You will be hurt, and you will be scarred. But no matter how many wounds you carry, don't ever, *ever* let this war steal that compassion from you."

Stanyard's next words echoed back to me loudly, almost as if he were sitting in the chair across from us.

"That—that compassion, that innocence—is why I believe in you. That's why I came back for you. That's why I..."

My chest ached as I relived that terrifying, exhilarating moment. *"Why, Stanyard? Why what?"*

"That's why I love you."

Jael rubbed my knuckles. "I can't promise I'll always be there for you. But as long as I am, I'll do everything I can to help you put the pieces of your life back together and manage your emotions. Remember that."

I took the implied invitation. "I don't feel like I've been managing my emotions very well lately," I admitted, thinking of the frequent panic attacks, violent tears, and constant doubt that followed me around like a shadow.

She paused. "You still aren't sleeping, are you?"

I winced. Was it that obvious? I hadn't slept consistently in weeks, not since Nic and I were separated. Losing Stanyard, my uncle, and then the Tangs had only made it worse. I got maybe a few hours a night in fits and spurts—and that was on a good day.

I was exhausted and almost always had a headache, but I thought I'd done a good job of covering it up. I used pain medication and caffeine to make it through the day, and I watched my words carefully, making sure not to snap at anyone even when I felt like committing murder. I didn't want Jael to—

She beat me to it. "You really need to take medication."

I shrugged out of her grasp; taking more drugs was the last thing I should be doing. "I feel all right," I said, hoping she'd buy that more than the textbook *"I'm fine."* "It's just been a lot lately."

"Using every ounce of willpower to hold it together is not doing 'all right,'" she chastised.

I flinched and glanced at her out of the corner of my eye. She arched an eyebrow. "Yes, I can tell, and no, I'm not mad."

I bit my lip.

"I want you to start taking these."

She stretched across the couch to grab her purse. She unzipped it and withdrew a pill bottle, setting the container in my lap. I took it instinctively, even though I wanted to drop it like a live snake. "But I—"

"Philadelphia. I know you're scared because of what happened last time, but I promise you, that incident was as much my fault as it was yours. I take full responsibility."

I wished it was that easy to wipe away the guilt. Last time I'd taken sleep medication, I'd only slept for an hour. Nic had tried to convince me to go back to bed, but I'd refused. Instead, I'd acted with impaired judgment and had a complete mental break, stealing a motorbike and *shooting* Jael in the chest.

It was a mercy the weapon had been set on stun.

Jael touched my arm. "Please stop punishing yourself. You *need* to sleep. You can't fight a war if you're fatigued."

I can't fight a war if I lose control.

"Take two a night about a half-hour before you go to bed. I promise, if you sleep at least six hours, it will not impair your judgment."

But what if I don't sleep? What if something happens in the middle of the night? What if—

"It will also help with your anxiety."

I jerked. "But I don't have—"

"Philadelphia. Stop lying to yourself. You've been kidnapped, separated from your family, had several near-death experiences, and witnessed multiple violent murders. You are not fine." She squeezed my arm. "Frankly, it's a miracle you don't need something stronger."

That's because it is a miracle.

Jael stood up, and I followed. "Just try it for tonight. It's a low dose. If you don't feel any better after a few days, we can do something different. All right?"

I just nodded, knowing that if I used words, the distrust would come out.

She smiled. "Get some sleep."

I hurried to my bedroom and locked the door behind me. Leaning against it, I waited until the lights in the living room shut off and Jael's footsteps faded before letting out a sigh.

I stared at the pill bottle in my hand and rolled her words over in my mind. She was right—it *was* a miracle I didn't need something stronger. I should be scarred beyond repair, but I wasn't, because I had God. The Holy Spirit had put me back together after each and every crisis. He'd healed me before; He would heal me again. I didn't need medication for this.

I *shouldn't* need medication for this.

I gripped the bottle and looked at the ceiling. "I am *healed*," I declared to the empty room.

Then I slammed the bottle down on the nightstand and turned out the light.

10: PHILADELPHIA

It took three hours for me to admit Jael was right.

I wasn't sleeping. And I was very, very anxious.

My chest was so tight that my ribs hurt. My nerves were so agitated that the very air felt thick, like it was oppressively humid inside my room. And every time I closed my eyes, my thoughts whirred louder and louder, growing bigger and scarier until I thought they were going to take form out of the shadows and devour me.

I prayed so hard. I repeated declarations. I recited Scripture out loud. I begged God over and over and over to heal me. Nothing worked. Not even listening to worship music helped, and every failure just made me feel weaker and more alone.

What was wrong with me? I'd seen a *dead man* raised to life because I prayed. Why couldn't I win the battle for a mere six hours of sleep?

What am I doing wrong, God?

If there was an answer, I couldn't hear it around the throbbing in my ears. Everything twitched and buzzed and vibrated, like there were a dozen ghosts vying for space on the bed. I could hear a thousand whispering voices, and none of them were the Holy Spirit. It was loud and dark and hot and *I couldn't take it anymore.*

I sat up and snatched the pill bottle off the nightstand, shaking two capsules into my palm. Jael was right; even being in a drug-induced stupor would be better than this.

I lifted my hand to my mouth, then hesitated. I glanced at the clock; it was after 1am. If I took the pills now, I wouldn't get a full six hours of sleep before my alarm went off. And we all knew what happened when I took medication and didn't sleep.

I sighed and shoved the pills in the pocket of my shorts. It was too late. I'd just have to fake it for another day.

Flopping back on the pillow, I grabbed my tablet and scrolled hopelessly through the empty home screen, searching for any distraction. But of course, there was nothing that hadn't been there five minutes ago.

I swallowed a lump of selfish grief. Stanyard would normally be awake at this time. Up until a week ago, he had always been there for me in the middle of the night, ready to pray or distract me or whatever was needed. He would faithfully send a message every hour, even when I wasn't responding. Sometimes that's all it took—seeing the screen brighten with a notification in the dark room and knowing, without looking, that it was him. The omnipresent feeling of someone praying for me was enough to muffle my anxiety so exhaustion could do its work.

Not anymore. His chat had gone completely silent; even Asia hadn't mentioned him recently. His file, like Nic's, was frozen. All it said was that he was "in custody," the location of his prison carefully redacted.

Where was he now? Did Asia keep him in America, or had she deported him somewhere else? The thought made me feel waterlogged with hopelessness, like driftwood washed up on shore. Tracking him down in America would be hard enough. If she sent him to another continent, we wouldn't find him until it was too late.

Jael had assured me that her people were on it, scouring the internet for any mention of him, but even her power had its limits. Her company had been searching for Nic for over a month without success. Both Nic and Stanyard were as good as dead to us.

I knew they weren't; Asia would have made a spectacle out of their executions. She would keep them alive like cards in her deck until I forced her to show her hand. But if this war didn't go the way she wanted it to—if the rebellion started to win—she might kill them. She might execute Nic and Stanyard and Lev and Bowen and everybody else before we had a chance to liberate them.

By then, it wouldn't matter who won the war.

"You may be alone."

I stifled a sob. Nic and Stanyard had sacrificed everything to help me. Nic wouldn't even have been on Earth if he hadn't come back to save me from Jayde. And Stanyard had been there for me like a rock on the shore, wading through death and unforgiveness and my own insecurities just to be my friend. The thought of leaving their bodies littered in my wake like sheep sacrificed to an unholy cause made me sick.

"I'm so sorry," I whimpered into the empty room.

I knew what Nic would say. Nic would tell me to do what needed to be done and never look back. But what about Stanyard? What was he thinking right now? Did he regret joining the operation? Or was he still worried about me and spending his lonely nights interceding on my behalf?

I knew the answer, and I owed it to him to have the courage to do the same.

I sat up and started a new message to Stanyard. I knew he wouldn't see it, but if—no, *when* he came back online, I wanted him to be able to read through my texts and know that I cared about him just as much as he cared about me.

HEY. I KNOW YOU WON'T SEE THIS FOR AWHILE, BUT I WANT YOU TO KNOW THAT I'M PRAYING FOR YOU.

I hit send and stared at the blinking cursor.

I KNOW GOD IS GOING TO PROTECT YOU.

I put a period on the words, even though I wasn't sure I had enough faith for them.

HE IS YOUR SHIELD. HE IS GOING TO DEFEND YOU, AND HE IS GOING TO DELIVER YOU FROM ASIA. HE'S GOING TO—

As if her ears were burning, Asia chose that moment to send me a text.

HAVING TROUBLE SLEEPING?

I resisted the urge to use a word Nic had taught me and quickly backspaced my message. I'd forgotten Asia had Stanyard's login.

YOU SHOULD BE IN BED, SWEETHEART

So should you. She must have had her notifications on loud, waiting for me to be stupid enough to contact Stanyard or any of our friends.

I KNOW YOU'RE HURTING. I KNOW YOU DON'T WANT TO DO THIS. YOU'RE BEING USED.

By you, I thought about texting back, but didn't.

YOU WERE NEVER MEANT TO BE A SOLDIER. YOU WERE NEVER MEANT TO BE A LEADER. THIS IS NOT WHO YOU ARE.

You have no idea who I am. But I didn't believe it, not really.

LET'S END THIS

Leave me alone! I closed the chat and tossed the tablet towards the end of the bed, but it did no good. She continued to message me, the screen flashing up notification after notification. The irritating *buzz, buzz* of the vibration against the comforter aggravated my headache and set my frayed nerves spinning again.

I growled and threw off the blankets. I couldn't stay in this claustrophobic room a moment longer. It's not like I was in any danger of sleeping, anyway.

Yanking on my shoes and a light jacket, I cracked open the door to my bedroom. The penthouse was dark, and there was silence coming from Jael's suite. The moonlight from the bay windows lit the way as I navigated around the artsy furniture to the front door. I pressed my thumb to the security panel to disengage the alarm. It flashed green and beeped, far louder than was necessary.

I flinched and quickly stepped out into the hall, softly shutting the door behind me. I hurried to the elevator and descended to the ground floor. Surely there was a gym or an empty conference room I could take laps in.

I stepped off the elevator—and shrieked as I walked straight into the broadside of a very large man.

"Sorry, sorry." He flapped his hands. "I didn't mean to scare you. I just saw you coming down the elevator and wanted to make sure everything was all right."

I squinted at his shiny badge and deduced he must be a security guard. "It's fine, I just can't sleep." At least that much wasn't a lie. I glanced around the lobby and saw double glass doors leading to a patio of sorts. "I'm going to get some fresh air," I declared, pointing.

He nodded and stepped back. "Do you want one of us to go with you?"

His partner waved at me from behind the security booth, providing the "us" of that statement.

I grimaced. "Do I get in trouble if I say no?"

The first guard chuckled. "No, Jael said you could go out in the garden."

"Thanks." *Glad to know I'm not a total prisoner.*

"There's security all around the perimeter, and I'll be watching the cameras," the guard behind the counter assured me. He pressed a button to page me through. "Just yell if you need anything. We'll be here all night."

I gave him a grateful smile and pushed the door open.

It wasn't much of a garden. The towering apartment cut off the sky on three sides; the fourth side was blocked by a brick wall so high you couldn't see the street—which was, I suppose, the only reason I was allowed outside. The patio was more concrete than greenery, and what few plants there were had clearly been transplanted against their will. It was austere and fake, but at least there was fresh air. I took a deep breath of the still-warm night and started taking laps.

They were short laps—it took maybe two minutes to get all the way around—but any motion was better than none. I focused on putting one foot in front of the other and counting every step. Around and around I went until I had completed ten laps or more. The repetitive movement drowned out the ringing in my ears, and I thought that maybe, just maybe, I might be tired enough to go back to bed.

That is, until someone disturbed my rhythm.

A noise broke the silence. It sounded like crunching gravel, or like someone had kicked a rock across the patio. I whipped around and scanned the garden, but there was no one there. The yellow lamps cast rippling shadows on the brick as the greenery shook in the hot wind.

"Hello?" I ventured, desperately hoping it was a security guard.

The answer came from behind me.

"Don't move."

I froze, but not because of the admonition. I knew that voice.

Oh God, no.

Very slowly, I turned and looked up. A figure crouched in the shadows on the garden wall. He jumped down onto the patio and stepped forward, bringing his face into the light.

Jayde.

11: PHILADELPHIA

He put both hands up. "Don't scream."

Screaming sounded like a great idea, but I couldn't get enough air as my heart and lungs panicked. *He's going to kill you he's going to—*

He cut off my crazed thoughts. "I'm not going to hurt you."

I wasn't about to fall for that. "How'd you get past security?"

He shrugged. "They'll come to in about twenty minutes."

Jesus, help! I had to alert the guards inside. A quick glance around revealed we were in a corner of the patio out of sight of both the security cameras and the door. I turned to run.

"Wait, please!" Jayde hissed. "I promise I come in peace."

"Prove it," I snapped.

Keeping one hand in the air, he reached towards his holster. Very slowly, he withdrew his electric pistol and held it out, showing me that it was off. Then he stooped, laid it on the ground, and kicked it towards me.

I snatched it and flicked it on. "What are you doing here?"

"I need to talk to you," he said, voice deliberately slow and quiet.

"You have thirty seconds." I braced my feet apart and mentally prepared myself to pull the trigger.

He put both hands back in the air. "It's about the guns that were delivered to the factory."

I hesitated, my grip slacking.

His eyes tracked my movements. "The Tangs weren't the only ones who got a shipment. Crates have been donated to groups all over the province."

"I know that," I snapped, my patience fading. The soldier who betrayed me had said General Jin received a donation and was redistributing the weapons across the city. "What's your point?"

"I know who paid for the guns," he declared, and then paused, as if wanting a reaction.

"Out with it!" *Why are you listening to him? Just shoot him already!*

He obliged. "The General Secretary."

The suggestion was so outlandish that I felt mocked. "What?"

"I can prove it. I've got text messages, money transfers, even a phone conversation." He patted the pocket of his military jacket. "More than enough evidence to prove that the General is funding Operation Blue Fire in Beijing."

"I don't believe that for a second," I huffed. "There is no reason on Earth or Mars that the General would want the rebellion to win. And even if he did suddenly have a come to Jesus moment, he wouldn't be so sloppy as to leave a paper trail that even *you* could find."

"I agree." Jayde lowered his hands. "That's why I think someone framed him and planted the evidence. Someone is forging his signature and using his credentials to pay for the guns."

"But who—" I didn't even finish the sentence. The information snapped together like colliding magnets: The sudden failure of the censors. The government's apparent indifference to my rising popularity. The generous influx of money and weapons being donated to rebel outposts.

And the one person who was guaranteed to have access to the General Secretary's credentials.

"Asia," I breathed, gagging on the realization.

I was right. Our victory *wasn't* God.

Jayde nodded. "That's my guess."

"But how? Why?" I struggled to maintain control of the gun as my thoughts whirled. "Why would she want the operation to succeed?"

"Same reason she wanted you to kill her father," Jayde explained. "She wants power. And the cleanest way for her to seize the throne while maintaining her popularity is for someone else to start the war. If she funds the rebels under her father's name, she can create unrest and scandalize him at the same time."

Operation Blue Fire would give her all that and more. All she had to do was add a little fuel to the fire *I* started.

She's still using you.

It all made wicked, horrifying sense—except for the fact that Jayde had figured it out before anyone else. "How'd you find out about this?"

"I'm military," he returned. "I can access the shipping manifestos for most of the bases in this province. I'm also part of the underground, which means I have plenty of contacts—despite Data's best attempts to excommunicate me."

A taste of bitterness seeped into his voice. I tensed.

He brushed past the transgression. "I also used to work for Thames," he continued. "I have access to a lot of Nolan's systems. And since Asia is using some of his—or should I say, *your* money to fund this venture, all I had to do was pull up your file and cross reference. You literally own the company that distributed the guns."

The thought of Asia using *my* inheritance for her schemes made me boil with rage. But even more disconcerting was the fact that Jayde had been tampering with my accounts.

I shivered. Jayde had worked for Thames and then for me, posing as my bodyguard for several weeks; he'd had intimate access to my devices and credentials as a Nolan. He knew my multiple identities better than I did—making me wonder why he hadn't tracked me down sooner.

"How'd you find me?" I demanded.

"I've been following you this whole time," he declared with absolutely no remorse.

I wished that revelation surprised me more than it did.

"It's not like I didn't know you were with the Tangs. All I had to do was track you from there to here." The condescension in Jayde's voice made me feel like I'd failed a math quiz. "And, if you're wondering how I knew you'd be in the garden, I was watching Stanyard's accounts. When you texted him a half hour ago, I figured you were up late and I might be able to catch you alone. I know you better than you think I do, Phil."

I tightened my grip on the gun. "Well, if I'm so predictable," I snarled, "why didn't you try to talk to me before?"

He snorted. "I'm not stupid. I knew Jael wouldn't let me get close."

"So why are you here now?" Even though he'd managed to get into the garden, he wouldn't have gotten much farther. If I didn't shoot him, I could easily scream and bring security racing to the patio.

"I'm not stupid," he repeated. "If Asia is funding the rebels, that means she knows where all the outposts are."

Lanzhou's morbid warning about Asia retaliating on operation day sent fear shuddering down my spine.

"We'll be worse off if the government slaughters hundreds of thousands of innocent people because we told them where to look."

"The Boston servers," I murmured.

Jayde nodded grimly. "I know what was on those servers— she could have traced the data to dozens, if not hundreds more allies. But she didn't. She just picked off a few big names to make it look like she'd done her due diligence."

"And sent weapons to the rest," I finished for him.

The dread in Jayde's eyes confirmed my fears. "She's orchestrating the whole thing. The entire operation will be a sham."

And a massacre, I thought but didn't have the stomach to say. I knew our sudden success wasn't God; it was Asia, controlling the chess game from a distance, just like she always had. I'd played into her hand yet again, and this time, I'd left the board wide open for her to checkmate.

Oh God, what do I do?

Jayde interrupted my prayer before I could find my courage. "Look, no matter what I think of you," he said, his tone filling in the blanks, "I want Operation Blue Fire to succeed. If we don't stop Asia, she's going to wipe out the entire resistance. We have to warn everyone—and you're the only one who can do that."

I focused on him and realized there was no malice in his expression—only respect.

I straightened. He was right. They wouldn't listen to him; there was no way he or anyone else could warn them in time. But they would listen to me.

I am Blue Fire. And this is my war.

There was, however, one piece of the puzzle still missing. "Why didn't you contact Jael?" I challenged. "I know she reached out to you. If you really 'come in peace,' you should have gone straight to her."

He arched an eyebrow. "Jael wouldn't have set that weapon to stun." He pointed.

I looked down at the weapon and realized he was right. Perhaps instinctively, I'd set it to stun.

I growled and considered changing the setting just to spite him. "You're a coward."

He spread his hands. "I'm your coward."

I *tched* and took my finger off the trigger, but I kept the gun aimed. "Fine. I'll take you to Jael. But I can't promise she won't shoot you on sight."

He indulged in a smile. "You'll make sure that won't happen."

How I wished he wasn't right.

12: PHILADELPHIA

As soon as we got into the lobby, the guards pounced on Jayde—literally. It took all my persuasive speaking skills to convince them not to strangle him. Unsurprisingly, I was the only one who believed him when he said he "came in peace." We finally settled on a compromise: Jayde got a pair of handcuffs while the guards paged Jael.

It took us a few minutes to ride the elevator to her penthouse on the top floor, and she must have used every second to prepare herself. She was staged dramatically right inside the door when we entered, looking as regal as ever, even though I knew we'd woken her up. She took one look at Jayde and then held her hand out to me.

"Gun, please, Philadelphia."

I obliged. She took it, strode up to Jayde—and then backhanded him across the face with the weapon. Jayde cursed and stumbled into the credenza, nearly sending a priceless African vase to the floor.

Jael leered over him. "Give me one good reason why I shouldn't set this to kill and shoot you in the heart," she hissed, barely raising her voice.

Jayde swiped his bleeding cheek on his shoulder and looked to me.

I sighed. "Please, hear him out. He has something to tell you."

"I'm sure he does. His first words better be 'Have mercy on me, for I am a fool.'" Jael put her free hand on her hip and took a step back, if only slightly.

Jayde, to his credit, took the hint. "Yes, I am a fool, but I'm not here to beg for my life. Operation Blue Fire is in jeopardy."

She aimed the gun at his chest. "Do tell."

I kept a wary eye on Jael's trigger finger as Jayde explained everything he'd told me. Jael asked a couple of clarifying questions, then retrieved the flash drive of evidence from his pocket.

"I'm going to cross reference everything. If I find you're lying…" She gestured vaguely.

He looked, for the first time that night, annoyed, if not utterly exhausted. "You think I'd risk turning myself in if this wasn't true? I'm not that dumb."

"No, I suppose not," she consented. She finally turned the gun off and handed it to one of the guards. "Get him out of here. And I shouldn't have to tell you this, but make absolutely sure he doesn't escape. If he tries anything, you know what to do."

"But don't hurt him," I ordered before I could second-guess myself.

The guards hesitated. Jael whirled on me. "Philadelphia, this doesn't concern you."

"Actually, it does." I took a deep breath and tried to find any semblance of autonomy. "He works for the Nolans, which means he answers to me."

Both of Jayde's bright-orange eyebrows shot straight up. The guards exchanged obvious glances. Jael glowered and looked like she was contemplating overruling me, then thought better of it. "Fine. Make sure he's taken care of. But he does *not* have to be comfortable."

I was too tired to argue on that point. The guards obeyed and prodded Jayde out into the hall. He went willingly, giving me one last glance over his shoulder.

I waited until the door had shut behind them before letting out my breath. I turned and looked up into Jael's frown.

"Why didn't you shoot him?" she demanded.

I shrugged. *I wish I knew.*

"He could have hurt you—honestly, the fact that he didn't is the only reason I'm taking his story seriously."

"I know."

She folded her arms. "I guess I'm just a little offended that you'll shoot *me* before you'll shoot him."

I managed a smile. She didn't return it, but she relaxed, her posture loosening. "If he's telling the truth..."

"I don't think he's lying. He's right—he wouldn't risk turning himself in if this wasn't real."

She didn't argue. "Then we have a crisis on our hands."

"Lanzhou was right," I whispered, finally allowing myself to admit it. "Asia is going to slaughter us all."

Grief gripped my throat as I thought of his fatherly smile. *We should have listened to him.*

Jael clucked her tongue. "No, that would be too kind. If she simply wanted to exterminate us, she would have done it before now. If she waits until operation day, everyone will question how she got the information—and why she didn't act sooner."

That made sense, which only made me feel more afraid. "Then what *is* she doing? Why give us weapons?"

Jael drummed her nails on the credenza and stared into space, as if reading invisible meeting notes. "My immediate guess is that she's planning to let us have a false victory. She'll let us gain control of a few population centers and make an advance on the council chambers. The people will question the government's lax response—and that's when she incriminates her father."

I sucked in a breath and felt the air jam inside my lungs. "And then she uses her knowledge of the underground to crush us and restore order."

"She'll be a hero."

"Then we have to warn them," I insisted. "We need to figure out where she sent guns and—"

"It's not that simple." Jael faced me again. "This isn't an organized army; it's a people's resistance. We have no way of tracking down all those guns, let alone the money she donated. And even if we could, the people who received those donations have already started sharing with their neighbors. If Asia does her job right, she'll be able to trace each outpost to a dozen more. There's no telling how many of our allies are potentially compromised."

"Then I'll blow her cover." I pointed at the TV. "Let me go on air and expose her. I'll reveal all of the evidence Jayde gave us, and then the government will take care of her for us."

It was the perfect solution—Asia's own father would murder her if he found out what she was doing—but Jael was already shaking her head, her earrings flopping about hopelessly. "She'll deny it. I'm sure all the evidence Jayde has is forgeable. Text messages can be faked and money can be laundered. If Asia is truly planning on incriminating her father, she'll have prepared a lot more than screenshots. She no doubt has a very intricate plan involving paid witnesses and a strategic reveal to the Council—all of which she'll abandon if she suspects you're onto her."

Jael's despondency weighed the room down, and I struggled not to lose my grip on my courage. "But at least I can warn everyone. They can relocate—"

"Philadelphia. We cannot reorganize the entire operation in less than two weeks," Jael sighed, sounding more exhausted than anything else. "And if you create a scare, we run the risk of losing the entire resistance. If you tell everyone that Asia knows exactly where they are, most of them will abandon ship. There won't be an operation."

I stared at her, begging her to tell me there was another way. "What are you saying?"

She stared back, expression vulnerable. "I don't know."

I gasped for breath as the defeated silence stretched between us. This was it—checkmate. Either I cancelled the operation and ended the resistance for good, or I gave Asia her victory with a failed war.

Either way the United won. The only difference was I might—*might*—save a few lives if I folded.

No. I felt determination shift in the depths of my soul, weak and fluttering like a candle caught in a draft. There wasn't a lot I was confident in right now, but there was one thing I would never deny: God was in control. Asia wasn't the only one playing chess.

Which meant I could not concede the game.

"There has to be another way," I murmured quietly, willing my thoughts to ignite. God had given me miraculous ideas before; He would do it again. I closed my eyes and reached out to the Holy Spirit. *I need Your wisdom!*

Jael was not convinced. "I'm sorry, Philadelphia. If I thought we had enough evidence to convince the government that she's orchestrating this, I'd let you go on air. But we don't…"

Her voice faded as Jayde's chilling words echoed back to me.

"I have access to a lot of Nolan's systems. And since Asia is using some of his—or should I say, your money to fund this venture, all I had to do was pull up your file and cross reference. You literally own the company that distributed the guns."

Asia wasn't the only one involved in this scheme. Thames had been her business partner.

And I was his daughter.

I looked up at Jael. "I know how we can get more evidence."

She stopped mid-sentence.

I took a deep breath. "I need to go back to the Nolan estate."

"What?" she exclaimed, the word barely forming.

"I need to go home," I repeated. "Jayde said Asia is using the Nolans' money to fund this venture. That means my family is involved. If I go home, I can find proof of what she's doing. I may even be able to talk to her and get her to confess—"

"Absolutely not." The bangles on Jael's wrist clacked like a gavel as she swung her arm. "Are you even hearing yourself? You can't just waltz in there and confront her. She'll shoot you on sight."

"But I know there's evidence on my family servers. Jayde said I owned the company that distributed the guns. If I can access my accounts, I can—"

She cut me off again. "Asia won't give you the chance. You'll be dead before you step over the threshold."

I knew that was a risk, but there had to be a way around that. "I know, but just listen to me, please. I know this will work. This has to be why God made me a Nolan. Nic said…"

I didn't finish. I could tell by the way her whole body heaved with a sigh that I was losing her. "Philadelphia. I am not having this conversation again. Enough with this foolishness."

But it's not foolishness! "No, you don't understand. I can—"

"We're done talking. Go back to bed. I'll let you know my decision in the morning." She pulled her phone out of her pocket and turned away.

I reached for her. "But I—"

The Holy Spirit breathed on me. *Stop.*

I pulled back. *No.* I was not taking us down this path again. I would not panic, and I would not argue. Jael and I were partners, which meant I had to treat her with respect—even if I didn't get the same in return.

I waited until my pulse slowed before speaking. "Jael?"

"What?" She continued to swipe on her screen.

"Remember the orders you gave me?"

She glanced up at me over her phone. "Yes, I told you to trust me. And I've decided—"

"You also told me to be honest."

She stopped typing.

I spoke slowly, tempering my tone of voice. "I'm going to be honest with you and tell you what I think. Please hear me out. After I'm done, if you still don't think it's a good idea…" I paused and rallied my courage before continuing, "…then I'll obey."

She turned her screen off and set her device on the credenza, giving me her full attention. "All right. I'm listening."

I took a minute to order my thoughts, determined to use as few superfluous words as possible. "I think we need to expose

Asia. You said yourself—we have no idea how much of the underground has been compromised. We have no way of knowing where those weapons were sent or how many demonstration sites she's tracked down. If we continued as scheduled, she'll slaughter everyone—and use the chaos to make herself general secretary."

Jael didn't argue. She just gestured for me to continue.

"It's impossible to warn everyone or reschedule the demonstrations. The only way to prevent this from being a massacre would be to cancel the operation."

I searched her face for consent. She said nothing, only staring intently into my eyes.

I straightened and forced myself to return her gaze. "But if we can expose her, if we can produce enough evidence that she's funding the operation, we can remove her from power. In fact, the Council will do the work for us. They'll execute her and then go on a witch hunt looking for her allies, and it will throw the government into chaos."

I stiffened when I remembered that Jayde had once said those exact same words to me.

"If you take out the General, it will throw the government into chaos. They'll be scrambling to replace him—and that's when we strike. That's when we launch Operation Blue Fire."

A shiver of raw possibility passed down my spine. Perhaps Jayde hadn't been wrong about everything.

I focused on Jael again. "*That's* when we strike. They'll be cannibalizing themselves; they won't be able to retaliate. And if Asia and her allies are gone, there will be no one to pull the trigger. We won't have to warn anyone—the operation can continued as scheduled."

Jael's gaze drifted elsewhere as she ran the calculations. *Please, God, help her see what I see!*

"And how do you propose we prove it?" Jael asked, but gently. Her eyes returned to mine. "I warned you, everything Jayde has can likely be faked. Asia is a wizard at covering her tracks, and she has plenty of powerful friends. If you want to convince her own father that she's a traitor, you'll need ironclad evidence. Even if she is using your money, simply pulling up your bank statements won't be enough."

I closed my eyes and prepared to reveal what I truly believed. *Holy Spirit, give me the right words!*

"That's why I need to go back to the Nolan estate. If I resume my identity as Andromeda Nolan, I'll have full access to my accounts and Thames's network. I can go anywhere Asia goes, talk to her allies, even show up at a company board meeting—all without raising suspicion. I can catch her in the act. Plus," I made myself talk slowly and clearly even though my mind was racing, "you can modify the router at the Nolan estate. You can bug my devices and the entire house. If she drops even a hint, you'll have video evidence."

I stopped and waited for Jael's response. She continued to stare at me, but her eyes were no longer defensive. She looked simply tired. Sad.

And that's when I knew I was right.

"Philadelphia," she sighed, using the name to brace us both. "I understand what you're saying. I want you to know that I respect your idea, I really do. But it's not that simple. If you go home, Asia will kill you. And that's not a sacrifice I'm willing to make."

I opened my mouth, but she put her hand up. "No, it's my turn to be honest with you. I know this is hard for you to accept, but you are far more valuable than you realize. You are the face of this revolution now."

I wrapped my arms around my chest and wished it wasn't true.

I am Blue Fire.

"If you go back to the Nolan estate, Asia will quietly kill you—or worse, expose your double identities."

That was a possibility I hadn't considered, but I doubted it. "I don't think she will," I calmly argued. "There is no direct evidence linking Andromeda Nolan to Philadelphia Smyrna. Philadelphia died on Rott—I haven't made a single mark on my file since then. The only way for Asia to expose Andromeda's real identity is for her to admit her involvement with Thames. She'd have to reveal that she's known about me this whole time—and she can't afford to do that anymore than I can."

Jael gestured her consent. "Perhaps, but it's far more likely she'd simply kill you and bury the evidence. Then your death will be wasted. I will not sacrifice my most important ally on fool's errand. I'm sorry, Philadelphia, but if you go home, even I won't be able to protect you."

I knew she was right. If I went back to the Nolan estate, I would be facing Asia alone and unarmed. But there had to be another way. There had to be something I could use as insurance, a trap I could set so that she couldn't quietly sweep me under the rug.

Suddenly, it came to me: the rook God had moved to the side of the board for this very moment.

"Unless…" I looked back up at Jael. "I invite her father over for dinner."

She frowned. "What do you mean?"

"At the state gala. I told the General I would love to host him for dinner—and he accepted."

I remembered the moment with all five senses. The Summer Palace, soaked in incense and bathed in the light of a hundred lanterns. The rustle of dresses and suits as Beijing's elite vied for favor. The clack of my heels on the wooden platform as I approached the General Secretary.

I had stared at him, wondering for one final moment if I should kill him. And then I'd lifted my skirts and bowed. My dress had glittered in the flash of a dozen cameras as the press captured the moment forever.

"We—I—would love to have you visit again. It would be my deepest honor to serve you."

The crowd had been appalled. Asia had been mildly impressed. The General had weighed my life in the scales—and found me worthy.

"I would be delighted to receive your invitation."

For the first time in weeks, I felt powerful—the power that came with influence and wealth. This, *this* was why I was a Nolan. This was why I had been allowed to go to the party, why the General had taken a liking to me, why the Holy Spirit had given me such audacious words. This was the plan all along.

For such a time as this.

"If I send the General an invitation, he'll accept—I know he will." I explained with both hands, drawing a battle plan in the air for Jael and I to see. "And if he does, Asia won't be able to just dispose of me. If I mysteriously vanish or drop dead right after inviting the General over for dinner, he'll ask questions. Asia will have to play along, at least for a few days—long enough for us to get the evidence we need."

Jael didn't respond. She stared out the balcony doors at the black night, silent.

I opened my mouth to make another argument, then stopped.

I'd said enough. I'd promised to tell the truth and then wait for her orders, and I meant it. The decision was hers now—and I could trust her to make the right one.

Give her wisdom, Father.

Jael took a breath, long and heavy, through her nose. "I have some calls to make. I need to verify all of Jayde's evidence and make sure everything he says is true." She turned back to me. "It will take some time."

I nodded. "Yes, ma'am."

"We'll talk in the morning," she said, and it was a promise. She tapped her phone and checked the clock. "Go back to bed. I know it's late, but I want you to get at least five more hours of sleep..."

She paused, and I knew what was coming.

She frowned at me. "Why were you even up wandering around in the garden? The medication should have kicked in hours ago."

I looked down, but I didn't deny it. My face would have told the truth anyways.

There was a beat. "Where are they?"

I pulled the two pills from my pocket and held them out.

She walked around the kitchen island and fetched a glass from the cupboard. "Why didn't you take them? We just talked about this."

Her voice was calm, but the patience was brittle. "I know," I mumbled, and didn't defend myself.

"Is it because of what happened a few weeks ago? I told you, nobody holds that against you, not even me." She filled the glass with water from the dispenser on the fridge.

"I mean, yes, but…"

"And I promise, it will not impair your judgment if you follow directions. If you have any negative side effects, we'll stop, no questions asked. Is that what you're worried about?"

"Yes, maybe, but…" I repeated, trailing off again. It was all of those things and none of those things.

She walked back over to me. "Then what is it?"

I stared at the floor, trying to mash the truth into words.

She set the glass on the credenza. "I promise not to be upset. But *you* promised to be honest with me."

I looked up into her face. "I don't know how to explain this, but… I just… I don't understand why prayer's not working."

She arched an eyebrow, and I almost lost my nerve. The rest of the truth gushed out in a puddle. "I mean, I saw Nic raised from the *dead*. I've seen so many miracles—I shouldn't have made it out of Rott alive, or Wing 74, or even that stupid state gala. I shouldn't even be standing here, and now I don't—"

"You don't know what you're doing wrong," she cut me off softly.

I flushed and nodded. At least she understood.

She studied me. "Did you ever consider that the fact you've survived so much is the reason you need medication?"

I frowned and waited for her to explain.

"Philadelphia, you have been through more trauma than any teenage girl should have to bear. All those experiences, miraculous or not, taught your brain that the world is not a safe place. You've been in survival mode for so long that your body doesn't know how to turn it off—that's why you're anxious."

The pinch in my chest told me she was right. Every time I thought I was safe, the people or places I relied on were taken away. What if it happened again? What if I lost Jael next?

She interrupted my thoughts before they could gain any more momentum. "All this medication does is help your body remember what 'normal' is. It's like giving you a blanket so you can get warm."

I looked down at the pills in my palm.

She held the water out to me. "Thank you for being honest and telling me how you feel. But now I need you to trust me when I say this will help you."

I took the glass. "But if I take these now, I'll sleep 'til noon."

"I'll wait. I promise I won't make any decisions without you, and I promise not to murder Jayde in a rage."

She smirked, and I found myself smiling—just a little.

She laid her hand on my arm. "Do you trust me, Philadelphia?"

The Holy Spirit echoed her question.

Do you trust her?

I did, I truly did. I firmly believed God had put Jael in my life.

Then do you trust Me?

I took a deep breath, then swallowed both pills and washed them down. They settled in the pit of my stomach like coal.

Jael squeezed my shoulder. "Get some sleep."

13: NIC

I'm not sure how long I knelt there. Long enough that the chemicals I'd spilled permanently scarred the linoleum, filling the room with the ripe scent of burnt plastic. I stared at the oozing cuts on my palms and wondered why I'd bothered. I felt crusty and drained and pathetic and generally worse than before.

Just then, the door opened. "Nic! Where you been? We got the new guy settled, and—*whoa!*"

I groaned. It was Ryan. And Vance, judging by the heavy set of footsteps that followed.

Great, I muttered, struggling to rise. *As if I didn't already hate myself enough.*

"What happened here?" Ryan squawked.

"Looks like he dropped some beakers," Vance brilliantly deduced.

"More like the whole cabinet," Ryan corrected. "Oh no, wait, he missed one on the top shelf."

"I'll clean it up." I waded through the broken glass to retrieve the spill kit from across the room.

Vance continued to lecture. "Why did you have that many beakers out at one time? You should only take out what you need for your experiment, in case of an accident like this."

Oh, it wasn't an accident. I grabbed the kit off the wall and turned around.

Ryan read my face, and his expression softened like melted butter.

Vance was oblivious. "Did you spill hydrogen peroxide?" He sniffed the air. "If that had combined with any of the iodides on that table…"

"Uh, Vance?" Ryan tapped his arm.

Vance didn't even feel it. "Even an errant splash of vinegar could have created peroxyacetic acid, and we all know how corrosive that is."

Ryan slapped him again. "Yo, *Vance*."

"Not to mention, you're not even wearing any personal protective gear. Honestly, you're lucky no one got hurt—"

Ryan jumped three feet off the ground to swat Vance in the back of the head. "Vance! Read the room, for crying out loud!"

Vance finally stopped and looked me in the eye. "Oh."

I opened the kit and pulled on a pair of gloves. "Just stay back."

Ryan ignored both interpretations of that order. He tiptoed around the mess and came to stand beside me. "What's wrong, friend?"

"Nothing…" I started, then clarified before either of them could object. "Nothing I can talk about."

The Voice in my head reentered the chat. *That's not true.*

I glared over my shoulder at the corner where He was figuratively standing. "Fine," I said aloud, "nothing I *want* to talk about."

Ryan leaned over to see what I was staring at. "Oh, is God here? Are we interrupting?"

"Yes," I snapped, and then was immediately convicted. "No."

Ryan waved in God's general direction, then looked back up at me. "So, what's going on? I need details."

I wasn't about to explain why I'd ended up sniveling on the floor of the lab surrounded by a thousand dollars' worth of broken glass, but I knew neither them nor the Voice in my head would accept an excuse.

I was quiet long enough that Vance felt the need to fill the silence. "We talked to the warden."

I grimaced. "What did she say?"

"That you're in *big* trouble for kicking her out of her own office and then ignoring her," Ryan quipped. "Bro, are you trying to get yourself sent to solitary?"

Being in solitary sounded like heaven right now. I stared at the bottle of sodium bicarbonate in my hand and contemplated turning myself in.

"Nic." Ryan elbowed me. "Talk to us. We can't help you if you don't tell us what's going on."

I slammed the bottle down on the table, viscerally remembering the time I'd said those exact same words to Philadelphia.

It was before she'd left for China on her suicide mission. She was training to kill and exerting herself to the point of passing out. Stanyard wisely inferred that something was wrong and alerted me.

I'd immediately called Phil and demanded answers. Admittedly, my first reaction was to come at her in a rage; I was so appalled that she'd lied to me, a sin I didn't know she was capable of. But when I saw how terrified she was, I got over myself and begged her to tell me what was going on.

My head throbbed as I recalled the fear, the heartbreak, the maddening knowledge that *I could fix it.* I knew I could help her. I knew I could save her. I knew I could spare her a world of pain—if she would just let me in.

The Holy Spirit hovered by my shoulder, no doubt feeling the exact same way.

I sighed and straightened. "Okay."

Ryan pulled over a desk chair and sat in it backwards. Vance walked across the room and joined us.

I stared at the ceiling and ordered my thoughts, trying to find the shortest path to the truth. "You know Blue Fire—Philadelphia Smyrna?"

"Uh, *yeah*," Ryan huffed. "We're not that sheltered."

"Who is she to you?" Vance asked. If the words hadn't been beleaguered by a coarse German accent, I would have thought it was the Voice in my head speaking.

I looked both of them in the eye and claimed my identity. "She's my daughter."

Vance, somewhat to my disappointment, just nodded, as if that was the answer he'd been expecting all along.

Ryan, at least, had the decency to give that declaration the slack-jawed, wide-eyed shock it deserved. "Wait, *you're* Dr. Smyrna?"

"What? No! My last name is Von Nieuwenhuyse—you know that." I glared down at him.

"Yeah, well, I didn't know if that was a code name or whatever. Why does Blue Fire call you Dr. Smyrna then?"

"I'm *not* Smyrna," I insisted, trying and failing not to be offended by the association. "That's her father."

Ryan squinted at me. "But you just said you were her dad."

I put both hands up to pause the conversation. "I mean, he's her biological father. I'm... adopted."

"Aww, that's great, buddy. Me too." Ryan folded his arms on the back of the chair and grinned. "So, how did you meet Blue Fire?"

"What do you mean, 'how did I meet her'? I'm the governor."

"Governor of what?"

"The base."

"Like a base for the resistance, or...?"

"No, the base on Mars! Have you not seen any of her videos?"

"Only clips," he admitted with a shrug. "And she definitely never mentioned you or Mars."

"She talks about Mars all the time!" I gestured at the empty space next to me, as if she were standing there, corroborating my story. "That's how this whole Shakespearean tragedy started—I summoned her family to Mars."

"Actually," Vance piped up, "Mars and Project 74 are a relatively small part of her story. A prologue, really. Rott was the incident that made her famous, and she's spent considerably more screentime discussing it. You've been featured in only about 13% of her original videos, not accounting for commentaries and reposts."

I whirled on him. "I assure you, I have affected way more than 13% of her life. Also, how would you know?"

He blinked. "I have access to personnel files in accounting. I've known who you are for about three weeks and have been doing some research."

"First of all, that's creepy. Second of all, how long were you going to let us carry on this asinine conversation?" I flicked my hand at Ryan.

He pouted. "Hey, it's not my fault you don't know how to use proper nouns, pal."

Vance shrugged. "I figured it was your story to tell."

I threw up my hands. "I don't need to tell you if you've already researched my whole life!"

"Well, this is all news to me, so I'd like to hear it from the beginning," Ryan inserted, scooting his chair closer.

"Yes, I think that would be very therapeutic," Vance agreed, and claimed his own chair.

I groaned. *Do I really have to do this?* I asked the Voice in my head.

Do I really have to answer that? He replied.

I rubbed my temples. *Please, anybody but them.*

No, exactly them.

Ryan yawned and drummed his fingers on his arm. "Let us know when you're done arguing with the Lord."

With a grunt that was ignored by all three of them, I dragged over another chair and surrendered.

I told them everything—or at least the highlight reel. I told them how I'd met Asia and attempted to create an apocalyptic superweapon. How Smyrna had finished it and Philadelphia had destroyed it. How I'd gone from wanting to kill her to making her my legal dependent—and how we were both stranded on Earth while various groups of people tried to either save or end the world in her name.

Both Vance and Ryan listened with rapt attention. Vance only interrupted when he thought I was omitting important details. Ryan, on the other hand, provided sound effects as he overreacted to every plot twist.

"Well," he declared when I finally reached the end, "that does explain a lot."

"Thank you for sharing," Vance said, and almost smiled.

I would have appreciated the gesture had I not still felt like a shipwreck. Wasn't therapy supposed to make you feel better?

Ryan rocked his chair and glanced around the ruined lab. "We need to get you a better anger management strategy, though. Have you thought about learning karate?"

"I took three years of it in high school," I admitted. "It had the opposite effect."

"What about yoga?" Vance suggested. "I lead a class every Thursday."

"He's a great teacher, too." Ryan put his arms behind his back and contorted in a way that shouldn't have been humanly possible.

"I'll check my calendar. In the meantime…" I brought my PhDs back online and tried to decide which of my insurmountable problems I should agonize over.

"Oh yeah, we gotta fix this Blue Fire thing first." Ryan spun his chair around and sat in it the normal way. "I think Philadelphia needs him more than we do, right, Vance?"

He nodded. "Arguably, we don't need him at all."

"Love you, too," I muttered.

Ryan pounded a fist on the table. "Then we have no choice."

"Agreed," Vance grunted.

Ryan stood and pointed a finger in my face. "We gotta get you out of here."

"You're… busting me out?" I gaped at them and wondered if I'd undervalued our friendship.

"Oh no!" Ryan put his hands up and slid back. "I ain't risking my promotion for you. Have you seen what she does to escapees?"

Several times. I glanced at the regeneration scar on my forearm.

"No, no, we gotta do this legally. You need to talk to the warden," Ryan declared.

"What's she going to do?" I scoffed. I may have earned some privileges by saving her factory, but I was still a prisoner—a fact she'd made abundantly clear.

"I think you underestimate the power of money," Vance inserted.

I turned to face him. His bushy eyebrows narrated as he explained, "Your reengineering of the factory has more than doubled profits. Her personal salary has increased by a factor of ten—and that's without me falsely reallocating resources. If you calculate in the fraud, you're looking at annual net gains in the millions."

I nodded and tried to pretend he hadn't just admitted to a crime.

"That kind of profitability doesn't go unnoticed. I've overheard some of her recent phone conversations. She is soliciting larger contracts, which creates a favorable supply and demand ratio, which under normal market conditions leads to better clients and more consistent profits..." Vance checked off boxes with his fingers.

"He's saying she owes you one," Ryan translated.

I doubted Ivanova had a healthy concept of justice, but maybe Vance was right—maybe the money would speak for me.

"At least try," Ryan pleaded. "What could it hurt?"

"I guess I've already bared my soul twice today," I growled, standing up. "Why not do it again in front of the woman who controls my life? Sounds delightful."

"That's the spirit!" Ryan crowed. "Besides, we kinda told her we'd find you and send you up, so... you have to talk to her anyway."

I shot him a glare. He shrugged. "I just do what I'm told."

Vance rose and laid a weighty hand on my shoulder. "This is the right thing to do. Trust us."

I didn't particularly trust them, but I did trust the One who had very obviously sent them.

And for Philadelphia, anything was worth the risk.

"All right," I consented, "I'll talk to her."

"Great! Let's go." Ryan took a broad step forward—and his boot crunched on glass. "Well… maybe we should clean this up first."

14: PHILADELPHIA

I was right: It was almost noon by the time I woke up.

It took over ten minutes for me to come to full consciousness. The first thing I registered was the warm light pooling at the bottom of the blackout curtains, then the sound of Jael talking softly on the phone in the living room. I rolled over and tapped my tablet, looking at the clock. *11:37.*

I sighed. A whole day wasted.

I sat up and tried to decide if I felt any better. My back ached and my head felt weighed down like a soaked blanket—but maybe that was because this was the first time in over a month that I'd slept for eight hours straight.

At least the medication worked.

I threw the covers back and reached for my tablet—then stopped. My leather-bound Bible sat on the nightstand. Stanyard had bought it off the black market as a gift for me. It was one of the few personal belongings I'd brought to China, and in some sinful irony, I'd barely read it since.

I picked it up and rubbed the water damage on the corner of the pages. I used to *love* the Bible. I wouldn't go anywhere without my reader, and I spent every spare moment scrolling through the digital pages. Now I had a gorgeous, rare paper edition, and it just collected dust on my nightstand. What changed?

The Holy Spirit sent the answer, gentle but firm. *You changed.*

I gripped the book to my chest and let the conviction break down something inside of me. I'd spent all this time running and hiding and surviving that I'd fallen out of the habit. I'd been so concerned about fulfilling the one message God had given Nic that I'd forgotten the Holy Spirit had given me a thousand other messages in this Book.

I sat cross-legged on the bed and spread the book in my lap. I'd already slept until noon—the world could wait another fifteen minutes.

I'd read Phillipians and gotten halfway through Colossians when I heard Jael's heels clacking on the kitchen floor and decided I'd better get up. I showered and washed my hair as quickly as I could, then threw on a clean sundress Jael had loaned me.

She met me in the living room with a cup of fresh coffee. "You slept well."

"Yeah," I admitted, and gratefully accepted the hot mug.

She gestured at the sofa. "How do you feel?"

I settled down and took a sip before replying. "Good, I think." My muscles were still sluggish, but I didn't have a headache.

And the anxiety's gone, I realized abruptly. My chest wasn't tight, and my nerves weren't frayed. I could take a full breath without feeling like I was swallowing water. I felt almost— almost—normal.

I stared at the dark brown liquid in my cup and wondered how much of that was the medication.

Jael sat down on the loveseat across from me. "Excellent. I, on the other hand, did not get any sleep, because as much as it pains me to admit it, you're right."

I jolted out of my thoughts, sloshing my coffee. "I am?"

She nodded, the gesture slow and final. "You're going home."

I gripped my mug as that declaration filled me with elation, then terror.

"I cross-referenced all the information Jayde had on his flash drive, and it appears legitimate. I was able to replicate almost everything." She picked her phone up off the coffee table and tapped the screen. "I also checked the recent activity on Andromeda's file, and he's right—the Nolans have been investing in some suspicious business ventures lately."

I bristled. *That's my money.*

Jael set her device aside. "I have no doubts now that she's the generous 'benefactor' who donated those weapons, which means our best hope of saving the operation is for you to expose her. If there's not enough evidence on Thames's servers, then ideally you can get her to admit her own guilt on tape. Even if you can trick her into sending a text while connected to your router, that might be enough for us to turn the Council against her."

"I can do it," I declared. That was one thing I was confident of: Asia would talk to me whether she realized it or not.

Jael put her own mug down and leaned forward. "I will not lie to you. This is incredibly dangerous. Asia may be desperate enough to kill you and accept the consequences."

She might be—but I didn't believe it. It would be too risky once I involved her father, and Asia would avoid an unnecessary mess until the last possible moment.

"And even if you succeed... I should say, *especially* if you succeed, she may kill you before I can get you out of there."

That I believed. If Asia thought the ship was sinking, she'd take me down with her.

"But by then we will have saved the revolution," I returned.

"I knew you'd say that." Jael smiled, but it was a pained gesture, like she was closing the door after saying a long goodbye.

I fought a wave of trepidation and returned the smile. "I am Blue Fire."

And the captain always goes down with the ship.

"That you are." Jael glanced away, and I saw her shuffle her emotions aside like papers swept off a desk. When she turned back to me, the determination had returned to her eyes. "I know I said I wouldn't make any decisions without you, but I took the liberty of drafting your guest list."

"My what?" My brain tried and failed to shift gears.

"For the dinner party."

I put my mug down. "But I only need to invite the General."

She shook her head and grunted. "No. First of all, that's terrible etiquette. Just because he thinks you're cute doesn't mean someone of your status can invite him over *alone*. He'd never accept, and Asia would correctly assume the worst."

She had a point; it would definitely look suspicious if I attempted to arrange a private meeting with Asia's father. "So, what are you suggesting?"

"If this is going to look legitimate, you need to throw a *party*." She shoved her device across the table towards me.

I picked it up and scrolled down the screen. She'd compiled a list of two dozen names; the only ones I recognized were Asia and General Secretary Mong.

"You'll raise fewer eyebrows if you throw a large dinner party and invite a crowd. We're stretching the bounds of propriety since you're giving them less than a week's notice, but I have a friend whose birthday is this month who will 'just so happen' to be in town—that's excuse enough."

I struggled to hold onto the phone as my palm grew clammy. The thought of entertaining the General was unnerving enough. But playing hostess for two dozen elites who were almost as powerful as he?

Holy Spirit, I need help.

"Honestly, I'm not expecting the General to attend—it's too short notice," Jael admitted. "The invite is a courtesy gesture, really. He will probably send back a 'regret to decline,' which will be enough to make Asia think twice about hurting you."

I tried not to let her logic disappoint me. "Who do you think will come?" I handed the phone back to her.

"Hopefully, almost everyone else will make the effort once they hear Asia is attending. I'm inviting some people I suspect might be her allies. If we're lucky, some *baijiu* will stimulate gossip, and we can pick up incriminating evidence on tape." Jael took a suggestive sip of her own drink. "There will also be several of your allies there, along with people I'm hoping to sway to your side. If this plan fails and we can't prove Asia's treachery, then we need more friends in high places."

I nodded even as I tried to sweep the despondent thoughts aside. *This is going to work.*

"Of course, I will also be honored to receive your invitation."

I looked up. Jael winked, and my shoulders relaxed. At least I wouldn't have to face this party alone.

"You'll have to pretend that we've never met, but I'm sure we'll hit it off right away. Let me make the introductions, and then just follow my lead. I'll make it clear who you should talk to who you should ignore."

I struggled to catch up as the plan snapped together—too quickly. "Okay, but what evidence should I be looking for on Thames's servers? Should I download company files, or...?"

Jael's diamond rings flashed as she flicked her fingers dismissively. "I'll handle that. Once I've modified your router, I'll have remote access to everything that belongs to Andromeda Nolan. I'll copy what I need and cover my tracks. I don't want Asia to get suspicious because you're suddenly showing an extreme interest in your financial investments."

I sighed. She was right—and that meant I was back to being a pretty face while everyone else did the hard work. "So, what *do* you need me to do?"

"Besides serve as hostess, provide the food and venue, and put together an entire dinner party in less than five days?" Jael smirked wryly. "I need you to do what you do best—make people love you."

I flushed.

"It's a compliment," she assured me. "I don't know if you've noticed, but you have an uncanny talent for making friends—the General himself being a prime example."

But that wasn't me, I silently protested. *That was the Holy Spirit.*

The response came like a breath of air. *So, use Me.*

I caught myself grinning.

"If all goes to plan, half of the people at the party will be your mortal enemies. Don't act like it," Jael ordered. "Treat them as equals. If anyone invites you to a function, accept. Every invitation is a potential alliance. I'll help you organize your calendar later."

I stiffened as Nic's words rattled around in my soul.

"I saw it all. You, in Beijing, as a Nolan, on even playing ground with Asia."

"I'll warn you—Asia *will* know you have ulterior motives. There's absolutely no way we can convince her you've gotten scared and quit the revolution, not after..." Jael stumbled over the silence, "...after all this time."

My heart autofilled what she'd been too polite to say.

Not after I left Nic and Stanyard for dead.

Jael clicked her tongue. "So, we're going to use that against her. I want you to waltz in there and pretend like nothing is wrong. There is no Blue Fire, you don't know anything about the revolution, and you and Asia are the best of friends. If anyone asks where you've been for the past month, tell them you were visiting family in America. I'll edit your file to match."

"Got it," I said, even as I began mentally rehearsing the words.

Jael leaned over to get in my line of vision. "If Asia questions you, play innocent. It will drive her mad—and that's when she'll make a mistake. If we're lucky, she'll confront you, and we'll get it on tape."

I nodded and took a grounding breath. I could do this—I could play chess with Asia.

I am Andromeda Nolan.

Jael reached across the table and found my hand. "Be careful. You're playing her game now, Andromeda."

I stared at the steam fading from our mugs as I remembered the ostentatious house, the costly dresses, the extravagant dinners. All the elites who fawned over me and told me how delighted they were to meet me. And the gracious Holy Spirit words that flowed off my lips as I smiled and bowed and blended into their ranks like I'd been born there.

And this is how I will fight my war.

"No," I said, looking up. "We're playing mine."

15: NIC

It took us most of the rest of the day to reset the lab. I'm not saying I stalled, but I am saying the lab hasn't been that clean in fifty years.

Vance and Ryan finally kicked me out. I ascended the elevator alone—humanly speaking.

I watched the floor number on the panel scroll up like a reverse time bomb. "You know how You said I could always ask for Your help?"

He didn't respond. He didn't need to.

I swallowed the last of my disobedience. "I need You."

He still didn't say anything, but His presence followed me out of the elevator and down the hall.

The door to Warden Ivanova's office was open. I approached the guards standing watch outside. "Is the warden—"

She answered for herself. "Von Nieuwenhuyse!" she bellowed. The shout echoed beautifully around the acoustics of the open factory until I was sure ten floors heard her.

I waited until my ears stopped ringing. "Well, it was nice knowing you," I said to the guards. "Please don't let Vance read the eulogy at my funeral."

One of them nodded. "I'll do my best."

I took a deep breath, smoothed my hair, and walked into the office.

She was posed behind her desk, fingers tented menacingly. "How do you take it?" she demanded.

I held back by the door. "Take what, my punishment? Anything but a freefall over the railing will be fine, thank you."

"No, your coffee." She reached for a carafe.

"Oh… uh, black."

She filled a mug and held it out to me.

I approached the desk and took it. "I feel confused and vaguely threatened."

She leaned back in her chair, crossing one leg over the other. "I figured after all those theatrics that you'd have a *great* story to tell me, so I brought refreshments. Sit."

I obeyed, flopping in a chair in front of the desk.

She picked up her own mug. "Start talking."

I downed half my coffee in one rallying gulp, then started from the beginning. I got through the story much more quickly the second time, mainly because the warden didn't interrupt me—or react at all.

"Is that the whole truth?" she said when I was done.

"Regrettably."

She picked at her teeth. "I'll admit, I thought you were being facetious when you said Asia sent you here because you dumped her."

"No, that's pretty much what happened." I finished the last of my coffee and set the mug on the desk. "So, can I go home now?"

She snorted. "Absolutely not."

What little hope I had came crashing down like a toy castle. I couldn't decide whether to be upset that I was still stuck here or annoyed that I even tried. "But—"

She put her hand up. "Trust me, if there was *any* way to get rid of you, I would have done it already."

"Charmed."

"But I don't know if you've looked at your file lately, but you've been flagged with the highest national security warning there is. The only people who could pardon you are Asia and the General Secretary himself."

I rolled my eyes; Asia always had to go the extra mile. "I'm not asking for a pardon. Just stage an accident and say I died or something cool like that, and I'll slip out the back door."

She was already shaking her head. "Asia's not stupid. Unless I have a body, she won't buy it. And then it will be my head on the chopping block."

The Voice in my head told me not to make a sarcastic comeback, so I didn't.

Warden Ivanova folded her arms on the desk and leaned forward. "Do you know why I'm so strict about discipline?"

"Because you had a bad childhood and your father never told you he loved you?"

"That too. But the main reason is because all the criminals here are security risks. If any of them escape and actually manage to make it down the mountain, I have to answer for it."

"And I take it they don't just slap your wrist and tell you to do better next time."

She nodded grimly. "I like you, but I'm not dying for you."

I groaned. A year ago, I would have gladly jumped ship and not cared who got hurt in my wake. But now I had too much integrity for such behavior, a fact that immensely irritated me.

She echoed the sigh. "I'm sorry, Nic. I mean it. But you're not getting out of here any sooner than I am."

There was a catch in her voice, and I wondered if I wasn't the only ex-friend Asia had earmarked for destruction.

The warden's flicker of humanity was gone as soon as it came. "Take the week off."

I shook my head. "Thanks, but I'd rather work."

"I wasn't making a request."

"Neither was I." I wanted—no, *needed* to work.

She arched an eyebrow. "I saw what you did to that lab."

I cringed. "You can take it out of my allowance?"

"You're lucky. We're rolling in profits, so the damage you caused is hardly a blip on my radar. Otherwise, I can assure you, this conversation would have gone *very* differently." She fingered her holster.

I swallowed. Maybe Vance was right; maybe I should take up yoga.

The warden stood up. "I'm not putting you in solitary because it's at capacity right now. But I don't want to see you anywhere near the lab or any of the equipment on the line—have I made myself clear?"

I could tell by her tone that arguing would be fruitless and potentially very painful. "Yes, ma'am."

She nodded and gestured at the door. I promptly saw myself out.

I hurried down the hall until I was out of sight of any guards. Then I walked up to the railing and braced myself on it.

"Now what?" I prompted the Voice in my head.

There was no response.

I knew what that meant. And it was the one answer I didn't want to hear.

Wait.

The factory continued to churn around me, unheeding. The concentric levels stretched as far as the eye could see, sparkling with lights and moving equipment. Elevators passed up and down the hollow center as the sounds of enterprise echoed in the open space. The building thrummed with activity, but I couldn't hear any of it.

All I could hear was thunderous, cavernous silence.

16: PHILADELPHIA

I stayed at Jael's apartment for one more night. She wanted to wait until the invites were received and word about the party got around before I made my appearance. We sent the gilded envelopes by private courier that afternoon, and several of my allies enthusiastically RSVP'd by nightfall.

Asia did not respond. She did, however, block me and delete her account on the messaging app, which I took as a favorable sign. I'd caught her off-guard by making the first move, and, for a brief moment, I had the upper hand.

We spent the rest of the afternoon recording. I went live and did exactly what Jael ordered: I pretended nothing was wrong. With a fierce glare and too much eyeliner, I shouted war cries into the camera and challenged people to the fight. Every word broke my heart; if this mission failed, I would be sending people to their deaths. But Jael was right; we had to fool Asia into thinking Operation Blue Fire was still on schedule. She couldn't know that we were on to her.

I then batch-recorded several hours of generic speeches for Jael to reuse while I was gone. As far as the rest of the world was concerned, Philadelphia Smyrna would be hard at work in the trenches for the next week. Only Asia would know that I'd switched identities, and I hoped the knowledge would drive her insane.

By the time we were finished, I was so exhausted that I didn't think twice about taking my medication. I retired early and slept for ten hours straight. Jael had to drag me out of bed in the morning, a fact she was immensely pleased by.

Even I had to admit that I felt better, but no amount of pills could suppress the rising dread as I packed what few belongings I had. As soon as I left this building, I would become Andromeda Nolan again, with nothing but my wits and social influence to protect me.

Jael escorted me to the elevator. "I want you to keep this on you at all times." She held out Nic's old phone.

I took it and rubbed the crack on the screen, fighting painful memories. This was the phone Nic had on him while we were running across Beijing. He'd registered it to Andromeda since my file wasn't flagged. I hadn't turned it on in almost a month, but now that Andromeda was back from "vacation," there was no reason I couldn't use it.

"I installed some advanced recording and location tracking software," Jael explained as she called the ground level. "Do not go anywhere without it, not even in your own house. I want to know exactly where you are and hear everything you hear." She stared at the floor number as it counted down. "Of course, I won't be able to help you if Asia pulls a gun, but if she says anything incriminating, at least I'll have it on tape."

I nodded and slid the device in my pocket. Guns were the least of my worries right now.

The elevator *pinged* and opened. Jael led the way to the front door, eyes on her phone. "When you arrive, you'll find the internet is out. One of my men will be there to 'fix' your router this evening."

I knew what she meant. She'd done the same thing to the Tangs' router, modifying the settings so most of their internet traffic bypassed the algorithm. With a little tweaking, my house would be safe from the surveillance state—relatively speaking.

"My tech is going to tell you that there's an issue with your wiring and he's sending an electrician tomorrow to run a diagnostic," Jael continued. "I want to make sure the house isn't bugged and then install my own surveillance. Until he's finished, don't say anything you don't want Asia to hear."

I shuddered but nodded.

"Now, listen carefully." Jael pocketed her device and glared at me. "If this is going to work, it has to be authentic. As soon as you walk out that door, you're no longer Philadelphia Smyrna—you're Andromeda Nolan."

I checked to make sure the thunderbird tattoo on my right shoulder—the brand that permanently marked me as Blue Fire—was covered by my shirt sleeve. I wore my blue contacts and had spent an hour putting on my makeup this morning. Andromeda Nolan was truly back from vacation.

"That means you act like her, talk like her, even *breathe* like her. I don't want you to think about the operation or worry about finding evidence. You are the lady of the house, and your job is to plan a dinner party, nothing more."

I fixed my posture and stood up straight. "Yes, ma'am," I said, my voice demure and smooth, the same way I spoke to Asia.

If Jael was impressed, she didn't show it. "From here on out, this is a blackout mission. You don't text anybody, call anybody, record any videos, or go online without my permission. The only people you talk to are your household staff."

I nodded, but the motion sent a weight dropping to my stomach. I knew I was walking into the lion's den, but I'd never once considered that I'd be unable to call even Jael. What if something happened?

My objections must have made it onto my face. "I'll be monitoring everything remotely," she assured. "And I'll be able to contact you if I need you."

"What if *I* need to contact you?" I returned.

"Then you'll send a message through him." She looked past me and flicked her finger.

I spun around. Jayde stepped out from a side hallway where he had apparently been waiting the entire time. He was uncuffed, and he'd shaved and put on his dress uniform.

He was also, notably, armed.

I clenched my fists as the sight of him ignited my fight or flight response. "What's he doing here?"

"He's your bodyguard," Jael replied.

Jayde bowed and tapped his heart with his white-gloved hand. "I serve the Nolan family," he agreed, voice devoid of emotion.

I had to admit it was a reasonable ruse. Jayde had been employed by the Nolans under false pretenses for as long as I'd known him. He'd come to Beijing under the guise of being a member of my security team, and presumably, that's what the official paperwork still said.

But that didn't change the fact that the last thing Jayde wanted to do was protect me. He wouldn't let me die; he needed me, at least for now. But he was not my friend, and I definitely didn't trust him to follow me around with a loaded gun.

Not after what he did to me.

My hands and face went numb—but then I remembered that the conversation didn't have to be one-sided. I took a deep breath and faced Jael. "I'm sorry, but I'm not comfortable being around him." I measured my words carefully, pulling the facts from the raw, unprocessed emotions. "I don't trust him."

"Neither do I," she declared. She jerked her head at Jayde. "Show her."

I glanced back at him. He hesitated.

"Show her," Jael repeated, all the politeness stripped from her voice, "or I'll demonstrate how it works." She pulled a shiny object about the size of a car key from her pocket and twirled it in her fingers.

Jayde grunted. With visible reluctance, he reached up and unbuttoned his starched jacket. He pulled down the collar of his shirt, revealing a flashing device implanted in the base of his neck.

"I'll be monitoring his position, heartrate, everything." Jael patted her phone in her pocket. "I can hear everything he can. And if I hear anything I don't like…" She shrugged.

I sucked in my breath.

"All the wiring's removable," she crooned. "Once a dog's been trained, it can walk off leash."

Jayde flushed a ferocious shade of red.

"Until then, you have the clicker." Jael held the slender object out to me. It was a keyring with a single button on it.

I didn't have to ask what the button did. I forced myself to take the device and put it in my backpack.

"Look." Jael put her hand on her hip. "He's not my first choice either. But running errands between us is going to be extremely dangerous. At least if he gets caught, he won't tell Asia anything she doesn't already know."

She had a point. Asia already knew Jayde was involved in the underground, and he didn't have any information that she couldn't scalp from the Boston servers—except for one fatal detail.

"He can tell her you're involved, though," I whispered, and hoped I didn't just give Jayde any sadistic ideas.

"What part of 'I'm wearing a shock collar' did you miss?" Jayde snarled. "I'm not stupid."

"He's not," Jael consented. "And in any case, he can't prove anything. There is absolutely no digital record that you and I have ever talked. You don't even have my phone number, Philadelphia."

I instinctively reached for Nic's phone in my pocket and realized she was right.

"I'm aware of the risks. But I am the one person in this operation most able to protect myself. No one can wipe a digital trail better than me—not even Asia." Jael's eyes glinted as she smirked. "Everything she knows about covering her tracks, she learned from me."

I searched her face and wondered, for the first time, how far back Jael and Asia went.

Jael stepped forward, closing the gap between us. She laid her hand on my arm. "I promise I will be watching. I can't control Asia, but I will know what everyone else is thinking before they do. For once, the algorithm is your friend."

I nodded and reminded myself who was in charge. *You do not have to be in control anymore.*

"Let me do the investigating. I know what we're looking for, and I can do it without leaving a digital trail. I just need you to open the door and buy me time."

We don't have much time. Operation day was in less than two weeks. If I didn't pull this off, it would be all-out war—and Asia would win.

Jael's acrylic nails dug into my arm as she gripped my elbow. "I'll be at the party and will give you further instructions. Until then, your job is to win friends. Every person you meet is a potential ally. I want you to think of nothing else besides impressing these people."

I took a deep breath and inhaled a wave of courage. They would love me—because I had the Holy Spirit.

I am Andromeda Nolan.

"Philadelphia."

I looked up into Jael's eyes.

She smiled. "Remember your orders."

Trust. Be honest. And do not give place to guilt.

I returned the gesture. "Yes, ma'am."

17: PHILADELPHIA

Jael hired a car to drive us across town to the Nolan estate. Jayde respectfully took shotgun next to the driver and religiously avoided looking at me. I sat alone in the backseat and watched out the window as the chaos of the inner city melted into the manicured affluence of Beijing's most elite district. After about fifteen minutes of driving past gated courtyards, we turned a corner and entered the Nolans' neighborhood.

The street was lined with everything from all-glass structures to miniature palaces that looked like temples. But the Nolan estate was by far the most beautiful home on the block, managing to be both elegant and tasteful. It was modeled after a traditional villa, with a square of two-story halls shielding a private courtyard. The glittering white stone walls contrasted with the black tile roof and the imposing iron phoenix statues that guarded the front door.

I stared at the gorgeous structure as we slowed to a stop, trying, yet again, to grasp the fact that I *owned* it. I'd grown comfortable with the label "Andromeda Nolan." I'd come to expect the surprise on people's faces when they heard my last name. I'd even gotten over the shock of looking at my bank account and seeing a mathematically improbable number of zeros. But I still hadn't gotten used to the *house.*

Ominously, the front gate was open. I failed to swallow the fear in my throat as the driver parked at the curb. Maybe Asia had been telling the truth when she said I could come home anytime.

I'm about to find out.

Jayde opened my door as I thanked the driver. I stepped onto the sidewalk and strode towards the house, struggling not to trip over my heels or my insecurities. Jael had loaned me a business skirt set and an assortment of diamond jewelry, so at least I was dressed like I belonged in this neighborhood.

The phoenixes cast their long shadows over me as I approached the front door. "My name is Andromeda Nolan," I whispered, more for the spirits that were listening than for myself. "And God has given me this house."

I pressed my thumb to the keypad—and it chirped and flashed green.

Jayde echoed the sentiment as he held the door open. "Welcome home, Miss Nolan."

I stepped into the foyer and was instantly greeted with a shout and harried footsteps. "Nolan *Xiaojie!* You've returned."

I looked up to see Peng, the Nolans' houseman, approach. He looked exactly like the butler from a classic movie, with his stout frame and pressed uniform, which I supposed was not an inaccurate description of his role in my life.

He bowed low. "It's so good to have you home. How was your trip to America?"

I faked a smile and wondered who had told him. "Pleasant, but it was much too hot." It actually probably wasn't that hot in Boston in early September, but it sounded like something a rich person on holiday would say.

"I wish I could say we're faring much better." He straightened and wiped his brow for effect. "But I've just had the pool serviced, so it's ready for you when you need a reprieve."

"Excellent," I said, even though jumping in the water was the furthest thought from my mind. I gestured at Jayde. "Will you see that the lieutenant is set up in his old quarters?"

"I can find my way," Jayde interrupted. He gave me a hasty bow. "If you need anything, just call." He hurried away before I could respond, apparently as eager to get out of my presence as I was to get out of his. I let out the breath I'd been holding for the last hour and hoped Peng didn't notice.

There was clattering as the driver dropped my luggage—most of which was borrowed from Jael—on the stoop. Peng scurried forward to collect it. "Shall I call the maid? You must be exhausted from your flight."

The last thing I wanted was for a maid to invade my privacy, but I knew that wasn't what Andromeda Nolan would say. *You are the lady of this house now.* "Yes, thank you. Will you tell the staff I'd like to meet with them in an hour? We have a party to plan."

Peng tipped his head to one side. "May I inquire of the occasion?"

"I apologize that it's such short notice," I said with authority, "but I just found out it's my friend's birthday and she happens to be in town this week, so I'm planning to host her and a few friends on Friday night."

More like her and two dozen of the most influential people in the world.

Surprise flashed across Peng's expression before quickly being replaced by joy. "What a delight! It's been so long since we've had an event—it will be an honor to host again."

I kept the plastic smile on my face. If only he had any idea *why* we were having a party.

"I'd be thrilled to help you coordinate the details, if you'd like the assistance," he offered.

"Please," I said, a little too desperately. "If you could also call Narissa and book an appointment for tomorrow, that would be very helpful. Tell her to expect it to take all afternoon." I tugged on my neglected hair self-consciously.

"Of course, ma'am," Peng replied, already pulling out his device.

"Thank you." I strode across the black-and-white tile foyer towards the staircase. I grabbed the curved iron railing and glanced back. "Oh, and Peng? Please tell the chef to set an extra place at the table. I'm expecting Councilwoman Mong for dinner."

*

Asia must have been across town at the council chambers, because she arrived precisely twenty-six minutes after I unlocked the front door. I heard the squeal of tires through my open balcony, followed by the slam of the front door and her screeched, *"Where is she?"*

She was livid. I smirked. *Forgetting our manners already, Asia?*

"Madame Mong!" Peng joined the conversation. "So good to see you again. Miss Nolan is resting in her room."

"I'm going up there." The announcement was unnecessary; the clack of her heels on the tile was so loud that it filled the entire stairwell.

"Ms. Mong, I must protest," Peng panted after her. "Andromeda is recovering from a very long flight. I simply cannot allow her to be disturbed."

Asia ignored him and stormed up to my bedroom door. "Andromeda!" She rattled the handle, but of course, I'd locked it.

"Beg pardon!" Peng exclaimed, sounding like a ruffled chicken. The door handle bounced as he pried her hand off of it. "Andromeda gave strict orders that she be left alone."

"I give the orders," Asia snapped.

"Not in this house."

The comeback was smooth and quiet, almost too quiet to hear. I stifled a laugh.

Asia, for her part, was speechless. I could only imagine the facial expression that went with it.

"Now, Andromeda will be down shortly. In the meantime, won't you join me in the courtyard for a sip of coffee?" Peng's soothing professionalism returned like an afternoon breeze. "I'd love your opinion on the azaleas I just planted on the east wall..."

Their voices faded as he guided her down the stairs. I turned away from the door with a grin, making a mental note to add a bonus to Peng's paycheck.

I had told Peng I would meet with the staff in an hour, and I intended to make Asia wait for every single second. In any case, it took me nearly fifteen minutes to find an appropriate outfit. Thanks to the benevolence of Thames Nolan, my suite contained a massive walk-in closet with more clothes than I could wear in a lifetime. I ruffled through the hundreds of hangers until I found a fashionable but relaxed black jumpsuit and a smart pair of sandals.

I twirled before the mirrored wall and briefly wondered what Mrs. Nolan would think. Cynthia Nolan had strong opinions about what my life as Andromeda Nolan should be—or she did, before her husband Thames's crimes were discovered and he killed himself. I shivered at the visceral memory.

Mrs. Nolan had refused Asia's offer of amnesty and chosen to join the underground instead. She'd accepted the fact that we would never be mother and daughter, but I knew she still thought about it. I could tell by the way she gave me long looks out of the corner of her eye when she thought I wouldn't notice.

I touched my reflection. In some strange irony, throwing this party was the closest I would ever come to fulfilling Mrs. Nolan's fantasy. I wished, not for the first time, that she'd come to Beijing with me; she could teach me how to host like a lady. But she'd chosen to stay behind in Boston and oversee my dad's revival, a sacrifice for which I was deeply grateful. Last I heard, she was hiding off the grid with my dad and Data.

I prayed for her safety, then hurried to the bathroom to put the rest of my costume together. A maid arrived and helped me salvage my hair and makeup. By the time we were done, I looked like a wealthy housewife ready to run errands—which was exactly the persona I wanted to project.

At precisely the turn of the hour, I left my suite and descended the stairs to the foyer. Peng's congenial chatter echoed from the inner courtyard. He was bustling around the planter boxes next to the pool, pointing out this blossom and that blossom with pride. Asia reclined in a chair on the patio. She had one leg crossed over the other and twirled an empty glass in one hand as she watched my houseman like he was a circus act.

I paused in the shadows of the empty living room and collected my courage. Once I walked out that door, there was no turning back. Even if Asia didn't try to kill me, I wouldn't be able to leave until this mission was complete. Either Andromeda Nolan would win this game of chess, or she would die trying.

I took a long breath through my nose. *Go with me, Jesus.*

Then I plastered on a smile and waltzed out into the sunshine to greet my mortal enemy.

"Asia!" I beamed, as if there were no one in the world I'd rather see.

She uncurled from the chair slowly, like a snake woken from a nap. She turned and stared at me, expression cold and suspicious.

She didn't say anything, so I took the lead. I flounced over and hugged her.

Her glass hit the tile and shattered.

"Oh my!" Peng exclaimed. "I'll get it."

I pretended not to notice. I gave Asia's shoulders a defiant squeeze and stepped back.

She leaned as far away as she could without falling out of the chair and gave me the same look Nic usually did when I hugged him.

I grinned. "I missed you."

She rebooted. "I missed you, too." Her voice held no pretense, and the darkness faded from her eyes. She stood up and nudged a shard of glass with her shoe. "I'm so sorry about the glass."

I waved off the transgression. "Don't even worry about it." Almost before I finished the sentence, Peng reappeared with a broom and dustpan and began cleaning it up.

Asia moved out of his way. "How was America?"

The question was casual, as was my reply. "Oh, it was a good visit, but I'm glad to be back. To be honest, I'm thinking of selling the house in Boston."

She arched one thin eyebrow.

I gazed at the pool as it sparkled in the noonday sun. "You were right—I belong here. Besides, there's nothing for me back in Boston… is there?"

I dropped my tone on the end of the sentence ever-so-slightly. Peng didn't notice, but Asia did. I cast her a hard glare out of the corner of my eye. *You hurt me, and I won't forget that.*

She stared back. She wasn't afraid, but there was one beat, two before she responded. "Indeed," she finally said.

Peng straightened with the dustpan in hand. "All better! The staff is ready, if you are, Miss Nolan."

"Oh, yes, perfect timing! Won't you join us, Asia?" I put my perky demeanor back on like a cloak. "I would love your input on the menu."

Peng led the way across the courtyard. Asia followed a few paces behind. "Menu?" she repeated.

"Yes! I'm having a dinner party this Friday. Didn't you get my invitation?"

"Yes—"

"Are you coming?" I spoke over her. "I didn't get your RSVP." I glanced over my shoulder and smiled sweetly.

She frowned, bloodred lips curled in annoyance. "Of course. I wouldn't miss it."

No. You wouldn't dare.

"Wonderful!" I waltzed into the house—and almost tripped on the threshold when I saw how many people were gathered in the kitchen. There were nearly a dozen uniformed employees standing around the island. I swallowed as my inadequacies caught up to me. I knew I had a staff; I didn't realize I had *that big* of a staff.

Asia brushed past me. "Everything all right, Andromeda?"

I roused myself. "Yes, just still dealing with jet lag. Would you make some coffee?" I glanced at my chef—or at least the man

I thought I remembered was the chef. I wasn't convinced coffee would actually calm my nerves, but at least holding the mug would give me something natural to do with my hands.

The chef obeyed me. While he clattered around in the pantry, I faced the rest of my staff. "Thank you for taking time out of your busy schedules to have this meeting. I know this party is horribly short notice, but it's for a close friend, and it will mean the world to me if we can show her a good time."

Asia claimed a seat off to the side. My employees simply stared at me expectantly. I twisted my pants in my fingers. What was I supposed to say now? Should I just tell them what to do? What *was* there to do? I'd never planned a party before in my life; there hadn't been a reason to celebrate when I was growing up in the containment camps.

I decided to start with the facts. "I'm expecting about twenty people. It will be an informal dress code for the guests, but I'd like all of us looking our best."

I received a few nods of acknowledgement. I found a breath of confidence—and then lost it when Jayde slid into the kitchen. He glanced at Asia and then took up station in the back corner, his eyes on me. I involuntarily stared back as my next sentence died on my lips.

The front door chimed, buying me a minute to gather my thoughts. "Beg pardon," Peng said, and excused himself to answer it.

The chef held out a mug, which I gratefully accepted. "I want my friend to see the best of China while she's visiting," I continued, making the words up as I went along. I intentionally looked at everyone except Jayde. "I'd love to serve a traditional family-style feast. I'm thinking an assortment of dumplings to start, then perhaps pork ribs for the main—"

I only got halfway through the list before Peng interrupted me. "Miss Nolan!" he called. "You'll want to take this."

Setting my mug on the counter, I apologized to my staff and hurried to the foyer. The annoying clack of Asia's heels followed me.

Peng held the door open. I stepped out onto the porch and was greeted by a soldier in dress uniform. "Miss Andromeda Nolan?" he asked. An SUV with the United seal idled on the road.

I reminded myself that Andromeda was friends with the law and smiled. "Yes, how may I help you?"

The tassels on his uniform fluttered as he bowed and held out a white envelope in one elegant motion. "His Excellency General Secretary Mong sends his regards."

He responded to my invitation! I took the card and slit the seal.

Asia hovered behind me, her strong perfume choking the air.

I deliberately ignored her as I pulled out the familiar embossed RSVP card. I skimmed the text, expecting a "regret to decline."

Instead, a bold checkmark decorated the box next to "honored to attend." In the margin, a note was written with a drippy fountain pen:

THANK YOU FOR THINKING OF ME. I LOOK FORWARD TO SEEING YOU AGAIN. —M

18: PHILADELPHIA

I stood there, staring at the brazen checkmark as that simple stroke of ink changed my life.

He accepted! Jael had been so convinced that the General wouldn't attend the party that I'd started to believe her. Surely, it was too short notice. Surely, I wasn't important enough.

I was wrong. The most powerful man in the world had cleared his calendar on less than a week's notice—for me. Why?

I rubbed my finger over his signature. *What are You doing, Holy Spirit?*

The soldier shifted, politely reminding me of his presence. I looked up and realized he was expecting a response.

"Tell His Excellency that I'm honored," I said, and hoped I didn't sound as shocked as I felt, "and I'm also very much looking forward to seeing him."

That must have been an acceptable reply, because the soldier nodded, bowed again, and returned to his vehicle.

I stumbled inside the house. "What is it?" Asia demanded, then snatched the card from my hand before I could even think about answering.

"Your father is coming to the party," I said, more for myself than for her. My thoughts restarted in a panic when I realized what this meant. *He's coming. The General Secretary is coming! Here! To my house! And I only have three days to get ready!*

Asia glared at the card as if she suspected it was a fake. Then, abruptly, she grinned.

"Oh, this is just wonderful!" she crowed. "I'm so glad you two will have some time together."

She sounded like she meant it. *Does she?*

"Come on, we have a party to plan! Goodness, there's so much to do." Asia grabbed my wrist and hauled me towards the kitchen. I tried not to trip over my own feet as I ran to keep up.

She pulled me around the corner, briefly out of Peng's sight. Before I could react, she spun me around and yanked me towards her. I was too startled to cry out as she gripped my shoulders and leered over me. Her sickly-sweet breath brushed my neck, and for a terrifying moment, I wondered if it was over.

"You want to play games, Philadelphia?" she hissed, her painted lips almost touching my ear. "Then let's play."

She shoved me away from her. I crashed into the wall, rattling a picture frame. Asia regarded the spectacle for a moment, then winked and led the way down the hall.

*

I spent the rest of the day fighting to keep Asia from taking over my life.

The old Asia—the one who gushed and crooned and suffocated me with compliments—returned in a blink like someone had changed the language settings on a device. She herded me back into the kitchen and seized control of the party planning with the enthusiasm of a drill sergeant. Suddenly, this was the most important event of the year, and she was going to make sure it was *perfect.*

While I secretly appreciated the help—since I had absolutely no idea what I was doing—I did *not* appreciate the fact that she started ordering my servants around and making decisions as if I wasn't there. This was my party—a fact I reminded her of several times with varying degrees of politeness—and I wasn't about to become a bystander in my own house.

Asia wasn't listening, but Peng was. Every time Asia gave an order, Peng would stop the conversation and look to me for approval. He even had the audacity to disagree with Asia's recommendations on several points. It drove her so mad that she finally decided to save time and start asking my opinion first.

The next few hours were a blur. I made so many decisions that I couldn't remember any of them. A menu was planned, musicians were contracted, and an assortment of flowers and lanterns were ordered. Of course, it wasn't just the house that needed to be decorated; I also had to look flawless, and Asia had strong opinions on that subject, as usual. In addition to my appointment with Narissa, Asia also booked three other beauty treatments she insisted I needed. By then, I was so tired of pretending to be an adult that I didn't have the energy to argue.

It was long past dark by the time she finally excused herself. I was beginning to worry that she'd never leave; maybe that was her plan, to haunt me like a shadow until she could safely dispose of me.

Much to my relief, however, she seemed to understand that I wasn't going anywhere. The General Secretary was coming to dinner; neither she nor I could make a move before Friday. Until the party was over, it was stalemate.

"See you tomorrow," she said as she flounced out the door, and it was a threat.

She left without eating dinner, leaving my chef slightly miffed that he'd cooked for two. I, on the other hand, was very grateful for the peace and quiet of the empty dining room—in part because Jayde finally made himself scarce. He'd hovered in my peripheral all day. He never spoke and never came close, but he was always *there*, watching me like a parole officer. Multiple times I thought about telling him off, but I didn't want to make a scene in front of Asia.

It was after eleven when I limped up the stairs to my suite. I kicked my shoes into the corner and flopped out on the bed. The mountain of purple-blue pillows caught me like a cloud, and I thought that maybe, just maybe, I could sleep without medication.

But I knew what Jael would say to that.

I rolled over and grabbed my backpack off the nightstand. I didn't relish the idea of taking medication with Jayde in the house and Asia a few minutes away, but I also knew what would happen if I didn't. I couldn't be anxious at this party; if I made a mistake in front of the General because I was jittery and sleep-deprived, the operation would fail.

I swallowed the pills with a prayer. *Protect me, Jesus.*

I leaned back on the pillows and waited for the pounding in my heart to slow. It would take at least twenty minutes for the medication to kick in, but I knew exactly what to do to pass the time.

I turned off all the lamps so the only light came from the fairy netting above my bed. Grabbing my Bible, I buried myself in the covers and fell asleep reading under the stars.

Eight hours later, I woke to the sound of my cat clawing at the door.

"Tommy, stop it," I groaned into the pillow. I rolled over, groping for my phone—and that's when I realized what I'd said.

I jerked upright. The sound came again; it was definitely an animal pawing at my bedroom door. *The Nolans don't have pets... and Tommy's back in America with John and Dowe. Isn't he?*

Of course, it wouldn't be the first time John and Dowe randomly appeared somewhere they shouldn't have been.

I slid out of bed and shrugged on a robe. The animal heard me coming and responded with whimpering and slobbery panting. *Please don't be John and Dowe.* I braced myself and threw the door open.

A fat, wrinkly pug sat in the hall.

We stared at each other. His tongue hung out of his mouth as he struggled to breathe through his flat nose. His bulbous eyes were nearly lost in the excessive folds of skin. He looked like a stack of pancakes, and he was so chubby that he could barely keep himself upright.

"Where did—" I started.

He took that as an invitation, yipping and jumping up on my leg. I jerked and almost fell backwards. "Off!"

"His name is Frank."

I whirled. A man about my brother's age stood down the hall, holding a steaming teacup. He wore a house robe and slippers and leaned against the railing like he owned the place. "Morning," he chirped.

I stared at him and tried to decide whether to feel scared or confused or question reality altogether. "What?" was the only word I could get out.

"His name is Frank," the man repeated. A light British accent coated his voice like butter on toast. "The dog."

That seemed like completely irrelevant information when there was a man I didn't recognize in my house at seven o'clock in the morning. "And your name is…?"

"Oh, my apologies, Cardiff."

"And you are…?"

"A lot of things. As far as what's relevant to you… I'm your 'older brother.'"

The quotes were audible, and I abruptly remembered what Mrs. Nolan had said when we first met.

"It's just us, only kid is grown, so we have the spare bedroom, all ready for you."

The man nodded at me with his teacup. "Cardiff Nolan," he repeated, in case I hadn't put two and two together.

I took a second look, and this time, I could see Thames written all over him. The broad shoulders, the dark hair, the chiseled face. He carried himself with the same posh confidence, movements slow and precise like he could bend time and space around him. The only difference was that Cardiff's lips were permanently curled, like he was on the verge of bursting into laughter.

Somehow, that was even more disturbing than Thames's cruel benevolence.

"I thought... I thought you were..." I stuttered and tried to come up with a reasonable explanation for why I didn't expect him to be standing in his own house.

"I've been on a science station in deep space for the last three years," he explained, pushing himself away from the railing. "And yes, I'm aware Mother and Father never talked about me."

His voice darkened, and his entire attitude changed like someone had snuffed out a candle. He seemed to grow taller and more intimidating as he scowled at some invisible ghost past my shoulder.

Suddenly, everything made sense and nothing made sense at the same time.

He blinked and almost dropped his teacup, as if he, too, were surprised by his mood. "But never mind that. He's gone and Mother won't answer my calls, so it's really a moot point. Here, I brought you something."

I felt like we should address one if not both of those statements about his parents, but he didn't give me the chance. He set his teacup on its saucer—*who wanders around the house with a teacup and saucer?*—to reach into the pocket of his velvet robe. He withdrew a jewelry box and held it out to me.

I walked over and took it, despite my better judgment. I opened it to find the most beautiful keychain I had ever seen. Nine charms shaped like planets dangled from a silver ring. The largest charm was a clear glass ball with orange-and-white gas suspended inside. It swirled mesmerizingly like the surface of a planet.

"It's real gas and particles harvested from Jupiter's atmosphere," he explained. "There's a magnet in the center that keeps it in motion. I thought you might like it."

I did, very much. I looked up into his face and saw he was grinning. It was a genuine smile, like he'd been waiting for years to give me this gift.

Maybe he had.

"Thank you," I said, closing the box. "Did they... tell you about me?"

"Of course. They've been planning to bring you home for over two years. What, you think they tried to convince me that my cousin had miraculously come back from the dead?"

I didn't know what I thought—but at this point, nothing would have surprised me.

He frowned. "I remember Andromeda. You're *nothing* like her."

I grimaced. It was easy to forget that "Andromeda" was a real person—or, she had been. Thames's brother and sister-in-law had a daughter who would have been about my age. The whole family had died in a car crash years ago. Except, according to the paperwork, Andromeda survived. Thames had modified her file and bribed witnesses to make it seem like his niece never died, all so that he could adopt me and give me a new identity out of her ashes.

"I know who you are." Cardiff swirled his tea. "I know all about Mars, and Red Rain, and Dr. Nic. I know Jayde isn't here just to be your bodyguard. I know you're responsible for this revolution—and doing a mighty fine job of ruffling some feathers, if I do say so myself."

"How did..." I didn't finish the question. I didn't need to. If Cardiff had access to Thames's servers on Mars—let alone my credentials as Andromeda—then he knew everything.

Including, perhaps, the real reason I'd come back to the Nolan estate.

He took a sip and smiled at me over the rim of his cup. "I'm delighted to finally meet you, *Philadelphia.*"

I slid back and almost stepped on Frank, who was hovering by my ankle. "*Don't* call me that."

He blew a raspberry. "Oh, pish posh. Don't be that way. Your secret is perfectly safe with me."

"Why should I trust you?" I demanded, and hoped he had a really good answer to that question.

"Because I don't fancy jail?" he replied, which wasn't the worst explanation ever. "Your alibi is my alibi. We're both Nolans. Revealing that I'm related to the United's most wanted criminal would soil the family name—not to mention, put quite a damper on our financial situation."

Regrettably, he was right. Thames was our father, which meant his crimes were our crimes. Cardiff would suffer just as much as I would if he exposed the truth behind my adoption. Until further notice, he and I were in this together.

Which was also, inconveniently, why I couldn't tell him to go back to his space station and leave me alone.

I folded my arms. "Why did you come home now?"

"Besides the fact that my science mission completed its orbit?" He shrugged and set his cup down on its saucer with a *clink.* "Someone has to run this estate now that the old man's gone."

I thought I was running this estate.

"On the subject of our mutual financial interests..." Cardiff pulled a phone out of the pocket of his robe and flicked across the screen. "Since you've been largely absent for the past several months, I took the liberty of having my financial advisor reinvest some of your shares. We can review the reports later, but I'm personally pleased with the returns."

I bristled. Apparently, Asia wasn't the only one who had been tampering with my inheritance. I started to object—but Frank decided he lacked attention. He rudely licked me on the leg. I squealed and almost fell over.

Cardiff applauded the spectacle. "Aww, you two are precious. He's so excited about the party—he can't wait to meet new people."

I not-so-subtly pushed Frank away with my foot. "Who says you're coming to the party?"

"I live here," he chirped. "Besides, I wouldn't miss this for the world. Speaking of... what time is it?" He pocketed his phone, then reached into the apparently bottomless folds of his robe and pulled out a pocket watch, of all things.

Why didn't he just check the time on his phone?

He popped the cover and squinted at the face. "Don't you have a hair appointment in an hour?"

I did have a hair appointment in an hour, but that was really none of his business. "How do you know?"

"Asia mentioned it."

"You already talked to Asia?"

"She's in the living room."

I groaned and hoped she could hear me from across the house.

Cardiff chuckled. "Welcome to the family, darling."

19: PHILADELPHIA

Frank insisted on following me back to my room. He followed me to the closet, around the bed, and then back to the closet again. The stupid dog even followed me into the bathroom. He chased my heel all the way down the stairs, nearly tripping me in the foyer.

Cardiff thought the situation was "positively adorable." I would have been more amicable had the dog's breathing not sounded like a car without a muffler.

Frank finally gave up on me when he spotted Asia lounging the dining room. He yipped and jumped straight in her lap, inducing an ungodly shriek. That made it *all* worth it.

Asia kicked him off and turned her attention to me. She rattled off a dozen updates that made it clear she had been up early modifying my itinerary. I was still disoriented from being dragged out of bed by a slobbering dog and a weird man who claimed to be my brother, which left me with no patience for her scheming. I glared at her and snapped, "Since when were you my secretary?"

I'm not sure who was more appalled by my attitude—me or her. Cardiff laughed so hard he snorted tea back into his cup. Peng salvaged the situation by stepping up and giving me the same information, just in a much more respectful manner.

Asia recovered and started whining about how I'd be late to my appointment with Narissa. I told her Narissa would wait, grabbed my Bible and my breakfast, and flounced out to the courtyard in defiance of them all. I'd be lying if I said I didn't do it partially to annoy her, but I was finally getting back into the habit of reading the Bible before starting my day, and I wasn't going to ruin it for a hair appointment.

Besides, I needed all the grace I could get if I was going to survive another day with Asia.

She insisted on coming with me to my appointment. Jayde appeared out of the woodwork and said he was driving, and then Cardiff decided a "family outing" would be delightful and joined the party. I tried to get one or all three of them to stay home, but they weren't listening to me.

I caught Jayde in the hallway as we were preparing to leave. "You are *not* coming with me," I announced in a tone I hoped was authoritative.

He glanced around. That's when I realized we were alone— too late to stop him from backing me into a corner. I stumbled and rammed into the wall. He blocked the way and leaned over me, face inches from mine.

I fumbled with my backpack, scrambling to find the clicker.

He pretended not to notice. "Jael sends a message," he whispered.

I stopped.

"Seoul called. Your father went through surgery last night. They haven't woken him up yet, but so far he's recovering well."

My breath caught in my throat as a grateful prayer struggled to break free. *Thank you, Jesus!*

"Lieutenant!" Asia screeched from around the corner. "Where is the car? We're late!"

Jayde stood back. "And yes, I'm coming with you. You're not leaving the house without a guard." Then he strode off before I could argue.

The ride to Narissa's studio was twenty-five minutes of pure agony. Asia's prattling was already torturous; Cardiff made it worse. He overreacted to all her comments and prodded her for details, which in turn made Asia even more dramatic. What's worse, I couldn't tell if he was doing it for the reaction, or if he actually enjoyed Asia's company. I wasn't sure Asia knew, either.

The only consolation was that Jayde hated it as much as I did. When we pulled up to Narissa's studio, he politely informed me that he would wait in the car.

He immediately regretted that choice when Cardiff also volunteered to stay behind.

Asia unnecessarily escorted me into the studio. The artsy salon was empty. All the black-and-chrome surfaces were polished to a shine, glinting in the morning sun that streamed through the bay windows. Soft zither music and the tinkle of the waterfall in the back of the room floated through the air, giving the salon the aura of a temple.

Asia shattered it when she banged on the bell at the front desk. "Narissa!"

"I heard the bell."

Narissa slid out from the back, wearing her usual all-black pant set. With her cropped hair and sharp winged eyeliner, she perfectly matched the aesthetic of the studio, almost as if the building had been modeled after her.

She gave me a *hmm* that I knew was the closest I'd get to a hello, then turned her glare on Asia. "Do you have an appointment?"

"She does." Asia flicked her hand at me, as if my presence weren't obvious.

"I didn't ask about her."

"I'll be staying…"

Narissa didn't even let her finish. She just turned and pointed at the sign on the door that said "no walk ins."

Asia bristled, looking like a hissing cat ready to scratch.

"Oh, calm yourself," Narissa droned. She walked over and grabbed a cape off the back of a salon chair. "It's not like you can't review the footage later."

I flinched. Narissa was blind—or she had been, until she'd received robotic eye implants funded by the government. Now, she could do more than just see; she could take measurements, match foundation shades, and communicate with her dress fabricator, all from her mind. The only drawback was that the algorithm heard everything.

Asia huffed her consent. "I'll be picking her up at noon."

"You'll pick her up when I say she's done. You put this child through a war and now I have to piece her back together. Miracles take time." Narissa turned the chair around and gestured for me to sit.

I obeyed. Asia fumed for a moment more, groping for last word, then stormed out.

Narissa waited until the car had pulled away from the curb before relaxing. "Insufferable."

I grinned.

My smile faded when she violently spun the chair back to face the mirror. She grabbed chunks of my hair with both hands and scowled at it with a look of utter disgust.

"What?" I managed after withering under her scrutiny for a solid minute.

"I still can't believe you bleached your hair without asking me. I absolutely hate this color on you." She tightened her grip on my hair, and for a moment, I feared she might rip it out of my head.

I braced myself. "I'm sorry." It had been necessary, in the moment. Philadelphia Smyrna was known for her long, dark hair; Andromeda had to be the exact opposite. So, before going back to Earth, I'd impulsively chopped my hair to my shoulders and bleached it almost white.

Evidently, Narissa still hadn't forgiven me. "I'm going to have to lift the roots again and..." She raked her fingers along my scalp, then stopped. Her frown changed to one of concentration as she pinched a strand of my hair and squinted at it. I couldn't see the flashing modules behind her contacts, but I knew the implants in her eyes were doing their work, scanning my hair and matching my exact shade.

With a *humph*, she strode over to the color bar and began grabbing bottles of product off the shelf. I daren't ask what she was doing, so I changed the subject. "I never got a chance to say thank you."

She mumbled an affirmative. When Nic and I first arrived in Beijing, Narissa helped us get a head start on Asia by giving us supplies and letting us out a back way. The only reason Asia didn't punish her for it was because Narissa was worth more alive than dead. It was hard to find a stylist who could be controlled remotely.

Narissa squirted a generous glob of brown dye into a mixing bowl. "I'll be over at 7am sharp on Friday to do your makeup and deliver your outfit. You'd best be ready for me."

"I will," I promised, "but I don't need any new clothes. I have a closet full."

"None you're wearing."

I knew better than to argue. Narissa had been my stylist since my very first video, working for Thames and then for Asia. The only reason the "thunderbird" had an image was because of her. She'd designed the dress I wore at the gala, and she'd even secretly sent clothes to the Tangs for me to use on my tour.

She was also the one who had asked me to visit the group home a few weeks ago.

I dug my nails into the leather arm of the salon chair as I remembered the note she'd taped to the white shirt box:

THERE'S SOME OLD FRIENDS OF MINE I WOULD LIKE YOU TO VISIT. CALL IT A FAVOR FOR ME—IT WOULD MEAN A LOT.

Everyone who lived in that home had been her friends. They were people just like her—people with conditions the government considered incurable, unfashionable, or illegal.

And now almost all of them were dead.

I blinked back tears. "Narissa, I..." I struggled to find words for everything I needed to say but couldn't, for fear the algorithm was listening.

She stopped with her back to me.

I sighed. "I'm sorry."

"So am I," she murmured, and that was all that could be said.

There was silence for a moment while she gathered herself. Then she resumed aggressively stirring the dye. "This had better work. I'm not going to have time to redo your hair."

"I'm sure it will be perfect. You always make me look good."

"You certainly don't make it easy," she snapped, which could have been taken any number of ways. She set the bowl on a tray and wheeled it over. "Eventually you'll learn to give me more than *three days'* notice before you need a custom order. You're lucky I was already working on designs."

I found her gaze in the mirror. "You knew I'd come back."

She returned the stare. "You have a job to finish."

I swallowed. *Yes, I do.*

"Then let's finish in style." She snapped on a pair of gloves. "Now hold still while I fix this atrocity."

20: NIC

Five hours and forty-two minutes. That was how long it took to walk a lap around each level of the factory, all eighty-seven of them, and that was information I wish I didn't know.

It had been five days since my little episode, and Warden Ivanova still refused to lift her moratorium on work. I was on my best behavior for the first two days, hoping to prove I was a changed man. On the third day, I went to her office and begged for mercy. She rejected me—and then promptly left the base on a trip. I decided to try my luck and go down to the lab, only to find she'd revoked my access to everything except the cleaning closet.

I'm not sure which was more unnerving: The fact that I was locked out of my own lab, or the realization that she'd outsmarted me.

Bested, I had no choice but to set a timer and calculate how long it took to walk the entire factory. The result was a highly inconvenient number. It wasn't long enough to fill a whole workday, but it was too long for me to get two complete rounds in. I would have settled for one and three-quarters, or one and a half, or even one and a third rounds. But no, the math worked out to something like 1.41 rounds. Which meant that when dinner was called, I was on some random level in the middle, and that made the whole thing feel even more pointless than usual.

I was aware the math was arbitrary. I didn't need anyone to tell me that I was literally going in circles. In fact, part of the reason I walked from one level to another, instead of picking a level and trying to beat my best personal time from Rott, was so that I could avoid anyone commenting on the futility of my existence.

There was one Voice I couldn't avoid, however, no matter how fast I powerwalked.

He didn't say much for three days. I knew what the radio silence meant: I was going nowhere fast, literally and spiritually. I'd opened a door during our heart-to-heart in the lab, and He wasn't going to let me shut it again. So, if I didn't want to keep going in circles until Jesus returned, I'd better start talking.

I did. I honestly gave it my best effort. I interceded for Philadelphia. I complained about Asia. I even, against my every inhibition, told Him how I was *feeling.*

It was a wasted effort. Don't get me wrong—He listened very politely. But nothing changed. There was nothing I could pray that He hadn't heard already, and all His answers were the same as they had been for the past month. It felt like I was jumping through a dozen submenus on an automated answering machine, only to get the response I didn't want to hear.

Wait.

I would have taken any instruction over that one. If He'd told me to stay up all night praying, I would have set my alarm. If He'd told me to fast, I would have gladly skipped dinner. If He'd told me to pull an Ezekiel and lie on my side in the middle of the cafeteria for 390 days, I wouldn't have asked questions. I would have done anything—literally *anything*—as long as it meant I was doing something.

But apparently, He didn't have any use for me. So, I continued to walk the levels, going faster and faster, until I tripped over the reality I was trying so hard to avoid.

Bowen.

He was on the 85th floor. The top levels of the prison were mostly forgotten storage and hence weren't well-lit. He was kneeling by the railing, completely hidden in shadow. I literally tripped over him and almost sent both of us plummeting to our deaths.

"Nic! I'm sorry, I-I wasn't expecting anyone to be up here."

I braced myself on the railing and waited for my life to stop flashing before my eyes. "In your defense, I *shouldn't* be up here."

"Guess we have that in common." He stooped and started gathering something on the floor.

"Why are you—" I stopped when I saw what it was: candles. He'd stolen a box from the storeroom and arranged a trio of them on the concrete floor, one of which I'd gracelessly snuffed out.

"Sorry," I mumbled.

"It's fine," he said, even though I could tell that it definitely wasn't. He'd made an alcove between two stacks of boxes and draped a white banner over the crates—half of a torn bedsheet, it looked like. Packing paper folded into the crude shapes of flowers and coins littered the ground.

And taped to one of the boxes was a picture of Lanzhou.

It was black and white and grainy, like someone had scanned a webpage on an old copier. The ghost of whatever was printed on the back bled through the paper, marring Lanzhou's stoic face.

I didn't have to ask what was going on. I'd been to enough Chinese funerals with my father to know what I was looking at. It was pathetic and homely—and it was the best Lanzhou would ever get.

Bowen picked up the fallen candle and relit it. He twirled it in his fingers, his eyes chasing the flame, before setting it with the others. He sat back on his haunches, stared at his makeshift memorial, and said absolutely nothing.

My stupid self had to fill the silence. "You... holding up okay?"

He mercifully didn't answer my dumb question. "It would have been my job to plan the funeral," he commented, as if that explained everything. "I'm the next oldest, and elders aren't supposed to grieve for the younger. My uncle wouldn't even have been allowed to read the eulogy."

I wondered if the very traditional Mr. Tang was observing that rite, grieving silently in whatever dungeon Asia had stuffed him in.

"I would have had to read it. What would I have even said?" Bowen turned and glared up at me, like he was actually expecting an answer to that question.

I didn't have one. I had absolutely no idea what to say.

Bowen filled in the blanks, his voice sharp and unstable. "That he was right all along? That it's my fault he's dead? That he should be the one running the company?"

I didn't know what to say to that either—because all of those statements were true.

What am I supposed to do with this? I demanded of the Voice in my head.

He was silent.

Bowen cackled, clearly aware he was coming unglued. "Not that there's a company to run."

He was three for three with irrefutable statements. The Tangs were ruined. Their factory was destroyed, and Asia had no doubt frozen their assets and revoked their rights. To add insult to injury, if the Tangs didn't exercise their patent for a year, the government would grant it to someone else. Even if Philadelphia managed to bail the family out of jail, they would have no fortune—and worse, no reputation.

The Tangs had weathered tragedy and financial hardship before. But through all their decades of resistance and civil disobedience, they had always maintained their honor. They were the most influential family in the district. Even the police—the ones who had been bribed to keep the church safe—respected them.

Not anymore.

"What do I do?" Bowen whispered, still begging for an answer from somebody.

Nothing. That was the answer. There was absolutely nothing he could do to fix this. The Tangs could recover their wealth, and they would, if they survived this war. But their honor was irreplaceable.

Bowen touched Lanzhou's picture. "I'm so sorry," he hissed, and then again, louder. "I'm so sorry!"

He blurted a stream of unintelligible Mandarin. Then he dropped to the floor, prostrate like he was making penance, and wept.

I stood there and panicked. I didn't know what to do. I couldn't help him. I couldn't comfort him, I couldn't reassure him, I couldn't even give him any wise advice. Me and my three PhDs were useless in this situation. Bowen's world was ending, and there was nothing I could do.

You don't have to do anything.

The command came like a gust of cold air—unwelcome, unexpected, and absolutely terrifying.

But I need to do something. Why else was I standing here? Why would God put me in this incredibly awkward situation if He didn't want me to fix it? In fact, why was I on Earth at all? Why would He give me visions and prophecies and a *living, breathing teenage daughter* if He didn't want me to do something about it?

I never asked you to do anything.

He knelt next to Bowen, His hand on the sobbing man's shoulder. His gaze pierced me, and I knew I had a choice.

I could walk away. I could maintain control over my life—and spend the next ten years fighting to fill the void.

Or I could obey... and do absolutely nothing.

He waited. I stared into His eyes like fire and decided which death I wanted to survive.

Taking a long breath, I settled on the floor next to Bowen. Then I stilled my hands in my lap and sat—in silence.

21: PHILADELPHIA

"Well, aren't you a doll!" Cardiff declared. He and Asia were crowding the foot of the stairs as I descended, like they were my parents about to see me off for prom.

It was the day of the party, and Narissa had truly worked a miracle. Instead of lifting my roots, she'd formulated a dye that matched my natural shade exactly and feathered it through my hair. When she was finished, it looked like I'd gotten an elaborate balayage, with my natural color on top and bright highlights underneath.

"Now I don't have to constantly fix your roots," she'd announced with pride. But I knew that wasn't the real reason.

Cardiff loved the new look, not that I'd asked for his opinion. Asia was critical, but it didn't have anything to do with the color. She knew what the hairstyle meant: Andromeda's days were numbered. If the revolution won, I wouldn't have to hide behind a false identity anymore. Philadelphia Smyrna could come back from the dead—and then I would most assuredly be growing my hair out.

Of course, Narissa's subtle rebellion didn't stop at hair dye. My dress also sent a clear message. The fitted bodice was modeled after a qipao, with a starched collar and three-quarter sleeves, but the full skirt had a loose fit and a high-low hemline that made it easy to move around in as I served. The black silk fabric was embroidered with the bold form of a phoenix, its flaming tail sweeping across my waist and down the side of the skirt. It would have been a very traditional design had it not been for the color choice: white and silver with flashes of blue woven into the tips of the feathers. It was subtle, but I knew Asia would understand the threat.

"Positively stunning!" Cardiff exclaimed as I reached the foyer.

I held out my skirt to show off the embroidery. "What do you think, Asia?"

She didn't reply.

Cardiff helped me off the last step. He held my hand for a beat too long, then bent forward to kiss the back of it. "Mother would be *so* proud."

I pulled my hand out of his grasp.

"It is missing something, though."

I turned to see Asia holding out an all-too-familiar blue velvet jewelry box.

My breath caught in my throat. *She didn't.*

I forced myself to take it from her. I opened it to find my pearl necklace. Asia had given it to me as a gift when we'd first met, as an invitation to join her in high society. I'd been wearing it defiantly ever since; it had been in my suitcase back at the factory.

Asia answered my unspoken question. "It was recovered from the wreckage."

I looked up into her smile, cold and cruel.

Memories of Lanzhou's kind face flashed before my eyes, but I willed myself not to grieve. *Don't let her get to you.* I brushed dust off the pearls. "How thoughtful, but you won't be able to see it under the collar."

Then I snapped the box shut and held it out to Cardiff, who took it with a wicked grin.

I excused myself before Asia could recover and went to check on the preparations, not that the staff needed my help. Peng had once again proven his worth and put on a fabulous production. The house was so alive with light and color that you could barely recognize it. An explosion of fresh-cut flowers adorned every surface, blanketing the rooms with their scent. The dining table was draped in red and decorated with fans and shafts of bamboo. Everything glittered with gold, while a trio of musicians filled the air with a hybrid of modern and traditional music.

The courtyard, however, was truly the crown jewel of the estate. Glowing lanterns hung from every balcony, bathing the patio in fire. Incense burned in the fire pits and sent smoke drifting into the air, like there were baby dragons curled up underneath the coals. In the center of it all, the pool shimmered in the moonlight as a hundred lilies and candles floated on its surface.

I paused in the doorway and admired the extravagance. Mrs. Nolan truly *would* be proud.

And so would Nic.

I gripped the doorframe. *Would he?* Nic had never once been proud of me, but he'd sacrificed himself so I could fulfill my calling. If we defeated Asia, would he be proud? Would he even find out?

I brushed the thoughts aside and kept walking. None of us would live to see tomorrow if I didn't pull this party off.

I hurried to the kitchen, where my chef was living his best life directing an army of temporary help as they prepared enough food to feed a hundred. Spice and sweet competed in the air as a dozen dishes were arranged on gold trays to be served. The chef gave me the obligatory taste test, then politely shooed me out of the kitchen with a stack of dessert plates to take to the dining room.

I bustled around the corner—and ran straight into Jayde. I shrieked and dropped all seventeen plates on the floor. The clatter of metal on the tile was terrific.

"Sorry," he grunted after the noise stopped. "Blind corner."

I sighed loudly. "Will you *stop* hovering!"

"Sorry," he repeated, kneeling down to stack the plates. "I've got orders."

"To do what?"

He shot me a sideways glance, and I stiffened. "What don't I know?"

"Jael didn't tell you?"

"Obviously not!"

He brushed aside the hem of his jacket, revealing his holstered pistol. "If Asia tries anything, I'm supposed to shoot first."

I stared at the weapon as this admission completely reframed our relationship. "But that's suicide," I murmured. It wouldn't matter if Asia came at me with a knife and everyone saw it; they'd still execute Jayde for touching the General Secretary's daughter.

He shrugged. "Better me than you." He stood up, balancing the stack of plates, and gestured with his shoulder. "Where are these going?"

I numbly pointed at the dining room, too stunned to respond. What was terrifying was that he sounded like he believed what he'd said.

Jael arrived a few minutes later, accompanied by a businesswoman I didn't recognize. "Oh, forgive me, are we early?" Jael said, glancing pointedly around the empty foyer.

"Not at all. Please, come in."

I waited until they had stepped inside and been relieved of their jackets and accessories before extending a formal greeting. I gave a short bow to Jael, then offered my hand, just as Asia had taught me. "Thank you for honoring my family with your presence."

Jael returned both gestures, then rattled off a gorgeous and lengthy African name I couldn't pronounce. "But I'd be honored if you called me Chidi," she added.

I smiled gratefully. Remembering not to call her Jael would be hard enough. "Since you're early, would you like the tour before the others arrive?" I suggested, and hoped she would pick up on my meaning.

She did. "I'd love to. Oh, Min," she turned to Asia, "have you met my friend Bristol?"

I hoped my eyebrows didn't expose my surprise. Not only had Jael skipped a formal introduction, but she'd also used Asia's given name, a privilege normally reserved for close friends.

Asia pretended not to be annoyed. "No, I don't suppose I have."

"Oh, you simply must hear about the labor riots they've been having in England. It's an absolute scandal." Jael grabbed her friend's arm and all but shoved her in Asia's face.

Bristol had clearly rehearsed for this moment and immediately launched into a tirade about what the ungrateful peasants were doing. Asia had no choice but to smile and nod.

I quickly led the way down the hall, leaving Asia stranded in the foyer. I waited until we were out of earshot before turning to Jael. "How long have you known Asia?"

"Long enough to get away with that." She followed me to the abandoned dining room and stopped inside the door, admiring the decorations. "This is gorgeous. You've done an excellent job."

I could tell she meant it. A little relief fluttered through me. "Have you found any proof?" I asked, dropping my voice to a whisper.

"Proof of what?" she remarked with a glare over her shoulder.

I flinched. I was Andromeda Nolan; I wasn't supposed to know anything about Blue Fire or the revolution. But Jael hadn't said a word since I'd left for the estate, and we were running out of time. The operation was in less than a week; if we didn't get enough evidence tonight, we wouldn't be able to expose Asia before shots were fired.

"Your only job is to throw a party," she reminded me. "Let me worry about the rest. Your router is doing the heavy lifting."

I nodded and checked to make sure my phone was still in my pocket.

She faced me and spoke quickly. "Your primary focus is the General—but don't crowd him. Let him spend time with other people. A good hostess doesn't have anything to prove, and it will confuse Asia."

She glanced past me, as if verifying that our enemy hadn't escaped from the foyer. "She knows you have ulterior motives for throwing this party. She's going to be watching you like you're watching her, waiting for you to slip up. The more you act like this is just a normal meal—that you don't have anything to gain from her or her father—the more you'll distract her."

I fixed my posture and took a slow breath. *Just look pretty, be polite, and make a good impression. I can do this.*

"There are a few 'friends' I want you to meet, though," Jael continued. "I'll do the talking. Keep the General and Asia busy, and I'll send people to you when the time is right."

"How will I know they're friends?"

"If someone says, 'It sure has been hot lately,' reply, 'Then perhaps it's time we had some rain.' That's your cue that someone is an ally."

I fingered the embroidered feathers on my skirt. "And if someone isn't an ally?"

Jael smirked. "Then convert them."

I closed my eyes. *Give me the right words, Holy Spirit.*

There was commotion on the street—the rumble of multiple vehicles and the clamor of a dozen people on the walkway. Peng called excitedly for me from the foyer, and I knew the General had arrived.

I skipped a breath as panic took one last shot at me. This man wanted me dead. He'd outlawed my religion, murdered my friends, and imprisoned my family. He was the most wicked man in the world—second, perhaps, only to his daughter.

And I was about to serve him dumplings and pork ribs.

"It's showtime," Jael murmured. "Remember, for the next three hours, he's not your enemy. He's your friend."

I nodded and cleared room in my heart for a peace that was not mine.

For such a time as this.

I turned and headed for the foyer.

"Oh, Andromeda," Jael called me back.

I glanced over my shoulder.

"Love the dress." She winked.

I grinned.

My top staff had arranged themselves in the foyer like they were prepared for a military inspection. Cardiff observed from the side. He carried Frank in his arms and was stroking the dog's back slowly like the villain in a kid's TV show. I could only hope he'd keep the animal in check; the last thing I needed was for that slobbering dog to ruin my dinner party.

Peng held the door open as Asia fussed on the step. Two armed guards entered, and then suddenly, the General Secretary of the United was standing in my house.

I was once again taken aback by how unassuming the man was. He wasn't tall; even Peng had a few inches on him. His hair was graying, his face was softly wrinkled, and his expression was calm. It wasn't a pretentious calm, either; not like Thames, who had used his cool manner to control and manipulate. No, the General seemed genuinely calm, almost gentle.

He didn't look like the kind of man who ordered genocide and criminalized religion. And, for the next three hours, I had to pretend that he wasn't.

I gave Peng a minute to collect the General's belongings, then presented myself. "Your Excellence," I said softly, "I'm honored." I delicately lifted my skirt and bowed as low as I could.

The General returned the bow and held it, with each second adding prestige to the Nolan name. Then he straightened and extended his hand. "The honor is all mine."

I looked up. He gave me a knowing smile.

"Next time I offer you my hand, don't refuse it."

Asia watched us, eyes narrowed.

I beamed and grasped the General's hand. Our palms contacted. "Thank you for making time on such short notice. I know it was an inconvenience."

"None at all. I'm glad you thought of me." He squeezed my fingers, then stood back. "Trust me, this will be far more enjoyable than anything else I was planning to do with my evening."

A polite chuckle rippled from the bystanders. The General scanned the crowd, and his gaze settled on Cardiff. "Oh, I didn't know you had returned to Earth." If there was any emotion attached to the statement, I couldn't decode it.

"Fresh off the space station. My apologies if I still reek of hyperdrive fumes." Cardiff forewent a bow and offered his hand.

The General accepted it, even though their palms barely touched. Frank squirmed and struggled to get down. The General hummed bemusedly and scratched the dog behind the ears. "I'd love to know how the mission is progressing," he said to Cardiff. "Have they had any success reaching the surface of Jupiter?"

I remembered what Jael had said about not crowding the General and seized the opportunity. "Yes, Cardiff, you should tell him everything. Show him the samples you brought back. There's a sitting room over here where you can rest until dinner is served."

I started to lead the way, but the General laughed. "You can't get rid of me that easily, Andromeda. I didn't come to talk to this old chap—I came to talk to you!"

The bold declaration silenced the room. I had no idea how to respond.

Asia did it for me. "Of course! Andromeda, you should give him the tour. Show him what you've done with the place."

"What a marvelous idea!" Cardiff echoed, not sounding the least bit offended. "You're going to love it. She's outdone herself—the courtyard is positively stunning."

He and Asia collectively herded me towards the hallway. I gathered my wits. "Oh, yes, of course. Cardiff, would you stay and receive the other guests?"

"With pleasure, sister." He winked.

I put my smile back on and gestured for the General to follow. His guards fell into place as I guided them out of the room. Jayde trailed us at a safe distance.

I did as I was told and took the General on a tour—showing him the dining room, the courtyard, the garden—but it was clearly just a front to avoid the other guests for twenty minutes.

He didn't want to talk about the house; he wanted to talk about me. He asked about my trip to America, my college plans, and Mrs. Nolan's health. I gave him what he wanted and answered his questions with as much detail as I could fabricate.

That is, until his questions became personal.

"How are you and Cardiff getting along?"

We'd stopped in a secluded corner of the courtyard. I busied my hands plucking a dead leaf off a bush to buy myself time to come up with a plausible response.

"It's been super awkward" would have been the truthful answer. Cardiff was nice—almost too nice, not unlike his mother. He had been helpful with the party preparations and had assumed management of the estate, reviewing investments and conducting employee evaluations and taking care of things I never would have thought of.

I would have been grateful if it weren't for the fact that he made everything weirdly personal. On paper, we were adopted brother and sister, and he wanted to live that fantasy to the fullest. He insisted we eat meals together, had an opinion about everything I did, and was generally up in my business at all hours. He was more annoying than Asia—not to mention, his dumb dog was constantly underfoot.

The whole situation was extremely weird and unpleasant, but the General couldn't know that. As far as the public was concerned, Cardiff and I were family.

"It's been strange having him home after he's been gone so long," I said, settling for a half truth, "but we're making it work."

"That's good." The General seemed genuinely pleased. "I was concerned it might be uncomfortable for you after what happened with your birth parents."

"What do you mean?" I said slowly. Andromeda's birth parents died in a car crash. There was no story behind it—unless, Thames didn't tell me the whole truth.

And if the General knew something I didn't, then my entire identity was about to collapse.

"I don't mean to be offensive." The General waved his hand, as if clearing the air between us. "I just worry about you now that Thames is gone. With Mrs. Nolan still in America, you're here alone, and… that's a lot for a young woman to handle."

I looked down and pretended to fidget with my skirt. "I do miss him," I said, which was the biggest lie I'd ever told.

"We all do," the General murmured. "Listen, Andromeda. I know all of this has been extremely difficult for you, but I want you to know that you made the right decision by coming home with the Nolans. I know it took courage to leave your birth parents."

Leave my birth parents? Andromeda hadn't "left" her parents; they were dead. I'd always assumed the original Andromeda Nolan was an elite, living a life of luxury until her parents' untimely demise put her in the care of her aunt and uncle.

And yet, looking back at my time in Beijing, I realized that all of the Nolans' friends had acted like they knew I came from a containment camp. Thames and Cynthia had bragged about me for almost two years before bringing me home, and everyone I'd met had crooned about how "lucky" I was to have been "plucked from the trenches." They didn't know I was Philadelphia Smyrna, of course, but they were aware that I came from poverty.

Suddenly, I wondered if Thames hadn't lied about my past at all. What if his brother and sister-in-law were unassimilated? What if the "car crash" that killed them wasn't an accident? What if they died in a containment camp—just like my mother?

I clenched my fists.

The General didn't notice. "I'm worried about you," he said, sounding disgustingly truthful. "No child should have to witness that."

Witness what? I thought, my blood boiling. *My classmates getting shot for refusing to go to school? My father being beaten and confined to solitary every other month? My own mother bleeding out on our doorstep?*

The General sighed and folded his hands behind his back. "You shouldn't have had to grow up in those conditions. It angers me that there are parents who will make their children suffer for their crimes."

It wouldn't be a crime if you hadn't outlawed religion!

I stared at him, and all at once, I remembered why he was the enemy. Why I blew up that factory on Rott, why I agreed to be Blue Fire, why I was risking my life to throw this stupid party.

The United was wicked. They hated choice, they hated freedom, and they hated God. They censored the truth and glorified everything that was vile and ugly in the world. The government was evil, and I would not let this godless man destroy another family without a fight.

I opened my mouth—but movement caught my eye.

Jayde stood across the courtyard, watching. He shook his head.

I snapped my mouth shut as Jael's words flashed across my mind.

"He's not your enemy. He's your friend."

I took a deep breath and closed my eyes. *Holy Spirit, help me. Help me see him like You see him.*

The General mistook my silence. "I'm sorry, I know it's a painful subject. I'm just concerned about you."

I forced a gentle smile and turned to face him. "You don't need to be worried about me. Peng takes great care of me, and Mrs. Nolan will be joining us soon, after she takes care of some affairs in Boston."

"Excellent." He beamed. "So, you're staying, then?"

"Yes," I lied. "Beijing is my home."

"As it should be. If you ever need anything, please don't hesitate to tell me or my daughter. We know how difficult it can be to adjust after having grown up outside of society."

I shook my head. "I don't have to be defined by my past."

And neither do you.

The thought came like a breath on the wind, and for a brief moment, I saw it. An infinite reality beyond this one, all made possible by one choice. One turn in the right direction was all it would take—and it was possible, right here, right now. One word, one Holy Spirit moment in time, and the General could change forever.

Just like Nic.

I stared at the General, for once not seeing him, but what he could be—what this world could be.

The image faded when he turned to admire the pool. "This truly is fabulous." He gestured at the courtyard. "I'm amazed you pulled this off on such short notice. Is this really your first time hosting?"

I blinked as reality settled back into place like a layer of dust. "Yes, it is, but I must confess that Peng did most of the work."

He chuckled. "All effective leaders have good staff underneath them." He glanced over his shoulder at me. "You could be a formidable householder—or a councilwoman, if you put your mind to it."

I tried not to laugh. *I'd make a terrible politician.* "I don't know anything about politics."

He winked. "Come to the council chambers sometime, see for yourself. Tell them I sent you."

I accepted the offer with a smile. "I will."

22: PHILADELPHIA

The rest of the party went off without a hitch. My staff ran like a well-oiled machine and presented a feast fit for royalty. Asia was unusually agreeable and supported my every decision. Even Cardiff made himself useful, dazzling the guests with stories from deep space and keeping Frank out of my way (for the most part). As for me, I spent the evening herding servants, deferring compliments, and spending a copious amount of time discussing the weather.

It was usually obvious which guests had talked to Jael. They would observe me from across the room, judging me and determining their place in this war. As soon as I was relatively alone, they would slide up, glance around to make sure no one was listening, and then whisper the code phrase.

They were all elegantly subtle about it. All of them except Ms. Ivanova, that is.

She told me to call her Sofiya, a name far too delicate for the brash and commandeering woman. She said she was the warden of "the most profitable work camp in Russia," which seemed like a weird thing to announce in polite company, but she was certainly proud of it. I overheard her bragging about the numbers at least five times before the turn of the hour—partially because all her conversations could be heard at least three rooms away.

It was obvious why Jael had invited her, though. She clearly had a history with Asia, and it wasn't pleasant. The two nearly got into a cat fight when Sofiya walked in the door. Asia was appalled and screeched, *"What are you doing here?"* before abruptly remembering her manners. Sofiya decided manners were optional and cooed, *"Oh, and I thought the Nolans had taste."* She then launched into some conceited spiel about how her increased profits had earned her an invitation into high society before Jael gracefully separated them.

What was amusing was how unnerved Asia seemed by Sofiya's presence. She immediately pulled me into the other room and then proceeded to hover for the next hour, much to Jayde's frustration. Anytime Sofiya would get within earshot, Asia would steer me away and force me into a conversation with one of her friends. I was just beginning to worry that I'd have to spend the entire evening at her side when one of her father's aides finally called her away. And that's when Jael struck.

I saw her and Sofiya talking from across the courtyard. Jael leaned in and murmured in her ear. Sofiya jerked her head up in a motion so sharp she probably sprained her neck. She glared at me for a solid minute, making no attempt to be subtle, then stomped across the patio and shoved her way into my circle.

"It sure has been hot lately," she announced, brazenly interrupting my current conversation.

I winced; at least the two people I had been talking with were known allies. "Then perhaps it's time we had some rain." I demonstratively lowered my voice, hoping she would take the hint.

She didn't. "Excellent." She downed the rest of her glass in one gulp, handed it to a very bewildered guest, and grabbed my arm. "Come with me."

She dragged me towards the house. I looked helplessly over my shoulder at Jayde. He frowned and followed.

Sofiya hauled me down the hallway to the room where the General Secretary was reclining. "Introduce me to the man," she demanded, and pushed me through the door ahead of her.

I tripped into the room, halting the conversation. The General looked up. "Andromeda, I was just asking for you," he chuckled, benevolently helping me save face. He patted the spot on the couch next to him, a seat that had been deliberately left empty by the other guests.

I accepted the honor and approached him, Sofiya on my heel.

The General gave her a onceover. "Who's your friend?"

Sofiya stepped around me and introduced herself. "Warden Sofiya Ivanova." She shamelessly offered her hand.

The General took it, barely allowing their fingers to touch. "Your reputation precedes you," he admitted. "I heard your institution has been very efficient this quarter."

She deferred with a slight bow. "It is, in fact, one of your most profitable ventures, Your Excellence."

I arched an eyebrow, noting the change of possessive adjective. Up until a moment ago, it had been "her" factory.

The General pulled his hand back and propped his elbow on the arm of the couch. "I'd be curious to learn more about your methods. Why the sudden increase?"

"Oh, it's a *hilarious* story. You absolutely have to hear this." She snatched a full glass from the tray on the coffee table and flopped down in the chair next to him without being invited.

"Do tell," he intoned, expression less than amused.

I gingerly perched on the edge of the couch and hoped I hadn't made an irreparable social error by introducing them. Jayde took up station in the shadows by the door and watched.

Sofiya took a swig before continuing. "The truth is, Your Excellence, I can't take credit for any of it."

There was a collective murmur from the others in the room. I had to admit that surprised me too, if only because she'd had no problem taking credit for everything five minutes ago.

"I'll admit, we were struggling," Sofiya confessed, voice dripping with drama. "Profits were plummeting, and morale was at an all-time low. I swear there was a prison riot every week. I was considering turning in my resignation, it was so shameful."

I doubted that, and so did the General. He patronized her with a raised eyebrow.

"But then you won't *believe* what happened." She gestured at the entire room with her sloshing glass, as if inviting the bystanders into the story. They obliged and collectively moved closer like a noose cinching.

"One of the inmates approached me, and do you know what he says?" She leaned forward and made eye contact with the crowd. "He tells me he can increase my productivity by fifty percent in thirty days, and it won't cost me a penny."

"Sounds like a scam," a businessman muttered.

Sofiya cackled. "That's what I said, but he was determined. He was so convinced that he could save the factory that he challenged me to a bet: If profits didn't double in thirty days, I could kill him."

It was such a heartless declaration that it rendered the room speechless. Even the General just blinked, as if he didn't know what to do with such gross social ineptitude.

I scrambled for a way to divert the conversation. *Holy Spirit, what do I do?*

One of the other guests finally recovered from the shock. "You didn't accept, did you?" she squeaked.

Sofiya just winked.

The businessman set his glass down with a mortified *clink*. "What happened? Surely it didn't work."

Jael silently slid into the room and joined the back of the crowd.

"Well, I'm enjoying tripled profits, and he's still breathing, so..." Sofiya twinkled her fingers in the air.

"That's insane," the General grunted.

"Utterly," she agreed. "But the numbers don't lie. He reconfigured my assembly line and restructured the workers' schedule, and profits practically doubled overnight. We're operating at over ninety percent efficiency and saving at least ten grand in resources every month." She glanced at me. "You should hire him to oversee your investments, Andromeda, now that you've inherited the estate."

I winced. Thames Nolan's abrupt demise was not a topic I'd planned on bringing up at this party.

The General intercepted for me. "I'm sure Andromeda has an excellent board of advisors."

Jael stepped forward and salvaged the conversation. "I might have a job for this miracle worker. You said he's an inmate? How did he end up in your institution?"

"That's the unfortunate part." Sofiya gazed into her glass. "I pulled his file, and he has absolutely no criminal history. No record of noncompliance. He's been a loyal, productive citizen his entire life—until he was walking home from work one night and got caught up in one of those 'thunderbird' riots."

I gasped, and too late realized I'd pulled the center of attention to myself. Jael shot me a glare.

"That's so sad," I fumbled, and avoided looking at the General.

"It really is," Sofiya agreed. "I have no reason to believe he ever intended to cause trouble—I mean, a real criminal wouldn't care about the government's profit margin, would they? He even turned himself in when officers arrived."

I struggled to keep my feelings in, knowing full well the grief and shame were burning on my face. *I did this. I put that innocent man in jail.*

Sofiya laid the guilt on thick, her eyes cruelly locked with mine. "It was just a matter of being in the wrong place at the wrong time."

I looked down at my lap. *I'm so sorry.*

"Well, now." The General shifted beside me. "That seems like an easy problem to fix."

I lifted my head.

"The whole purpose of the justice system is to help people assimilate back into society," he recited, soliciting a murmur of agreement from the crowd. "After all, people don't have to be defined by their past, do they, Andromeda?" He turned to me.

I sat up straight. "No, sir."

He smiled, crow's feet wrinkled with affection. "Well, what do you think? Should we give this young man a second chance?"

"Yes!" I exclaimed, too quickly.

He chuckled. "Then it's done."

The group whispered. I looked around and realized they were regarding me like I was an adorable puppy performing tricks in exchange for treats.

I blushed, suddenly second guessing my behavior. I glanced at Jael for reassurance.

She grinned.

"You can handle the paperwork, yes?" The General nodded at Sofiya.

"Of course. Thank you, Your Excellence, this makes me so happy," she praised, for the first time that night sounding completely sober.

He waved dismissively. "Have Asia review it. She has my authorizations."

If only you knew, I thought to myself.

"Wonderful. Let's get it taken care of, Andromeda." Sofiya stood up and yanked me off the couch before I could object. "Don't worry, I'll bring her right back," she promised as she hauled me out of the room.

The General winked.

I struggled to stay on my own two feet as Sofiya barreled down the hall. "So, who is this guy, exactly?"

"I can't believe that actually worked," she crowed, completely avoiding the question. She halted in an abandoned vestibule and pulled out her phone. "Good thing I had his pardon pre-drafted."

"Wait, how long have you been planning this?" I demanded.

She ignored me. She swiped a few commands into her phone and then shoved it at me. "Give this to Asia, tell her to sign it. Do *not* tell her it's from me. If she asks what it is, just say the General is donating money to a project of yours."

I stared at the device and reconsidered the entire situation. "I—"

"Andromeda!" Asia screeched from around the corner.

"We never talked," Sofiya hissed, and darted out of sight into the next room.

Asia's heels popped on the tile as she stomped towards me. "What are you doing?"

"I just… I just came from the General." I quickly composed myself and held the phone out to her. "He wants you to sign this."

She took it. "What is it for?" she said with a healthy amount of skepticism.

I put on a sweet smile. "He's donating money to a little project of mine."

She frowned at me, and for a terrifying minute, I was sure she wouldn't believe me.

Then her bloodred lips parted in a murderous sneer. "Oh, isn't that just *wonderful.* How kind of him." She signed the file without reading it, then pressed her thumb to the screen. The device chirped.

She handed the phone back to me. "Is he still in the east wing?"

"Yes. I'll join you there in a minute—I just need to talk to the chef about dessert."

"Excellent." She swept down the hall, the grin still on her face.

Sofiya waited until she was gone before creepily reappearing at my elbow. "I have waited my entire life for that moment."

"Care to tell me what's going on?" I grumbled.

She didn't, apparently. "Well, I'm going to go deliver the good news. Pleasure doing business with you, Philadelphia." She snatched the phone from my hand and waltzed towards the foyer.

I cringed; thankfully, no one but Jayde was within earshot. "But I—"

She wasn't listening. "You can thank me later!" She waved her fingers over her shoulder and then let herself out before Peng could even make it to the door.

"You realized she used you, right?" Jayde muttered from behind me.

I folded my arms. "I'm aware."

He snorted. "You're so gullible."

I ignored him and watched out the window as Sofiya's cab pulled away from the curb. I could only pray I didn't just pardon a criminal mastermind.

23: NIC

I knew I was in trouble when Warden Ivanova came back early from her trip.

I was eating lunch with Ryan, Vance, and Bowen when she found me. "Von Nieuwenhuyse!" she bellowed across the cafeteria.

I glanced at the giant clock that was mounted on the wall. She wasn't supposed to be back until Tuesday, which meant she was a full three days early. And, presuming the train was running on schedule, she'd just disembarked an hour ago. That meant the first thing she'd done after getting off the elevator was yell at me.

That couldn't be a good sign.

"Nieuwenhuyse!" she shouted again. She stood at the railing three floors up, giving her the perfect vantage point to project her voice with maximum efficiency. "My office! Now!"

Her screech ricocheted around the cafeteria. The entire room silenced and looked at me.

Ryan stood up on the bench to survey the crowd. "Wow, the acoustics in here are amazing! We should definitely organize the next riot in here."

Vance grabbed his shirt and pulled him back down. "You, sir, are not allowed to organize any more riots without the express permission of the warden."

"She said she might let me do one in October!"

The warden had even less patience than usual. "Von! Don't make me come down there!"

I swung my legs over the bench and stood up. "Well, gentlemen, I think this is goodbye forever."

"Oh right." Ryan picked up his spoon and resumed shoveling gruel into his mouth. "Can you see if she'll hold off on the execution until 2:30pm? I've got a meeting with my floor managers after this that I can't miss. If you can get her to move it, Vance and I will definitely be there for you."

Vance checked his calendar on his communicator. "I can't do 2:30pm. 3pm would be ideal."

"I could make 3pm work," Ryan consented. "Bowen, you're free all afternoon, right?"

"I-I..." Bowen stuttered. He'd been doing a lot better over the past few days, but he still hadn't assimilated to Vance and Ryan's existence. "You write my schedule."

"Oh, good point." Ryan gestured at me with his spoon. "Make it 3pm, and we'll all be there to support you."

I saw guards moving in my direction and figured I'd better start walking. "I'll do my best, but I don't think she's in a waiting mood today."

I hurried to her office, flanked by an unnecessary entourage of guards. She was standing in front of her desk, tapping her boot impatiently, which I found highly unnerving. She wasn't normally this eager to see me.

I halted inside the door. "I didn't do it."

She stopped tapping. "Do what?"

"The equipment fire. It wasn't me, I swear."

She scowled. "What equipment fire?"

"The one on Level 56. I'll have you know, I was on Level 32 when it happened, so I had absolutely nothing to do with it. However, if you want my opinion, I think the autoregulator on the interdimensional plasma fabricator is off again and needs to be replaced."

She shot a glare at the guard standing next to her. He cleared his throat. "It was on our agenda to discuss, ma'am."

She shook her head. "Never mind. I've got more important things to deal with. You, thumbprint." She thrust a tablet at me.

I stumbled forward and took it. "Since when did you need my consent for anything?"

She snorted. "It's a form stating that you acknowledge your crimes, recognize the justness of the government's ruling, and will not commit a repeat offense."

I held the tablet back out. "Yeah no, I can't sign that in good conscience."

"Well, it's either that, or your pardon is null and void."

I dropped the device. Thankfully, it had a protective case on it. "What?"

She grinned maniacally. "You're going home."

I blinked. When she didn't recant her statement, I ventured, "I thought you couldn't pardon me."

"I didn't. Asia did." She kicked the tablet towards me.

Picking it up, I scrolled down the screen and saw a signature I knew all too well:

MONG SHI MIN TAI

I stared at the document as the Holy Spirit made His presence known. I looked up to see Him standing in the corner, smirking.

Wait and see the salvation of the Lord.

"Thank you," I said to Him after I'd collected enough of my wits to formulate a sentence. I turned to the warden. "I'm assuming there's an epic story behind this."

She folded her arms and leaned against the desk. "Andromeda Nolan sends her regards."

I froze. If Philadelphia had returned to the Nolan estate, that meant something had gone very, very wrong—or very, very right. "Well, that creates more questions than it answers."

The warden shrugged. "All I know is that she's posing as a Nolan. She's working with a woman named Jael, and they put on one killer party. Even the General Secretary came."

I stared into the void as all the dreams and visions I'd had about Philadelphia flashed across my mind in one terrific blur.

"I saw it all. You, in Beijing, as a Nolan, on even playing ground with Asia."

I glanced at the Holy Spirit. He gave me an *I-told-you-so* look. Well, it wasn't so much a look as it was a general conviction that I should have spent a lot less time panicking and a lot more time trusting and praying over the last month.

"I don't know what trickery Phil pulled," the warden continued, oblivious to the conversation going on over her head, "but the General *loves* her. I think he would have given her half the kingdom if she'd asked. All I did was make up some sob story about the poor, falsely accused prisoner who helped save my factory, and he pardoned you just to see her smile."

"I take it you didn't mention my name."

"He didn't ask."

I tried to imagine how that conversation had gone down. I could believe the General was that gullible; men will do immeasurably stupid things to please a woman, speaking from experience. I did not, however, believe Asia was that gullible. "And how'd you convince Asia to sign it? She knows who you are."

The warden cackled. "She didn't even read it. Phil told her that the General was donating money to a project of hers, and Asia signed it without looking."

I studied Asia's ornate signature. It wasn't like her to be this careless, which either meant she had an ulterior motive, or she'd been blinded by the Holy Spirit.

Both, He answered, *both is good.*

"How long's it take you to sign a form?" the warden chided. "The train leaves in two hours. If you're not on it, you'll have to wait three days for the next one. Hurry and pack your things."

I swiped my signature on the tablet and handed it back to her. "The fact that you think I have something to pack is mildly offensive."

"Then go say your goodbyes. You have twenty minutes to be on that elevator." She sat down behind the desk and returned to her computer.

I stared at her, struggling to close the book on one of the most bizarre chapters of my life. "Thank you."

She winked. I turned and headed for the door.

"Oh, and Dr. Nic?"

I glanced back.

She grinned like a crocodile. "Tell Blue Fire: I'm *so* in."

*

After fielding several congratulations, farewells, and high fives from the guards, I hurried back to the cafeteria. As soon as he saw me, Ryan waved both arms above his head like he was an air marshal signaling my landing.

"Hey, you're still alive! Did you convince her to move it to 3pm?"

I stopped at the table. "No, I… I'm here to say goodbye."

He deflated like a popped balloon. "Aww, buddy, I'm so sorry. What did you do?"

I put my hands up. "No, I mean, I'm being released. I'm going home."

All three of them stopped and stared at me.

Ryan was the first to reboot. "Now I *really* need to know what you did."

There was no way I was going to attempt to explain the warden's story, which I only partially believed myself, so I summarized. "Philadelphia arranged my pardon."

Vance smirked, as if he'd seen this coming all along.

"So, she's safe?" Bowen demanded.

If Phil really had resumed her identity as Andromeda Nolan, she was less safe than ever, but he didn't need to know that. "She's fine. She and Jael are still heading the operation."

He let out his breath, releasing a thousand pounds of guilt with it.

"Go Team Blue Fire!" Ryan whooped. "When do you leave?"

"Now." I glanced at the clock. "I have to make the next train."

Ryan whined and thumped his fist on the table. "But I was almost done planning your going away party! I'm just waiting for the balloons to come in. They were backordered."

I'd spent enough time with him to know that he was being completely serious. "You've been planning a party?"

"I knew God was going to free you sooner or later," Vance explained, "so I advised him to plan ahead."

I stared at him, feeling mortally ashamed that Vance, of all people, had had more faith in my release than I did.

"Well, I guess I'll just reuse the decorations for the warden's birthday party. We're going to miss you, buddy." Ryan climbed up on the table and stepped over our trays to give me an unsolicited hug.

I resisted the urge to pry him off and drop him on the floor; I owed him this one. "I'll miss you, too." It was mostly the truth.

Vance walked over and clapped me on the shoulder. "Don't forget us."

I met his gaze. "I won't," I said, and realized, much to my chagrin, that the statement made me sad.

A guard jogged up to the table. "Dr. Nic! We need to leave."

I separated myself from Ryan and handed him back to Vance. Bowen stood up. "Tell Phil I'm sorry."

We made a brave attempt at a manly slap-on-the-back hug. "She forgives you," I said as I pulled away and restored my personal space. "When this is all over, she'll get you pardoned."

Such an optimistic word: "when." And for the first time in a long time, I believed it.

He smiled, but the gesture was agonizing. "Tell her not to worry about me. But if she can do something for my aunt and uncle…"

"She'll find them," I promised. "She'll bring you all home."

Home to what? I remembered with a punch to the gut. The Tang family was ruined. Their factory was destroyed, their home was burned to ash, and their reputation was tarnished. Even if Phil did bail them out, they'd be homeless and penniless.

Unless...

I remembered the other vision God had sent me—the one about Bowen and Warden Ivanova presiding over a board meeting—and realized this was one problem I *could* fix.

I gestured at the guard. "Call Warden Ivanova."

He squinted but reached for his communicator.

"Ask her if she'd like to manufacture something far more profitable than powercells."

The guard stopped with his finger on the screen. "Pretty sure the answer to that question is yes."

Bowen frowned at me.

I smiled. "Tell her I know someone who holds the patent to an interstellar space station part—and he's looking for a new supplier."

24: PHILADELPHIA

For the sixth day in a row, Frank woke me up.

The rattling at the door ripped into my dreams like a toddler shredding wrapping paper. I moaned and rolled over, fighting to hold on to either consciousness or sleep, but both eluded me. Darkness and light competed like I was caught at the bottom of a whirlpool, unable to pick myself up. The room swam, my joints were swollen, and the only thing I was confident of was that I had a massive headache.

"Go away," I snarled.

He didn't.

I forced myself to sit up—and that's when I realized it was pitch black outside.

The breeze from my open balcony door fluttered the curtains, revealing the moon high overhead. I swiped on my tablet screen and checked the clock: 4:32am.

I groaned. It was way too early for me to be up. Besides the fact that this was an obscene hour of the night, I'd only been asleep for about four hours—and that was bad news considering I'd taken my medication the night before.

The last two days had been a whirlwind, even more exhausting than the party itself. As Jael had predicted, I'd been invited to at least a dozen other functions before the night was out as my guests vied to secure their position in my social circle. Jayde had forwarded all the invitations to Jael, who told me what to accept—starting with breakfast with the owner of a bank the following morning.

So, before the decorations were even cleaned up, I dragged myself out of bed, put on a fresh layer of makeup, and started the game all over again. I had three engagements on Saturday, which led to four more on Sunday. I visited a factory, toured one of the capitol buildings, and ate every meal with someone important. I was grateful Peng was managing my calendar, or I wouldn't have survived past Saturday afternoon.

I knew each visit was forging a link in my network, even though most of the politics happened behind my back. At almost every event, Jael or one of her friends "just so happened" to be there. I would trade handshakes and pleasantries while my allies forged contracts in the shadows. It was weird to think that a war was being waged when all I was doing was smiling and looking pretty, but I trusted Jael. So, I went where she told me, wore what Narissa sent me, and said what the Holy Spirit gave me as I fraternized with the most powerful people in the world.

Asia haunted me as much as she could, following me around and appearing even when she wasn't invited. She tried to commandeer my calendar, insisting I accept her friends' invites over others. She even went so far as to sign me up for a Sunday night dinner without asking. I wanted to tell her off—mainly because I couldn't stand the thought of another social engagement—but Jael encouraged me to go.

I swapped outfits yet again and became the daughter Asia needed me to be—demure and overwhelmed. I pretended to be starstruck by all the wealth as her cohorts swarmed around me like flies, crooning about how "precious" and "adorable" I was. I loathed every minute, but I knew the phone in my pocket was doing the work as it recorded conversations and scalped text messages, compiling evidence against Asia.

Jayde said we were close. What that meant, I didn't know. Operation day was on Thursday. Under Jael's orders, I hadn't been online or looked at the traction on any of my videos, but I knew the movement was reaching a breaking point. Fear gripped

Beijing as even assimilated civilians began to realize violence was imminent. Schools and businesses announced closures for Thursday while people boarded up windows and barricaded apartments.

It broke my heart to think that innocent people were afraid of us. Operation Blue Fire was never supposed to be a violent demonstration. But if I didn't expose Asia, it would be.

And I had less than three days to bring her down.

With every hour that passed, I felt the panic closing in like a gathering shadow, but I would not move until Jael ordered me to. So, I let Asia's friends fawn over me like I was some caged parrot and gleefully accepted all their invitations for the following week. I didn't get home until after eleven on Sunday and didn't take my medication until nearly midnight.

That meant I absolutely, positively should not be up before seven. If I didn't get a full night's sleep, I'd be a wreck all day, and I couldn't afford that.

I heard movement in the hall. "Get lost, Frank!" I yelled.

A nervous voice answered me. "Actually, it's Peng, miss."

I struggled to recalibrate. I had no preset for being woken up in the dead of night by my houseman. "What do you need?"

"I'm sorry, miss, but it's important," he stuttered, which didn't at all answer the question.

What could be so important at 4:30 in the morning? I grunted and climbed out of bed—or tried to. My stiff muscles and groggy nerves got the better of me, and I tumbled to the floor. Now I had an aching shoulder on top of being in the worst mood ever.

Snatching my robe off the chair, I limped over to the door and threw it open. "What?" I snapped, cramming all my displeasure into one syllable.

He took a healthy step back. "There's someone here to see you."

I squinted at him and began to wonder if I was still dreaming. "And you let them in? Tell them to go away! What do I pay you for?"

Peng started to respond, but someone else spoke first. "Watch your attitude, young lady," a familiar voice called from downstairs.

The drowsiness evaporated from my mind. *No, it can't be.* I shoved past Peng and ran to the top of the stairs.

Nic stood in the foyer, grinning.

I stared at him, for one terrified minute convinced the medication was playing tricks on me.

Then he arched his eyebrow in that bemused gesture I had missed so much. "He said it was important."

"Nic!" I screeched, all my joy and disbelief and elation colliding.

I hurtled down the steps and practically fell into his arms. "It's you," I gasped. It was a stupid thing to say, but I had to be sure. I had to be sure it was really him, here, alive.

He braced himself on the railing. "The one and only," he replied, the sarcasm in his voice as comforting as a warm blanket.

I grabbed him and gripped his shirt with both fists, trembling as the world crashed and restarted. I knew I'd get scolded for giving him a hug, but I didn't care. I wasn't about to let go.

The reprimand never came. Instead, he did the unthinkable: He hugged me back.

Well, "hug" was a generous term for the amount of physical contact he was giving. But he did wrap one arm around my shoulder and lean over to whisper in my ear. "Phil," was all he said, and that was all he needed to say.

I buried my face in his chest and burst into warm, happy tears. "Oh God, You brought him back!" I cried. "You brought him back!"

Nic tightened his grip and muttered three words I never expected to hear from him. "Thank you, Jesus."

I pulled away. "Wait, are you…?"

"Did I kiss and make up with the Voice in my head?" Nic shed his jacket and held it out to Peng, who stood petrified at the foot of the stairs like a coatrack. "I didn't really have a choice after He spawned me back in."

I wasn't sure which excited me more: the fact that Nic was home, or the fact that He'd come back to God. I didn't know whether to shout for joy, cry from relief, or ask a million questions. Instead, I just got really overwhelmed and sobbed even harder.

"Maybe we should take this one step at a time," Nic suggested. "Got any coffee?"

Peng roused himself. "I'll put a pot on."

"No, I'll get it." I pulled myself together and wiped my eyes. I needed some time alone with Nic before the rest of the house woke up. "This way."

Nic followed me to the kitchen. I listened to the familiar *squeak* of his Oxfords behind me and struggled to push past the muddled emotions. *Nic is here. He's really here!*

I flicked on the light in the kitchen and finally managed to formulate a coherent question. "How did you get here?"

He settled on a stool at the island. "Heard you met Warden Ivanova."

I gasped as everything snapped into place. "*You* were the prisoner she was talking about!"

"What?" he scoffed. "Some crazy Russian lady concocts a story about a mysterious prisoner and you don't automatically assume it's me?"

"She said you were compliant..." "Innocent" and "compliant" were never words I'd use to describe Dr. Nic.

His eyebrow returned to its locked and loaded position. "It's called lying, sweetheart. Have I taught you nothing?"

I folded my arms. "In my defense, I'm not sure you ever actually *lied* to me. You just got really upset when I started opening random doors."

He smiled, as if it were a pleasant memory. In a way, it was.

Neither of us said anything as I hunted in the gigantic pantry for some coffee grounds. The dribble of liquid into the carafe was the only sound in the sleepy house. I filled our mugs, handed one over to him—and stopped.

"What?" he finally broke the silence.

I stared at the liquid rippling in my mug, thinking of all the times I'd refilled Nic's coffee on Mars. Of the time his father gave me my first cup. Of the time my brother laughed at me because I took my coffee the way Nic took his, black as dirt. Of the time I got us coffee while we were running across Beijing, when we sat in the park and stole a moment of peace.

Nic set his mug on the counter. "Phil."

I looked up. "I missed you."

He met my gaze and said exactly what I needed to hear. "I missed you, too."

I blurted the next most important thing. "I'm so sorry."

"It's not your—" He stopped, as if realizing that *wasn't* what I needed to hear. He took a deep breath. "I forgive you."

The tears started all over again as a thousand broken things were made whole. I slammed my mug down and threw myself in his arms.

He caught me with a grunt. "You're going to milk this, aren't you?"

"For the rest of your life," I mumbled into his shoulder.

He patted my head awkwardly. "I guess I did sign up for this."

"You literally volunteered." I squeezed him for good measure, then stepped back. "Oh, I did get my chip removed." I showed him my right hand, not that you could tell it had ever contained a bomb.

"Thank you for establishing that *after* you hugged me— twice."

I blushed.

He picked up his mug. "So, did you figure out who tried to kill me? Was it just a happy accident, or…?"

I pulled up another barstool. "No. The chip contained two sets of DNA—yours and the General's."

Nic's mustache twitched as he considered that.

"It wasn't Data—the guy who programmed my chip," I clarified. "He bought the code off the black market. He tried to track the source, but... something about an evolving proxy chain."

I tried to remember what else Data had told me about the code, but I could barely string a thought together. The adrenaline was wearing off, bringing the effects of the sleep medication crashing back down on me. The world blurred as my head began to throb.

"Are you all right?" Nic asked.

"Still groggy," I mumbled. "You talk—tell me what happened."

He obliged, recounting the wildest story I had ever heard. It sounded like the lead-up to a bad joke—*a Mexican rebel, a German accountant, and a Martian scientist are all sentenced to the same prison*—except there was no punchline. Perhaps the craziest part was that Nic actually *had* saved the factory and doubled profits.

"Is Bowen going to be okay?" I stared at the bottom of my empty mug and tried to decide which of my dozen emotions was most relevant.

"Don't worry—the warden will treat him like royalty once she finds out how much that part is worth. He'll be fine until this is all over. On that subject..." Nic reached for the carafe, then changed his mind. He shoved his mug aside and leaned towards me, folding his arms on his knees. "What are *you* doing here, Andromeda?"

I closed my eyes and tried to gather my thoughts, but it was like trying to chase bats out of a dark attic. My half of the story was even more complicated—and it didn't have a happy ending. "Well..."

A slamming door and approaching footsteps interrupted me. Jayde stumbled into the kitchen, looking barely awake. He scratched his tousled hair as he glared blearily at his device. "What are you doing up so early?" he grunted. "You shouldn't be awake."

"Jayde..." I tried to warn him.

He looked up and spotted Nic. "Oh—"

The word he started to say wasn't nice, but he didn't get to finish it. Faster than anyone could react (least of all me), Nic had Jayde pinned to the floor on his back with his own gun aimed at his face.

It took everyone a full ten seconds to recalibrate. Jayde looked more perplexed than afraid. "How did you—"

Nic jabbed him in the chest with the weapon. "I ask the questions, punk. First question: What are you doing here? Follow-up question: How would you like to die?"

I grabbed Nic's shoulder and tried to haul him back. "Nic, stop, it's okay. He's with me."

Nic whirled on me. "He's *with* you? Oh no, don't tell me... You *forgave* him?"

I put my hands up. "Jael vetted him, it's fine."

"That's a cute way of putting it," Jayde muttered.

Nic used one hand to keep the gun in Jayde's face and the other to shake a finger at me. "I can't believe you just forgave him! Nope, never mind, poor choice of words. I *can* believe it, and I hate that."

"Sorry to disappoint," I sassed, "but a lot has happened. Which I would tell you if you'd put the gun down."

He didn't take the hint. "You can't just keep letting people off the hook like this, Phil."

"Yes, I can. That's kind of how Jesus works. Also, you're one to talk—I forgave you." I put my hands on my hips.

"She has a point," Jayde quipped. "Can I get up now?"

Nic kneed him in the ribs, his eyes still on me. "I think you had best start from the beginning."

I obeyed, explaining about the guns that had been donated to the underground and Asia's plot to undermine the operation and overthrow her father. About halfway through the story, Nic let Jayde up, but he kept the gun. He wandered over to the door and stared at the pool as the sun began to warm the sky. He refused to make eye contact with me until I finished talking.

"What are you thinking?" I prodded when he still didn't react.

"You want the literal answer?" he muttered, then didn't wait for an affirmative. "I'm livid that you had to go through all that without me."

Silence blanketed the kitchen except for the *tick, tick* of the ornamental clock.

"You're here now," I finally said.

He glanced back at me and almost smiled.

Jayde shifted uncomfortably on his barstool. "I hate to break up the moment..."

"Then don't," Nic snapped.

Jayde ignored him, even though I could see he was starting to sweat. "But we need to talk." The statement was directed at me.

Nic took a step forward. "She doesn't *have* to do anything as far as you're concerned."

Jayde held my gaze. "I think you should consider recording a video."

"What?" both Nic and I said at the same time.

"I think you need to go online and address the underground. The operation is in three days—they need a call to action. One that *isn't* prerecorded."

I didn't disagree, but it wasn't my call to make. "I'm not doing anything without Jael."

"Jael still hasn't contacted me." Jayde tapped the screen of his device, as if verifying that was still true. "If we don't have enough evidence to turn the Council against Asia, then we're going to have to do it ourselves. You need to warn the people that the government's coming and tell them to shoot first."

Nic looked ready to lunge, but I put up my hand to stop him. Jayde answered to me. "Jayde, I'm not telling a bunch of schoolkids and factory workers to open fire."

"Then why do we have weapons?" Jayde pointed at the gun Nic still had clenched in his hand. "Phil, it's now or never. We won't get another chance. You started this—you have to finish it."

I opened my mouth, but someone beat me to it. "Personally, I agree with the lad."

I whipped around. Cardiff loomed in the doorway, almost as if he had teleported in. I certainly hadn't heard him approach.

Nic was, of course, the first to react. He flicked the weapon on and aimed it at Cardiff's face. Jayde cursed and dived off the stool to get out of the line of fire.

Cardiff was unbothered. "Dr. Nic," he greeted, taking a sip from his inexplicable teacup. "Please to finally make your acquaintance."

"Nolan," Nic snarled, clearly not pleased to make anyone's acquaintance. "I thought you were dead!"

I glanced at Jayde. "Is that what I sound like when people randomly resurrect?"

He brushed himself off. "Yeah, kinda."

"Oh, my apologies, you're clearly confusing me with my father." Cardiff set his cup on its saucer and extended a hand to Nic. "Cardiff, the younger Mr. Nolan."

Nic didn't accept the handshake *or* lower the gun. "Nope, definitely still thought you were dead."

I reached for him. "Nic, put the gun down, please."

"Come now," Cardiff whined, "I think it makes introductions much more exciting."

"What are you doing here?" Nic demanded.

Cardiff shrugged. "I live here."

"Nic, turn the weapon off!"

He continued to ignore me. "Last I checked, Andromeda was the only name on the deed."

Cardiff's expression flatlined. "Trust me, I'm aware. But she's been very kind to let me stay in *my* rooms."

"Well then, take your British self back to bed, because this conversation doesn't involve you."

"On the contrary, as her 'brother,' I'm deeply involved." Cardiff slurped his tea pretentiously. "Certainly more so than you, doctor."

Nic took two whole steps forward and jabbed the weapon at Cardiff's chest. "Don't pull that card on me. She's already got one annoying older brother—I'm not putting up with two. I don't care what the paperwork says—"

I put myself between them. "Will you stop arguing about the paperwork! Nic, seriously, drop the gun."

He just leaned around me to get a clear shot at Cardiff. "And how much do you know about the operation, anyway? Give me one good reason why I—"

"Nic!" I yelled. "Gun! Now!"

He finally looked at me. I gave him the best glare I could conjure. With an incoherent mumble, he reached down to turn the weapon off.

"As we were saying," Cardiff continued seamlessly, "I agree with the lieutenant. The reward clearly outweighs the risk. I recommend you move forward with the operation."

I frowned at him, a little unnerved that he had an opinion on the whole ordeal. Of course, he knew I was Blue Fire; he was more involved with my alternate identity than I cared to admit. But he'd been off planet for years. How much did he really know about the operation? Whose side was he on?

Jayde didn't give me a chance to ask. "Just listen to him, Phil," he pleaded. "I know you respect Jael, but the people don't follow her. They follow you. You need to go online and rally everyone before it's too late."

"Precisely my thoughts," Cardiff concurred with a wave of his teacup.

I took a step back. "I'm not having this conversation with either of you," I insisted, and hoped my tone of voice was understood. "Nobody's doing anything until we talk to Jael. Now if you'll excuse me, Nic and I…"

I turned and realized Nic had gone completely silent. He was staring at the gun in his hand, face rigid.

"Nic...?" I ventured.

He jerked his head up and glared at Jayde. "Where did you get this gun?" he demanded.

Jayde put his hands up. "It was in one of the shipments Asia sent. Why?"

"Is this the powercell that came with it?" Nic tapped the charge bar.

"Of course. Why?" Jayde repeated.

"Were all the guns that were donated from the same manufacturer?"

Jayde glanced at me, as if I had any idea what was going on. "All the shipments I tracked were, yeah. Why's it matter?"

Nic tightened his grip on the weapon. He was shaking.

I stepped closer. "Nic? What's wrong?"

He drew a sharp breath and faced me. "We have a problem."

25: NIC

I stared at the cursed weapon in my hand. The world bled black and red as hopelessness and rage turned my mind into a hailstorm.

Oh yes, there was a very good reason why I had been sent to Russia. But I was too late to do anything about it.

"Nic?" Phil appeared beside me. "What's wrong?"

I took a deep breath and tried to put a cap on the hurricane. "We have a problem."

She stared at me with those wide, watery eyes. How I wished I wasn't about to destroy her world—not after I'd just put it back together.

The Voice in my head stirred. *Let Me help you.*

I faced the group and spoke slowly and clearly. "If you fire these guns, they will explode."

"What?" both Phil and Jayde exclaimed with equal amounts of horror and disbelief.

Cardiff slammed his teacup down on its saucer.

I carefully pried the casing off the side of the gun and showed them the powercell. "This brand of powercell has a faulty design. The conductive core reacts at high heat and melts, causing it to mix with the coolant. The result is extremely explosive."

Phil stood rigid as all the courage drained from her face.

"How do you know this?" Cardiff challenged.

I glanced at him. "We were manufacturing them in Russia. We realized there was a problem when all the batteries that had been subjected to high-voltage testing started detonating."

Jayde gripped the back of a barstool. "And an electric pistol shot…"

"Is the perfect amount of energy to set off the chain reaction," I finished for him. If the weapon was set on stun, it might take two or three shots to reach the needed temperature. If the weapon was set on kill, it would be nearly instantaneous.

A disgusting thought seized me. If I'd shot Jayde—which I'd strongly considered doing at least a dozen times in the last hour—I would have killed us all, including Philadelphia.

Jayde didn't give me time to wallow in that horrific universe. "How big of an explosion are we talking about?"

Phil answered before I could. "Enough to bring down a building."

We all turned to her. She stared at the floor, shivering, not seeming to realize she had spoken. When she finally looked up, her face was running with tears.

"Lanzhou," she whimpered.

Jayde swore.

"What?" I demanded.

"The factory…" Phil struggled to explain, her voice shaking as hard as she was. "There was an explosion, and we thought Asia had bombed us, but… Lanzhou. He-he'd taken one of the guns to defend us. There were shots, and… Oh God, *no.*" She broke off, muttering in tongues, and hid her face in her hands.

I watched her weep as I acknowledged the truth she was too afraid to say: Lanzhou would still be alive, and the factory would still be standing, if he hadn't fired that gun.

Cardiff set his teacup down on the counter. "Do you suppose Asia is aware these guns are defective?"

"She has to be," I insisted. If there was one thing I was confident of, it was my ex-girlfriend's ability to be cunningly evil. "It's a proprietary design, and the source company is a shell. She had them manufactured just for this purpose."

Phil sucked in a breath. "Didn't you say the Nolans owned the company that distributed the guns?" she asked Jayde.

He whipped out his phone and scrolled in a panic. Cardiff walked over, read the screen, and said something incredibly impolite, at least for a British person.

"It's true," Jayde admitted. "You and Cardiff own the majority of the shares—and it's made you a *lot* of money lately."

"You're welcome," I groused, even as I wondered if we'd be in a better situation had I *not* saved the factory and expedited production.

The Holy Spirit didn't move. *Trust Me.*

"There goes the family fortune," Cardiff muttered.

Phil wiped her face on her sleeve. "How many of these guns have we received?" she asked with a sniff.

Jayde hesitated a beat too long. "At least one hundred thousand, that I know about."

"We manufactured around a quarter million powercells," I added, "and that's assuming she doesn't have another supplier."

Phil winced; that wasn't the answer any of us wanted to hear. "Can we replace the powercells in the guns we have?"

"It's not that simple." Jayde pocketed his device. "It's a specialized part for a restricted weapon—you can't just buy them at the corner store. It's also not that easy to replace a powercell. It's a rechargeable battery; it's not meant to be removed. I could do it, because I have military training, but your average civilian isn't going to know what wire to cut."

I glared at him, only because I wished he wasn't right.

Phil closed her eyes. Her lips moved, but no sound came out. About thirty seconds too late, I realized I should join her.

And that's when the Holy Spirit moved, saturating the air until He was the only authority left in the room.

Phil tipped her chin back and squared her shoulders, as if she had to brace herself for what she was about to say. Then she opened her eyes and looked straight at Jayde. "We need to call it off."

"What?" It was Jayde and Cardiff's turn to react with equal measures of shock and anger.

"We need to call it off. We need to cancel Operation Blue Fire." She glanced at me, looking for support.

Jayde didn't give me the chance. "Phil!" he exclaimed, the name ripe with disgust. "You can't just 'cancel' the operation! We'll lose the war!"

"I concur—it's much too late to pull back," Cardiff moaned. "This is a preposterous idea."

"I didn't ask for your opinion." Phil silenced him with a glare before turning back to Jayde. "And we don't have a choice. If the underground uses those guns, we'll lose the war anyway."

"But—"

"Don't you see? Asia's not planning to track us down. She's planning to slaughter us."

No one argued with her, because there was nothing to debate. Anyone who used one of those guns would become a suicide bomber—and would take out everyone around them within a quarter-mile radius. Asia wouldn't even have to deploy the military.

Maybe that was the real reason the government's response had been so lax. Asia had already done the work.

I looked down at the weapon I still had in my hand. I rubbed the manufacturer label on the powercell, finally appreciating just how cruel my ex-girlfriend had been. I would have found out about the guns eventually; word would have gotten around once the weapons started blowing up in people's faces. By then, blood would have been spilled, and I would have rotted in prison with the knowledge that I'd indirectly helped massacre the underground—no doubt killing Philadelphia in the process.

I slammed the gun down on the counter.

Jayde took a deep breath but made no effort to temper his tone. "So, we recall the weapons, swap as many powercells as we can, and warn the people we know got shipments. We can't just call off—"

"And what about the people we don't know about?" Phil didn't raise her voice. She didn't need to. "Jayde, if even a hundred people use these guns—"

"It would be worth it to take Beijing," he snapped.

Almost anyone else would have agreed with him. Anyone but Philadelphia.

She stared at him, fresh tears brimming in her eyes. "If we use these guns, there won't *be* a Beijing."

No one said anything. She picked up the weapon and flipped it over in her hand. "You saw what it did to the factory—and that was just one shot. If there's a thousand explosions—never mind a *hundred* thousand—all across the city on the same day, it will reduce this province to rubble. We'll kill *millions* of innocent people."

I imagined apartment buildings falling, the subway caving in, crowded streets turned to bloodbaths, and realized she was right. If the underground used these weapons on operation day, it would wipe Beijing off the map.

"We might as well have used Red Rain," I murmured.

"Honestly," Cardiff grunted. He picked up his tea and resumed swirling it aggressively.

Jayde clenched his fists and looked ready to do something stupid. "They're not innocent, Phil."

To my surprise, Phil didn't argue. "Enough," she declared, setting the gun back on the counter. "I'm not having this conversation with you. I need to meet with Jael."

"But they're part of the problem! If they're supporting the system, they're the enemy."

He took an insolent step forward. I prepared to knock him down a peg, but Phil beat me to it. "I said enough," she repeated. Her whole body stiffened.

Jayde missed the warning signs. "No, you listen to me! This is war, and we have to do what it takes to win. Now you need to—"

"You are not in charge!"

Her shout silenced the room. Everyone froze. Even Cardiff held his teacup above its saucer, as if he were afraid to put it down and make a noise.

Phil collected herself. "You are not in charge anymore," she repeated. She lowered her voice, which was somehow even more damning. "I am Blue Fire, and I answer only to Jael."

Jayde bristled, and I began to very much regret not killing him thirty minutes ago.

Phil merely frowned. "I have made my decision, and I do not want to hear another word on it until I've talked to Jael. Furthermore, this is my house, and I will not tolerate any more disrespect. So, you can either do your job, or I can send you back to Jael and let you explain yourself to her."

The threat hung in the air like ice. I stared at her and realized that a lot had changed in the month-and-a-half I'd been gone—and some of it was for the better.

Jayde considered his options and wisely chose life. "Yes, ma'am," he mumbled, and pulled back.

"Thank you." Phil sagged, as if the fight had taken everything out of her. She rubbed her temples. "When am I supposed to meet Jael?"

Jayde checked his phone. "You're scheduled to tour one of her facilities this afternoon and then have dinner with her."

"Move it up. I need to speak with her as soon as possible." Phil walked around the island and searched in the cabinets for a glass.

"With all due respect," Jayde said, for once in his life sounding like he actually had some, "I don't think that's wise. If you cancel your other appointments and move up your meeting with Jael, Asia will be suspicious."

Phil scowled, but she didn't argue. "Fine. But contact Jael and tell her what we know—the facts only—so she's prepared." She filled the glass at the sink and gulped it down with a grimace.

Jayde was already typing with his thumbs. "That said, I think you should skip your breakfast appointment."

She glanced up at him.

He met her gaze. "You should go back to bed."

I didn't like the look he was giving her; it said he knew something I didn't.

Although, in his defense, Phil did look awful. If it had been under any other circumstances, I would have regretted waking her up at the bewitching hour of 4:30am.

"But you're supposed to have breakfast with Asia," Cardiff complained.

"All the more reason to cancel it," Jayde argued, and for once, I was in total agreement.

"But she'll be here in less than an hour." Cardiff withdrew a pocket watch from the folds of his house robe, as if he couldn't get any more ostentatiously annoying. "She's going to expect you to be ready."

Now *this* was a problem I could solve. "Oh, you need someone to tell Asia off?" I chirped. "I volunteer as tribute."

Phil didn't share my enthusiasm. "Nic, no, when she finds out you've escaped, she'll—"

"Throw a hissy fit and start hurling empty threats? Yes, I'm quite looking forward to it."

"Nic!" she objected, and then winced, as if her own voice were giving her a headache.

I lowered my volume to help her out. "Stop worrying, Phil, I'll be perfectly safe. She can't do anything as long as Andromeda Nolan is in good standing with the General. Just let me have this one. I feel like I've earned it after spending six weeks in a Russian freezer."

She eyed me, as if debating whether or not I could be trusted with such power. "Okay, but show some discretion. Asia doesn't know we suspect her—she can't even know that you've discovered the fault in the powercells."

I threw a salute. "Don't worry, I know how to keep a secret. I kept your brother 'dead' for two years, remember."

She rolled her eyes, but I saw the tiniest sparkle of a smile in them. She refilled her water and walked towards the door. "Send a maid to wake me up at ten. And I don't care what you have to do, but do *not* let Asia disturb me. And keep Frank away from my room."

The last bit was directed at Cardiff with a glare. "It's not my fault he loves you," he whined.

"Who's Frank?" I demanded. *If she picked up another boyfriend, I will shoot him, exploding powercell or not.*

She either didn't hear me or chose to ignore me. "And Jayde?" she called over her shoulder.

He tensed.

"Get your gun fixed."

He nodded. "Yes, ma'am."

I still didn't love the idea of him having a weapon, but given the circumstances, I suppose at least one of us needed to be carrying.

We all waited until Phil was out of sight before resuming our lives. "Wow, did you see that?" I gestured down the hall where she had gone. "She handled both of you with perfect grace."

Jayde scowled. "I've got calls to make," he grunted, and then stormed out onto the patio.

"As do I," Cardiff added. "It was a pleasure finally meeting you face-to-face, doctor." He gave a curt little bow and waltzed out of the kitchen like some unseen director had told him to clear the stage.

"The feeling's not mutual," I muttered. I didn't like him, although the bar was set really low in that department. In theory, he was no more a threat than Mrs. Nolan was, and he had ample incentive to stay quiet. But he was deadweight, and Phil didn't need any more conflicting voices in her life. I was sure Jayde had provided more than enough unsolicited commentary over the past few weeks.

Peng rapped on the doorframe, interrupting my stewing. "May I show you to your rooms, doctor?"

I decided I'd better stop plotting Jayde's murder and focus on one enemy at a time. "Please. When is Asia supposed to be here?"

He checked his watch. "If she's running on schedule, she'll be here on the hour. Mind if I observe?"

"Please do," I encouraged. "The more people who witness her epic downfall, the better."

He showed me to a suite on the second floor that was, thankfully, only a few doors down from Philadelphia's. I took ten minutes to cull my hair and return my mustache to its former glory. Then I refilled my coffee cup and staged myself dramatically in the foyer. Peng and half of the staff gathered to watch.

Asia didn't arrive until almost fifteen minutes past the hour. She bustled in without knocking. "Andromeda!" she screeched, not looking up from her device. "We're going to be late!"

"And whose fault is that?" I chided.

She screamed—an immensely satisfying shriek of pure terror—and dropped her device. Of course, she was too perfect to put a case on her phone, so it shattered immediately.

Peng gave us ten seconds to savor the moment before he stepped forward. "Allow me to clean that up."

Asia gaped at me, apparently unable to breathe.

I took a slow sip of coffee. "Good morning, sweetheart."

She gripped the door handle. "You… you…" Suddenly, her anger returned like a lightning strike, chasing the panic out of her expression. "What are you doing here?"

"Enjoying my first day of freedom. Why? What's on your calendar?"

"But how—"

"If I had better manners, I would thank you." I let the silence hang just long enough for the sarcasm to ripen. "That was such a nice thing you did for Andromeda. Too little too late, if you ask me, but still, the gesture was appreciated."

She finally caught on that she was the brunt of a joke. "What did you do?" she slurred. She sounded like the demon from a B-rated movie.

"That's the beauty of it, *Min*," I taunted. "I didn't do anything. You're the one who signed the pardon."

"I didn't—"

"You didn't? Well, then you might be the victim of identity theft." I scratched my mustache. "It was your signature and thumbprint on the paperwork."

I watched the blood drain from her face and smiled. I had been waiting nearly ten years for this moment, and it was everything I hoped it would be.

I returned to my coffee and gave her a minute to cycle through all the requisite emotions. She eventually rotated back around to anger, but her voice was more squeaky than threatening. "You tricked me!"

I rolled my eyes. "I wasn't even there. And don't go blaming Andromeda—she was clueless, bless her heart."

She growled and stood on her toes, fluffing herself up like a little frilled lizard. "You won't get away with this!"

I pinched the bridge of my nose. "Seriously, I'm going to need you to stop looking at the bad guy Tumblr for your one-liners. You're a highly educated woman—this is embarrassing."

She didn't take my advice. "I'll have you killed!"

"Go ahead."

She jerked.

I blew on my coffee cup. "Knock yourself out. I can't *wait* to see how you explain yourself when Andromeda goes crying to the General that you killed her favorite person."

"He doesn't care about you," she sneered.

"Of course not. He might wonder who signed my pardon, though."

She choked on her next threat.

"I'd say you should have read the fine print, but that wasn't even the fine print. My name was in big, bold letters at the top."

She tried pitifully several times to form a word, like an engine failing to ignite.

I set my empty coffee cup on the credenza. "Tell you what, I'll make you a deal. I'll stay here and keep my mouth shut so you don't get executed for your laziness, and you go away."

I strode towards her. She stumbled back out onto the front step. "But—Andromeda and I have a breakfast appointment."

"Oh, didn't I tell you? She's cancelling. She wasn't feeling well—on account of me waking her up in the middle of the night and all." I yanked the door from her grasp and blocked the way. "I'll have her secretary let you know when she's free."

"But you can't—"

"*She* can. You have no authority here."

It was only after the words left my mouth that I realized they were true in more ways than one.

Asia tipped her chin back and stared at me, for once having the decency to look afraid.

I leered over her. "I just want you to remember one thing, sweetheart."

She glowered.

I smiled. "You could have prevented all of this."

And then I slammed the door in her face.

26: PHILADELPHIA

Jael's Beijing headquarters was a gorgeous and imposing building—not unlike the woman herself. The skyscraper was at least fifty stories tall. Its asymmetrical floors were staggered, making the whole building curve like a human spine. The endless windows flashed in the dying sun, while a giant digital sign cycled through the company name in a dozen different languages.

Jael didn't join us for the tour, which was just as well; I wasn't sure I could have kept the emotion off my face. Nic and I followed an excited staffer around as we visited massive server rooms that glittered like caves of diamonds. But even more impressive was the control panel for the algorithm. It was a behemoth piece of equipment, not unlike the original computers of the pre-2000s.

I stared at the thrumming machine. This program had ruined so many lives, including my own. Now, it might be our only hope of saving millions.

Finally, the staffer led us to the top floor of the building—a floor that didn't exist, according to the elevator. The windowless space was lined with rows of servers, no doubt the ones that held all the incriminating data for my revolution. A guard took our electronics and locked them in a case with a dampening field. Even "Blue Fire" couldn't be too careful in the room that contained the secrets of war.

Jael was waiting in a meeting area off to the side. She rose when we entered. She approached me without greeting and dropped something small and sharp into my hand.

I looked down at it: It was the remnant of a powercell. Only the first letter of the company logo was still legible; the rest of the fragment was charred and pitted.

"So, it's true," I whispered. I'd believed Nic, of course, but some part of my soul had clung to a shred of hope. Maybe there had been a miscommunication; maybe only some of the powercells were defective. Maybe there was still another way out.

She nodded. "I tested it myself."

I pinched my eyes shut. *Then there's only one thing we can do.*

Jael turned to Nic and offered her hand. "Glad to have you back. I only wish you had brought us better news."

He accepted the handshake. "I only wish I had gotten here sooner."

"I'm not sure it would have mattered," Jael said in a tone too bitter to be consoling. She faced me again. "I've spoken with General Jin and Warden Ivanova. I have reason to believe all the guns we received from our mysterious donor are defective."

I swallowed and tried to gather the courage to say what needed to be said.

She kept talking before I found it. "Unfortunately, it gets worse. I reached out to Data and was informed that several outposts in Boston also received munitions. Different company, but... I'm having him run some tests."

I clenched the fragment in my fist. It was one thing to set fire to Beijing, but now Asia was trying to destroy my hometown, too? What if she sent these guns to our allies all across the world?

Nic had the same thought. "Do you suppose any of our other friends have received a 'donation'?"

"I'll make some calls, but my guess is she concentrated her efforts around Beijing and Washington. It will be much easier for her to restructure the United if she destroys both seats of government."

Jael tapped a tablet that was sitting on the coffee table. The screen brightened, and a small hologram projected from the surface. It was a map of the world, speckled with dots—the sites of known demonstrations for operation day. Most of the dots around Beijing and Boston were red, making the world look like it had been stabbed in the chest twice.

It all made wicked sense, and I briefly wondered why Asia *wasn't* using Red Rain. If her plan all along had been to wipe cities off the map, Red Rain would have left no survivors. It had been within her power; she could have scalped the formula from my father's broken brain months ago, and manufacturing the acid would have surely been quicker than planting the defective powercells. The only benefit to using the guns was that the resistance—and, by extension, her father—would be blamed for the destruction.

I suppose that was reason enough.

"General Jin is recalling all the weapons within his regiment." Jael gestured at the projection, as if she could just wipe the red away with her hand. "We're working to track down as many shipments as possible."

"And what about the guns we can't track?" I asked. "You said yourself—even if we could find all the original shipments, people have already distributed the weapons among their friends. Those guns are all over the city." I searched her face, begging her to contradict me, to provide a different explanation, to conjure another solution.

She hesitated, and I had my answer. There was only one choice.

Sliding the powercell fragment in my pocket, I took a deep breath. *Jesus, help me save this city.*

"I'm hopeful we can recall most of the guns," Jael continued without optimism. "We have two days before Operation Blue Fire launches. If we can pull most of the weapons—"

"It won't be enough."

She stopped. I glanced at Nic.

He nodded.

Courage finally flooded me. I straightened and raised my voice. "Recalling the weapons won't be enough. We have to cancel the operation."

She didn't even hesitate, making me wonder if she'd already considered the possibility. "That's out of the question. First of all, launch time is in less than 72 hours. It would be impossible to pull people back."

"Not for me, it isn't," I argued. "You said yourself—they follow me. If I go online and warn everyone, they'll listen."

"They absolutely will—and that's exactly why I can't let you do it." Jael sighed, her voice soaked with condescension. "Philadelphia, this isn't just about Beijing or Washington. This is a global movement. We have managed to galvanize resistance in every sector of the world. If we strike together, the government will not be able to maintain control."

Jayde's voice haunted me. *"If we all stand up together, they can't make us all sit down."*

"We will not be able to organize that level of resistance again," Jael continued. "Even you would not be able to rally the people a second time."

I didn't fully believe that, but that wasn't what I was afraid of. "We won't *have* any people left if we use those guns. You saw what it did to the Tangs' factory—imagine a hundred, a thousand explosions like that across the city."

"I'm fully aware of the situation we are in," Jael returned. "That's why we're going to recall as many guns as possible."

"And then what? Leave those groups defenseless?" I stepped forward and pointed at the red blur on the map that represented Beijing. "They're not going to be able to find enough replacement weapons in two days. If we recall the guns, Asia will simply send the military to slaughter them. She still knows where everyone is."

"She's right," Nic spoke from where he hovered on the sidelines. He leaned against the wall, arms folded, observing. "Either way, you lose Beijing."

"I'm willing to sacrifice Beijing if it means winning the war," Jael returned, the words cool, slicing. "We need the global momentum of operation day to break the system. If we can disrupt the government's network of control, we can form regions of independence and fortify ourselves. We'll take Beijing later by force if need-be."

I didn't like the sound of that, but I struggled not to get lost in a hypothetical reality. "And in the meantime, what about our allies here?" I demanded. I thought of the dozens of churches, safehouses, and underground hospitals I'd visited. All the poor, underprivileged, and oppressed citizens who believed in me. The citizens I'd been telling, in video after video, that I would fight alongside them.

"I'll do my best," Jael promised.

That's what you always say.

"I'll contact my network and warn them to destroy the guns and relocate. I won't be able to reach them all, but I'll save those I can."

"So, we'll abandon the rest?" In my head, the words were angry, but my voice came out heartbroken and frail. No matter how many guns we pulled, there would still be hundreds in the field, enough to collapse half of Beijing. I couldn't abandon a city of thirty million people. I couldn't walk away—not like I had with Nic, and Stanyard, and all the other people Asia had executed.

I could barely hear Jael over the ringing in my ears. "They knew the risks."

I backed up. "No, they didn't." No one had committed to becoming a suicide bomber with a rigged gun, and I couldn't let them die when I had the power to save them.

Jael closed the gap, her clacking heels loud and irritating in the silence. "Philadelphia. I promise I am not making this decision lightly."

"But I told them—"

"You did what you were ordered to do. This is my call to make."

But I can't go along with it.

"I know this is hard for you to understand." Jael gripped my shoulder. "But this is a sacrifice we have to make. And your orders are to trust me."

"You also told me to ask questions." I pulled away and faced her. "You told me heroes save life when they can. What happens when people find out we knew the whole time? Someone else is going to figure out the truth about the guns. What are we going to tell them when they realize I left them to die?"

Jael shook her head. "That's my problem, not yours."

No, it was mine. It was very much my problem.

"I will handle the damage control. I'll give you a script—"

"Covering up what happened isn't damage control," I snapped. "I won't lie to people."

Her face tightened in a gesture I knew all too well. "You'll say whatever I tell you to say."

"No."

The declaration ripped out of me before I could censor it. Jael frowned, her hand poised midair, as if giving me a chance to recant.

I didn't. This was a line I wouldn't cross.

"I can't go online and lie to people," I repeated, slowly, firmly, struggling to keep my emotions under control. "I won't sacrifice an entire city just to win the war. This is wrong."

This time, Jael did hesitate, and the silence was a threat. "Philadelphia, this is not your decision to make. Your job is to trust me."

"I do trust you," I insisted, and believed that, maybe, it was still true. "But I can't do this."

"I didn't ask for your—"

"I *won't* do this!" I shouted, then caught myself. I lowered my voice even though everything was shaking. "Jael, please, just listen to me. If I don't warn them, millions of people will die. If

Asia sent these guns to other countries, we could kill *billions* of people."

She sighed, the sound dangerous. "It's a sacrifice we have—"

"No, it's not! Don't you see? If I let those people die, I'll be no better than Asia or Thames or anyone else." The realization hit me with a rush of cold memories. "If I'm willing to sacrifice millions of people just to win, I should have stayed on Mars and let Nic finish Red Rain."

I turned to him. He tugged on his mustache and said nothing.

I kept my eyes on him as I reached for the Holy Spirit. "This is not who we are," I insisted, and I'd never held a statement with more conviction in my life. "The way we win matters. I blew up that factory on Rott because I refuse to fight with their weapons. I will not be the next dictator—that is not what Blue Fire stands for."

"Blue Fire stands for whatever I tell her to."

I whirled. Jael stood at the coffee table with her back to me. "I created Blue Fire, and she works for me. That means she does what she's ordered to do."

The room began to pitch and blur; I knew what was about to happen. "Jael, I—"

She didn't let me finish. "Any disobedience will be treated as insubordination and punished accordingly."

I stared at her as she drew a line between us in bloodred. I had a choice. I could do what I knew was right and fracture the underground by alienating Jael. Or I could obey her orders and allow the deaths of millions of people.

And that was a choice I couldn't make.

My eyes burned. "Jael, please, don't make me do this."

"Enough," she declared, passing judgment with that one cruel word. She tapped the tablet and turned off the projection. "I've made my decision, and now you need to do as you're told."

I can't, I can't!

She glared at me over her shoulder. "Am I understood?"

I couldn't answer. *This isn't right!*

She turned. "Are we going to have a problem, Philadelphia?"

"I've got a problem."

Nic's sudden declaration cut through the noise like a knife. He unfolded himself from the corner, straightening to his full height. "This conversation is not helpful." He frowned at Jael.

She wasn't intimidated. "This conversation doesn't involve you, doctor."

"It does now. Go home, Philadelphia, and Jael and I will discuss this."

Every nerve crackled with panic. I was *not* going to be shut out of the room while other people decided my fate again. "Nic, please, you don't—"

He caught my arm. "Phil."

I looked up into his face. His expression was stern but not unkind. "Let me handle this."

I stared back as a new emotion invaded the chaos.

"Let me help you."

I took a deep breath and stepped back. "Okay."

He let go. I turned to the guard standing by the door, not trusting myself to look at Jael. "Please bring the car around."

27: NIC

The guard moved to obey her without a word, and she followed him out of the room. I waited until they were both safely beyond earshot before turning to Jael. "Let's talk about this."

"We were talking about this. I don't know how you expect this conversation to go any differently." She put her hand on her hip and fixed me with that condescending stare that made me feel like I'd forgotten to shower.

I did my royal best not to return the look in kind. "Well, seeing as I'm not a seventeen-year-old girl, I'd expect this conversation to go very differently. We're adults here."

She wasn't convinced. "If that's the case, then you should know that she's being immature and impulsive."

"And *you* should know that you're being cruel and insensitive." I sighed. "Were all the death threats necessary? You're killing her."

"Better me than someone else. I cannot allow her to entertain such foolish ideas."

"Forgive me," I drawled, "but I'm something of an expert on foolish ideas. And I have to say, turning a quarter million of your most loyal followers into suicide bombers without their consent tops anything I've ever come up with."

"I told you both," she enunciated loudly, like she was overexplaining herself to a toddler, "we'll do our best to minimize the damage. We'll warn those we can—"

"And what about those you can't? Philadelphia made a good point. Several, in fact."

"They knew the risks." Jael picked up the tablet and started scrolling, as if she weren't being rude enough already.

I crossed my arms and scowled, not that she was looking at me. "I don't know what that phrase means to you, but I think the average civilian would disagree. 'We'll give you a defective gun that will blow up in your face' was nowhere in the fine print. I looked."

She continued typing. "These things happen in war."

"Okay, pause for a second." I put both hands up. "The fact that you keep giving me textbook answers is a little insulting. So, I'm going to need you to drop the pretenses and tell me what's really going on."

She arched an eyebrow. "I don't 'have' to do anything."

"No, but if I stand here and harass you long enough, you're going to wish you'd taken the easy way out."

She finally glanced up at me and looked like she couldn't decide whether to laugh or punch me in the face.

I shrugged. "I just spent six weeks dealing with Warden Ivanova. You're easy."

That did the trick. She hurled the tablet on the coffee table with a thud. "You want the truth? Fine." She paused, breathing sharply through her nose, like she had to go digging in the back of her closet for the words. "The truth is, I wasn't expecting to win Beijing in the first place."

I froze. My brain had autofilled several explanations, but that wasn't one of them.

"I never expected to win the front in Beijing," she repeated. "The military presence is too strong here. Resistance is suicide, exploding guns or not."

That statement was more than a little concerning coming from the woman who was supposed to be leading said resistance. "So... what *was* your plan?"

"My plan was to cripple their infrastructure and disrupt their communications, then retreat to strongholds in the countryside. They would have driven us out of the capital, but if we gave them enough internal problems, it would have made it difficult for them to retaliate on other fronts."

It wasn't the worst plan ever, except for one minor detail. "That's not what Phil said in her videos."

She didn't even blink. "Would you join an army if the leader was prophesying failure?"

"As someone who knows a little bit about prophecy, I would prefer the truth."

She scoffed. "This world hasn't operated on truth in at least a century."

"No, but Philadelphia does."

And that's what makes her different than you.

"Look," Jael sighed, and for once, she didn't sound like she hated me, "I'm not saying we wouldn't have tried. If anyone can rally the people to overthrow the Council, it's Philadelphia."

I could tell she believed that statement with every fiber of her being, as did I.

"But when I found out Asia had planted the guns and was tracking the underground, I knew it was a losing battle." Jael looked away, and I could tell by the creases around her lips that she had spent many long nights calculating failure. "Even if Philadelphia could turn the Council against Asia, it wouldn't have saved everyone. Asia's information is on a server somewhere. The government would have just seized her devices and found her map of the underground, and then our allies would be worse off."

She was right. The underground had been exposed, and it was impossible to fully erase that data. "The only way to save them all *would* be to call off the operation," I said, finally understanding what Phil had seen all along.

Jael nodded, the gesture slow and final.

Asia truly had created an inescapable trap—but that still didn't answer one question. "Then why did you let Philadelphia go back to the Nolan estate? If you knew it was a lost cause, why put her at risk like that?"

"Because Asia is still our greatest enemy," Jael confessed. "If I can take her out—and send the government on a witch hunt—then we just might have a chance of winning the war. It was worth the risk to potentially expose Asia."

I didn't agree, but I knew Philadelphia would—if she had been given the truth. "Why didn't you tell Philadelphia?" I asked, and genuinely hoped she had a good answer.

She didn't. "Do you think she would have gone through with the operation if I did?"

My general aversion for this woman returned, thick and slimy. "So, you sacrificed *my daughter* just to get intel on Asia, and you didn't even tell Phil what you were doing?"

"She wouldn't have understood."

"I beg to differ, but she'll never learn if you just yell at her instead of explaining your actions. Why'd you threaten to court martial her?"

"Because I'm not stupid. I know I'm playing with fire. If she'll defy Asia and Thames, she'll certainly defy me."

Under any other circumstances, it would have been a compliment. "So, your solution is to scare her into submission? I believe they call that manipulation, and it's usually what bad guys do. I've tried it a few times. Do not recommend."

"I can't risk it!" She swiped her hand like a murderer slashing a knife. "She has no idea how much damage she'll cause if she goes online and scares everyone off."

"She won't know if you don't explain it to her!" I shouted back, fully aware we were going in circles. I struggled to be the better person and lower my voice. "Please, just try talking to her. She's more mature than you give her credit for. If you explain it to her, she'll follow you."

For better or for worse.

Jael turned away from me. "No. I can't do that to her."

"Do what? Treat her like an adult?" I mocked. "Yeah, because no teenager ever wants to be treated with respect."

"Enough!" she shouted, as if that word could end all wars. "I will not put her through that!"

"Through what, Jael?" I demanded, and then realized what wasn't the question. "What are you afraid of?"

She flinched, and I knew I'd finally broken past her defenses. She stood with her back to me, silent.

I waited.

Finally, she drew a sharp breath and whispered, "Seventy thousand."

"What?"

She stared at the wall, like she was having a conversation with someone else. "71,632." She turned and looked at me again. "That's the estimated number of people the United killed when they bombed the border of my country. The casualties were mostly the elderly, women, and children—including every single member of my extended family."

"I'm sorry," I said, and then wondered if it would have been better if I'd kept my mouth shut.

She twirled one of the bangles on her wrist. "I had to make that decision. There was no one in the room when I intercepted the transmission, no one I could reach in time. I had to decide between saving the two million people in the capital or saving my family."

I stared at her. I of all people knew that you couldn't judge by appearances—and I had definitely judged this woman too swiftly.

"I am responsible for every single one of those deaths!" she screeched. "Sixteen years old, and I had to decide who lived and who died." She jabbed her finger in the air, as if making a case for an invisible jury.

What verdict she received, I'll never know. She sighed and lowered her arm. "I don't want Philadelphia to have to make the same choice. That's why I demand obedience—because if she's just following orders, she doesn't have to bear the consequences."

The Voice in my head muddied the silence. *That's not true.*

"She's going to bear the guilt whether you sign off on it or not," I murmured.

If Jael forced Philadelphia to go through with this, Philadelphia would live with not only the guilt of causing the deaths of millions of people, but also the knowledge that she violated everything she ever stood for. That after a year of running and fighting and sacrificing everything, including her family, she'd become what she hated most and handed the baton to the next dictator.

I couldn't let that happen—and the only way to stop it was to prevent Jael from taking that role.

I spread my hands. "Jael, listen to me. I think you need to consider what Phil is saying."

"Don't you think I have?" she snarled, her voice still too loud for the room. "Don't you think I've spent every waking hour studying predictions and looking for another solution? Every simulation I've run says that if we save Beijing, we lose the war."

"Then maybe it's a war you need to lose."

"You can't be serious," she scoffed.

I was—and so was the Voice in my head. "I think you're underestimating how dangerous this plan is. Phil is right. If the people find out she knew about the guns, they'll turn on her— and your newly-forged democracy or whatever will crumble."

"Don't you think I've thought of that? I have a whole PR campaign planned—"

"Oh, so you'll cover it up with the media? Sounds like the United."

She had enough character not to deny it. "You have no idea how to lead a war."

"You're absolutely correct."

She froze, which was what people usually did when I admitted they were right. I continued before she could reboot. "I *don't* have any idea. I've spent the better part of the last decade either off-planet or in prison. And if it were up to me, I'd still vote that we set up a colony on Mars and let this place burn." I paused. "The Voice in my head says I'm not allowed to say that."

She backstepped. "The Voice in your…"

"Never mind. The point is, I'm out of my league, and I'm not afraid to admit that."

Actually, you're terrified, the Voice in my head corrected.

I laughed cruelly. "You're right. I have three PhDs, and none of them prepared me for parenting a traumatized teenage girl while also trying to save the world. I have absolutely no idea what I'm doing."

Jael was silent, perhaps because she, too, abruptly realized how underqualified I was for this.

You're going to make me unpack this baggage later, aren't You? I challenged the Voice in my head.

He smiled. *Whenever you're ready.*

I bookmarked the conversation and turned my focus back to Jael. "Listen, I'm not here to stage a mutiny. I refuse to drag Phil into another custody battle. If this is what you decide, then fine. You won't get any trouble from me."

She paused, as if making sure I wasn't going to take it back. "Thank you," she said finally.

"Just promise me one thing."

She tensed.

"Promise me you'll do what I didn't."

"And that is?" she returned, the distrust creeping back into her voice.

"Talk to her."

She frowned. "Meaning?"

"Meaning, if this is your decision, sit her down and explain it to her."

"I thought I just did."

"No, that was called issuing an order like a heartless despot. I mean you need to tell her the truth, no matter how ugly it is. Tell her the real reason you sent her back to the estate. Tell her your plan for the war. She may not agree with you, but at least you'll save your relationship."

She pulled back like an eel into its den. "This is war. I don't have time for feelings—"

"Then make time, because this isn't about you. This is about saving Philadelphia."

She hesitated. I took a deep breath and pulled on the Holy Spirit every way I knew how. "Look, I know you don't see it yet, but she needs you. And not all these military-general-court-martial vibes. She needs *you*, the woman who's survived a war."

The Holy Spirit answered the call, and I saw a fragment of what the woman was inside, beneath the cold attitude, ruthless morals, and heavy jewelry. "You know what it's like to sacrifice everything and be the last woman standing. You know what it's like to have blood on your hands and ghosts in your closet. You are the one person who best understands what Philadelphia is going through, and you're the only one who can help her put her life back together when this is over."

Jael looked away. Perhaps because she realized that she, too, was grossly underprepared for the burden that had been handed to her.

"She needs you," I repeated, "but if you don't tell her the truth, you'll lose her. You'll join a long list of adults who never listened to her, myself included."

My name was on that list a dozen times. I should have encouraged her to stay on Mars instead of letting her make her own decision; I should have helped her find her father instead of leaving her to fend for herself; I should have taught her how to be a leader instead of watching her fail. I'd had so many opportunities over the past six months to make her a friend instead of an enemy, but I'd chosen to stay walled up in my prison because I didn't want to be responsible for her life—or my feelings.

I was a pathetic, inadequate, wholly dysfunctional excuse for a father. But by God's grace, I wouldn't make the same mistake again.

"Jael."

I waited until she looked at me before continuing.

"Please don't do this. Don't force her to choose between your respect and doing what she thinks is right."

"I don't need her respect," she returned, but there was no conviction behind the words.

"Maybe you don't, but she does. She needs your love—and right now, you've told her that she has to blindly obey or lose that love. She's probably on the floor back at the house right now, praying her guts out, begging God for another solution."

Jael winced. There was no denying it; she knew Philadelphia as well as I did.

I took a step forward, desperate to close the gap over the one person we both cared about. "Please don't make her go through that again. Don't force her to choose between your relationship and her conscience."

She didn't respond, breaking eye contact once more.

I opened my mouth, but the Holy Spirit got there first.

Enough.

I obeyed and turned to go. I'd made my case; the power of life and death was in Jael's hands now.

She didn't stop me. I stepped out into the hall, then paused.

"Besides," I called over my shoulder without looking back, "I think we both know what she'll choose."

28: NIC

I was right. When I got back to the house, Phil was on her face in the courtyard, sobbing.

"She's outside," Peng said unnecessarily as he collected my jacket. The information was superfluous; I could hear her crying through the half-open patio door.

Jayde stood watch in the shadows of the living room. He looked up at me as I approached. "Fix this," he hissed, "or the war is over."

"I'll handle it," I snapped, and hoped he could read the threat in my tone of voice.

He obeyed and disappeared. I waited until he was out of sight, then opened the screen door silently. I needn't have bothered; Philadelphia was in no danger of hearing me. She was splayed out on the tile next to the pool like she'd been shot and left for dead. A Bible lay open beside her, its pages crumpled. Her gauzy house robe fanned around her like a prayer shawl as she beat the ground with her fists.

"Jesus, Jesus, *Jesus*," she wailed, as if that name was the only thing keeping her head above water. She scratched at the tile with broken fingernails. "I don't know what to do. I can't let them die! I can't destroy this city!"

I took a step towards her. She jerked upright, the motion inhuman, but she was facing away and didn't see me. "This isn't right! This isn't what You called me to do!" It was almost a question as she stared at the stars, begging for an answer.

She hugged her knees and fell silent, long enough that I almost said something. But then she spoke again—and she said exactly what I didn't want to hear.

"Please don't make me do this," she rasped like there was a hand around her throat. "Not again."

As if realizing words were insufficient for the crisis, she broke off in weeping and tongues. There were more tears than the latter as she curled into a ball and quivered, completely unaware of me.

I stared at her as regret after regret crushed my lungs. I'd had a dozen opportunities over the last six months to prevent this horrific universe, and I'd missed them all. Now the weight of the world was on her shoulders, and I couldn't fix it.

You don't have to fix it.

The Holy Spirit rippled the waters of the pool.

You don't have to do anything.

I walked over and sat down cross-legged on the patio beside her. She didn't hear me. I watched her shake and sob and wondered if I should speak up.

And that's when I realized there was one thing I *should* do.

I knew exactly what she needed. I knew what one simple act would keep her world from collapsing.

And it was the one thing I couldn't give.

I clenched my fists. Everything in me told me that I didn't want to open this door. That if I did, Philadelphia would never let me shut it again—and I would be responsible for her in more ways than one.

Religion was all well and good when it was just me and the Voice in my head.

A breeze gusted across the courtyard. *I didn't give you a gift so you could save yourself.*

I closed my eyes and let the cold air wrap around my shoulders. Then I took a deep breath, looked out across the pool, and prayed.

"God," I started, and then almost didn't go any further—because I abruptly realized I had nothing to say.

Philadelphia started and almost fell into the pool. She hastily wiped her cheeks. "Nic?"

I kept my gaze on the moving water. "Phil needs You. She needs Your wisdom, and she needs Your presence."

Philadelphia fell silent. She gripped her knees and stared at me with those wide, vulnerable eyes.

I had no idea where to go from there, so I just started listing the facts. "You brought her here. You connected her with Jael. You gave her this position of influence and power—and now she needs to know what to do with that power."

I hesitated when I realized Philadelphia wasn't the only one who needed intercession. "Give Jael wisdom. You put her in a place of authority for this very hour—show her why. Show her what You showed me."

I trailed off. There were a dozen other things I could ask for, but I felt like I'd said too much already. It was definitely the lamest, dumbest, and most theologically pedantic prayer I'd ever prayed, and putting an "Amen" on it felt even dumber.

The Holy Spirit did it for me. *Amen*, He breathed, and then smiled.

Philadelphia sniffed. I finally turned to face her. Her breathing had returned to normal as she dried her face on her sleeve. "Thank you," she whispered.

Saying "you're welcome" seemed weird, so I just smiled.

She adjusted her robe and turned to dip her bare feet in the pool. "Did you talk to Jael?"

I leaned back on my hands. "Yeah."

"And?" The word was tiny, fearful.

"She's going to call us in the morning."

Phil hugged herself. "And if she says we're going through with the operation?"

I'd been asking the Holy Spirit and my three PhDs for an answer to that question and hadn't gotten a solution out of any of them. "I think you need to give her a chance to speak for herself before you plan alternatives."

She nodded, but she barely made it all the way through the motion.

"But… if she refuses, *we* will talk."

I put the emphasis on the plural. I couldn't promise a solution, but I could promise that she wouldn't go alone.

She looked up at me. "Thanks, Nic."

Her eyes were watering again, but this time, she wasn't afraid. And in that moment, I realized I had absolutely no regrets.

The breeze danced across the patio again, ruffling the pages of her Bible. I picked it up. "Where did you get this extremely illegal piece of paper?"

Her lips twitched. "Stanyard gave it to me."

How I wished that name inspired anything but utter disgust. The kid deserved better from me, of course; he was in jail because he'd risked his life for Philadelphia. But if I was being honest, I wasn't entirely mad that they'd been on separate continents for the past month. At least I didn't have to worry about him kissing her or hugging her or, heaven forbid, *proposing* to her when he was halfway across the world.

I flipped through the crinkled pages. "Have you heard from him?"

"No." Her voice shuddered. "Asia hasn't mentioned him in several weeks. She won't tell me where he is."

I slammed my fist on the tile. *Can I please kill Asia?* I begged the Voice in my head.

No.

But it would solve so many problems!

I said no.

I grumbled out loud. Phil gave me a look.

"Sorry," I said, "just arguing with the Voice in my head." I closed the Bible and tried to find a clean way to end the conversation. "You should get to bed. It's late." *Wow, taking this "old man" role a little too seriously, are we?*

She sighed. "I guess I should take my pills."

"Pills?" I repeated, and my suspicion made my voice way too loud for the acoustics of the veranda.

She reached into the pocket of her robe and pulled out a prescription bottle. She held it in both hands and stared at it in the moonlight. "I've been taking anxiety medication."

"Jael put you on *medication*?" I tried to figure out why that thought made me so irrationally angry. I would have recommended the same thing, had I been there. But I wasn't there, and now someone had put *my daughter* on medication without asking me.

Phil was oblivious to my parental crisis. "It's supposed to help me sleep, too."

I brushed the feelings aside. "Is it working?"

She shrugged. Her eyes wandered elsewhere, looking anywhere but in my direction.

"What?" I prodded.

"I just..." Her fingers tightened around the bottle. "I don't... I don't understand why Jesus won't heal me."

The anguish in her voice sent my soul to my throat. "What do you mean?"

She finally turned to me. "Nic, He *healed* you. I've seen a dead man raised to life, and now I can't even sleep without taking a dozen pills!" She drew her arm back and looked like she was about to hurl the bottle into the pool, then reconsidered. She dropped her hands back in her lap. "I just... don't know what I'm doing wrong. Why won't He heal me?"

There were a dozen possible answers to that question, none of which she needed to hear. Good theology wouldn't save her, but I knew that if I didn't say something, she'd have a wound that medication couldn't heal.

I turned my thoughts inward and let the Voice in my head speak first.

"Sometimes God fixes our problems," I repeated slowly. "Other times, He gives us the wisdom to fix it ourselves."

Phil stared at the bottle in her hands, reconsidering.

"And, don't take this the wrong way, but... if you stop praying just because you're on medication, that seems like a personal problem."

She jerked, and I knew I'd saved a life.

I stood and led the way to the house. "Let's get some sleep."

She scrambled to follow. "Nic, wait."

I glanced over my shoulder. She fidgeted.

I groaned and held one arm out. "Make it quick," I said, even though I didn't mean it.

She darted over and grabbed me around the waist. "Thank you," she sniffled into my chest.

I squeezed her shoulder. "It's our little secret. If you tell anyone, I'll deny everything."

That worked. She giggled and let me go.

"Now, bedtime. I'm not telling you again." I shoved the Bible at her.

She pushed it back. "I want you to keep it."

"Why? Because I need it more than you do?" I snarked.

You said it, not Me, the Voice in my head commented.

She tried and failed to laugh. "No, I… I just want someone to take care of it."

She avoided my gaze, and I realized what she was implying.

I gripped the spine. "I don't think Pizza Boy will be happy when he finds out you regifted his love offering."

She shrugged.

I decided not to push it. "I'll keep it safe."

She gave me a smile, then ran for the step. I stood on the patio and watched her disappear into the shadows of the house.

I looked down at the Bible in my hands. Phil didn't expect to get out of this alive—and even if she did, she didn't believe she'd ever see Pizza Boy again. And that was a future I couldn't let her live in.

Someone had to save that boy.

29: NIC

I went back into the house and fetched the phone Jael's people had given me. They told me it was fully secure—not that it would matter after I sent this text.

I opened the app and typed in a number I wished I didn't have memorized.

IT'S NIC. CAN WE TALK?

She left me unread for an indecent amount of time. I was quite sure she saw the message immediately, but she didn't respond for almost twenty minutes, just to be petty.

YOU MUST BE DESPERATE IF YOU'RE COMING TO ME

WHAT DID WE SAY ABOUT THE ONE-LINERS? OF COURSE I'M DESPERATE

WHY SHOULD I MEET WITH YOU?

BECAUSE YOU'RE CURIOUS. LET ME BUY YOU A COFFEE. OUR FAVORITE PLACE IS STILL OPEN.

Back in the good old days when Asia and I were dating, we'd both been incredibly busy—me, a decorated scientist and her, a scheming politician—so we'd mapped out several places in Beijing that were open late. There was a coffee shop close to the council chambers with a quaint upper room that Asia would rent out so we'd have our privacy.

The thought of being alone with Asia gave me about as much joy as an aneurysm, but if I was going to save Phil's future husband, I'd have to make a deal with the devil.

Thankfully, the devil was willing to play.

I'LL MEET YOU IN AN HOUR

The coffee shop was in a kitschy shopping district, the kind of neighborhood they showed on the news to make it look like communism was working. Everything was clean and sparkly and perfect. The shops were all gimmicky, with plastic tile roofs and neon signs styled to lure tourists. Even the people seemed fake as they posed for selfies under the archways.

The coffee shop was vacant when I entered. The only person in the room was a soldier guarding the foot of the stairs. He bowed and gestured for me to follow.

Asia sat at our usual table in the balcony. She'd dressed down—relatively speaking—for the event, which I found somewhat threatening. She wore a simple top and slacks and had no lipstick on. On the table in front of her were two mugs of black coffee.

"It was my turn to buy," I groused.

She didn't respond. She picked up a small metal case off the floor and opened it. "Phone, please."

I obliged, turning off my device and tossing it on the dampening field. She added her own phone to the pile as a gesture of goodwill, then latched the case and set it aside.

I sat down across from her. I exchanged eye contact with the soldier standing watch in the corner, then turned my focus on Asia. "Thank you for meeting me," I said, and I actually meant it.

"Curiosity killed the cat." She slid a mug across the table towards me. "Besides, I think we can make an equal exchange."

I took a rallying sip. "Name your price."

She picked at the chipped laminate on the table. "Let's keep it simple tonight. I'll answer your questions, and you answer mine."

"Fair enough. You first—because then if you ask a question I can't answer, I still have time to back out."

She smirked. "What is Philadelphia planning?"

"Besides the overthrow of your government? Narrow the search parameters, please."

She swirled her mug. "Why is she here?"

I stalled by gulping down half my drink. Asia clearly still didn't realize that Phil knew about the guns, and I had to keep it that way. Unfortunately, Asia wasn't stupid, and she knew me better than I cared to admit. She would know if I lied.

So, don't lie, the Voice in my head commented, as if it was that easy.

Maybe it was.

I set my cup aside. "Why do you think? To get close to your father."

She tapped her acrylic nail on the handle of her mug like an irritated typewriter. "She had her chance."

"And she blew it. Jayde almost killed her, I had to swoop in and save her, it was a whole thing."

"You did look good in that suit," she consented. "But why now? She could have come home anytime. I've given her plenty of... incentive."

"Yes, I heard you two did a lot of bonding while I was gone," I hissed, letting a bit of the distaste into my voice.

She liked it. Her tongue frisked the edge of her teeth. "I'll admit, I really thought the stunt with your fake trial would work. I'm still surprised she left you out to dry."

As was I, although I was more proud than anything else. "I guess you misjudged her motivations."

"Apparently so." Asia propped her elbows on the table and tented her fingers. "So, educate me. What's inspired our little princess to come home?"

I hesitated a beat too long. "Don't avoid the question, doctor," Asia cooed. "You promised. Why didn't she just take the shot when she had the chance?"

"She wasn't ready," I mumbled, and as soon as the words left my mouth, I realized they were the complete truth. "The assassination was a childish plan from a very childish man. If she'd gone through with it, she would have handed the world to you on a silver platter—and she knew that."

Asia flicked her fingers in a gesture of vague consent.

"But now she has real power. Your father is obsessed with her. She doesn't need to bargain with you—he'll give her anything she asks for. She's playing with the big boys now, and if she deals her cards right, he'll hand her the keys to the kingdom and never even realized he's been fooled."

Asia arched one eyebrow. "I almost believe you're telling the truth."

"You wish I was," I returned, "because that's what you want to happen, isn't it?"

It is, the Voice in my head whispered.

Asia winked. "Is that the question you want an answer to?"

"Nah, that was just a rhetorical statement for dramatic effect. I have bigger problems than dissecting your evil schemes."

"Very well." She crossed one leg over her knee and leaned back in the chair. "What can I do for you, Dr. Nic?"

Unlike her, I had no reason to be catty, so I came right out with it. "Where's Stanyard?"

She paled, and I lost all courage. "Is he alive?" *Dear God, please don't let me be too late.*

"I... I don't know," Asia fumbled.

"What do you mean, you don't know? Last I checked, he was rotting in *your* prison. Where is he?"

"I don't know," she repeated.

I slammed my hands on the table, and the guard tensed. "I'm going to need a better answer than 'I don't know,'" I hissed. "I answered your questions, and now you'd better keep your end of the bargain. Tell me where he is."

"How many times do I have to say 'I don't know' before you believe me?" She sat up and punctuated with both arms. "He was being held in Boston. They were transporting him here, but we lost contact with the plane. The signal cut off over the middle of the ocean."

I searched her face for any signs of guile, but she seemed just as panicked as I was. "Do they think the plane went down?"

"Maybe," she said in a way that suggested she had her own theories. "But no distress signal was sent out, and they haven't recovered any wreckage."

A flicker of hope flashed across my mind, but Asia promptly snuffed it out. "But if they survived, the plane would have landed somewhere—or surely my pilot would have made contact. Everyone who was onboard has dropped off the grid."

I could tell by the pace of her breathing that she was telling the truth. And for once, I wished she wasn't.

"I'm sorry," Asia whispered, and I realized that was the only genuine apology she'd ever given me. "If I hear anything, I'll tell you."

I gripped my coffee mug with both hands and resisted the urge to throw it across the room. What was I going to tell Philadelphia? That her boyfriend vanished into the Bermuda Triangle and wasn't coming back?

The Voice in my head shifted. *Trust Me.*

"Thanks for not lying," I sighed. "We should have tried this ten years ago. It's surprisingly efficient."

She propped her chin on her hand. "Would things have been different?"

I stiffened. She didn't need to clarify, but she did anyway. "If I'd left your parents alone."

I wanted to say no. I wanted to believe that even if Asia hadn't gone on a killing spree, it still wouldn't have worked between us. That there was no universe in which she and I ended up together.

But that was not, in fact, the truth.

"Maybe next time you should ask these questions before you commit murder." I stood to leave.

She stared at me. I knew that look. It wasn't a conniving stare. It was a gentle, thoughtful, affectionate stare. She used to look at me like that all the time.

And that's when I remembered why I hated her so much. It wasn't the betrayal. It wasn't the lying and the bloodshed and the cruelty. It was because I could never, after all these years, figure out if she'd truly loved me, or if she'd just been manipulating me the whole time.

I would have preferred the latter. But that was a mercy she would never give me.

I stormed to the stairs.

"I enjoyed this, doctor," she called after me. "I'll miss you when they send you back to jail."

"I would say the feeling is mutual," I cast over my shoulder, "but we've been weirdly honest with each other tonight, so I think I'll continue that trend."

She cackled. "You know I'm over you, Nic. But I don't think you're over me."

She's right, the Voice in my head agreed.

I glared up at the ceiling. *Excuse me?*

If you were over her, you wouldn't be so angry.

He was annoyingly correct. I was *furious.* It was moments like these when I remembered why I wanted to end the world. Why I avoided friendship like the plague. Why I never wanted to be a husband or boyfriend or significant other to anyone ever again.

It was because Asia had stolen the one thing that couldn't be replaced, and now she didn't even have the decency to say *"I never loved you."*

She doesn't need to apologize.

I gripped the railing as I remembered what I'd said to Philadelphia this morning.

"You can't just keep letting people off the hook like this, Phil."

"Yes, I can. That's kind of how Jesus works."

She'd forgiven so many people—her father, the Nolans, Jayde, even Pizza Boy. She'd erased the debts of a dozen sinners, most of whom had never asked.

Including, I realized with some embarrassment, me.

She hadn't waited for permission. And maybe I shouldn't, either.

I inhaled through my nose. "Min?"

Her chair scraped on the floor. "Yes?"

I faced her. "I forgive you."

I descended the stairs before she could respond. And then I walked out the door a free man.

30: PHILADELPHIA

Where is Nic?

It was nearly ten o'clock, well past the time when he should have been up, and I still hadn't heard a word from him. Jael had arrived unannounced before breakfast, much to my alarm. Thankfully, Asia had informed me that she would be busy all day. Cardiff had also left the house early, claiming he would be supervising maintenance on his private transit—because apparently an interstellar spaceship was also something the Nolans owned. I was grateful, especially since he took Frank with him; Cardiff may know about Blue Fire, but he definitely didn't need to overhear this conversation.

I stalled as long as I could, serving breakfast, delegating staff, and fielding Peng's usual morning litany of messages. I knew I was making Jael wait in the sitting room much longer than was proper, but I didn't want to meet with her alone.

She finally pulled me aside. "Philadelphia, sit, please."

I'd run out of excuses, so I was forced to oblige. I took the armchair next to her.

She slid down the couch to be closer to me and leaned over so we were eye to eye. I struggled to hold her gaze.

"We need to talk," she announced.

I clenched my fists in my lap. *Please, God. I can't do this.*

She gently pried my hands apart. "I want to apologize."

My heart restarted.

"I am sorry for how I handled our conversation yesterday. I told you that I never want you to be afraid to ask questions, and I mean that. I always want you to feel like you can come to me with your opinions and concerns." She rubbed my knuckles. "Even if we disagree, I want you to trust me as much as I trust you."

A flicker of hope beat in my chest. "You trust me?" Jael had never asked for my trust; I just followed orders.

She smiled. "Why wouldn't I? I asked you to be honest with me, and you have been. You've handled yourself with maturity, and you've followed orders even when it's hard. I know that when you say you'll do something, you'll do it. This whole time you've been at the estate, completely on your own, and I haven't once worried that you'll endanger the operation." She let go of my hand to gesture at the room.

I straightened as her words patched the cracks in the bridge between us.

"You can't imagine how valuable that loyalty is to me, as a leader. There are not many people I can trust with the amount of power you have."

I frowned. "What power?" I didn't have any power; I wasn't in charge of the operation and never had been. I was just a figurehead.

She arched an eyebrow. "You have immeasurable power, Philadelphia. You could command this army if you wanted to. With one video, you could convince even my top advisors to follow you instead of me."

I squirmed. The thought made me royally uncomfortable—in part because it had never occurred to me.

"But I know you would never do that, even if we disagreed," Jael continued, as if reading my mind. "And I do not want to take that loyalty for granted. Which... is what we need to discuss."

I braced myself.

"You were honest with me yesterday, and for that, I am grateful. However... I was not honest with you."

She shifted on the couch, and the room swayed, like the Earth had gotten knocked off its axis. I closed my eyes and gripped the chair to keep from being thrown overboard. *No, not again. I can't do this again.*

"I told you I was willing to sacrifice the front in Beijing. There's a reason for that." She paused, as if this conversation was just as terrifying for her as it was for me. "I never expected us to take control of Beijing in the first place."

I opened my eyes. "What?"

She bravely met my stare. "The military presence is too strong here. We never would have been able to fully break the government's control. I was planning on them driving us out within the week. It was always a suicide mission—even without the defective guns."

"But..." I thought of all the hours I'd spent on air telling people that we could win if we acted together—reading from scripts Jael had written.

I lied to them... You lied to me.

"My plan was to cripple their infrastructure and break down communications, then retreat. That would have prevented them from retaliating on other fronts, so we could liberate regions of independence and hold them. We don't need to control Beijing to end the United—we just need to break the monopoly."

She was right; it would only take one free country to change the future. "Then why aren't we doing that in the first place? Why not liberate Africa or South America and advance from there?"

"Do you know how many have tried that and failed?" she said gently.

I remembered what she'd told me about her home country— and the war crimes the United had committed to force them to surrender—and winced.

"We need the global momentum to break their system of control. We need Operation Blue Fire—and that's why I needed the thunderbird to promise victory."

I wanted to argue, but there was nothing to debate. Jael had done exactly what any military general would have done: strategize to win the war. But she'd won the same way the United did: by manipulating the truth with propaganda.

And Blue Fire had been her mouthpiece.

"That's also why I sent you back here," Jael continued before I could formulate an objection.

"I don't understand," I said, and wondered if I really wanted the truth.

"Asia is our greatest enemy—and that was before she donated a shipload of bombs. I knew that if you could expose her, the government would turn to cannibalism, making it impossible for them to regroup. It would make them weak—and we just might be able to topple the giant."

"Why didn't you tell me?" I blurted. Everything she was saying made sense—and that made the wound sting all the worse. If she had told me what she was planning, I would have obeyed without question. I would have given her what she wanted. Instead, she'd stolen my loyalty through lies and false promises.

And now I wasn't sure I could continue to follow her.

She didn't hesitate. "Because I didn't want you to have to make the same decision I did."

With a flash of regret I could taste, I remembered the other half her story.

"I didn't tell anyone that I knew about the plan to attack the villages. I didn't want anyone else to have to make that decision."

"I won't sugarcoat it, Philadelphia." Jael looked out the window and tapped her foot, her heel drumming the rhythm to a doomed war. "There is no right answer. Whether we go through with the operation or not, someone loses. Either people risk their lives in a fight we cannot win, or we yield the floor and the government continues to execute your followers one by one."

My vision blurred as the tiny flicker of hope in my chest snuffed out. Either I could sacrifice an entire city to end the government, or I could retreat and condemn the universe to another hundred years of tyranny.

I knew what the right answer was. But either way, Asia won.

Jael touched my knee. "There is no happy ending where we save everyone—and I didn't want you to have to decide who lived and who died."

I tried to blink away the tears and focus on her face.

"I am sorry I yelled at you yesterday," she whispered, her own voice cracking around the edges. "I thought that if you were just following orders, I could spare you the guilt. But I know now that's not true. You still would have been responsible for your decision, because you would have had to decide whether or not to follow me."

I felt the Holy Spirit moving between us. *Obedience is always a choice.*

Jael found my hands again. "And I know that if I'd asked you to obey, you would have."

Would I? I thought of all the times I'd told her I trusted her—the overwhelming conviction that God had placed her in my life—and thought that, maybe, I would have.

"But that's not the kind of relationship I want to have with you." She tugged on my hands, pulling us closer. "Soldiers are a dime a dozen. I have plenty of people who will blindly follow orders. But I want to be more than a commanding officer to you, if you'll let me. I don't want our relationship to end when the war does."

Breath rushed back into my lungs when I realized what she was implying, offering.

The smooth metal rings on her fingers brushed my cheek as she cupped my face with one hand. "You are going to have regrets after this war, Philadelphia. But I don't want trusting me to be one of them. From now on, I promise to be as honest with you as you have been with me. Will you forgive me for lying? Will you help me fight this war—together?"

"Yes," I whispered, and then broke down into gentle tears.

She drew me in and kissed my forehead. "You'll always be my Blue Fire."

I hugged her. *Thank you, Jesus.*

"Hold on, time out."

I jerked back. Nic waltzed into the room, followed by Peng with a breakfast tray.

Nic halted in front of us and pointed at my face. "Are those Jesus tears, or I-need-to-kill-someone tears?"

I started to laugh, but the sound caught on the sob in my throat and came out a garbled mess. I snorted through my nose and shot goopy snot everywhere.

Nic arched an eyebrow. "Better out than in, I guess."

That just made me laugh and snot harder. Peng set his tray on the coffee table and magically produced a handkerchief from his pocket.

I mumbled thanks and mopped my nose. "Yes, they're good tears."

"Excellent. I don't fancy murder before breakfast." Nic pulled up another chair.

"Where have you been, anyway?" I accused.

He poured himself a cup of coffee, then leaned over to refill mine. "I overslept my alarm."

"Seriously?"

"What? I haven't slept that great since before you were born." He grabbed his plate and began devouring his breakfast with enthusiasm.

I eyed him. He seemed... different, not that I could have identified why. He wore the same neutral expression he always did, and he was using an acceptable amount of sarcasm.

"So, what did I miss?" He glanced at Jael.

"Nothing you and I didn't already discuss, doctor." She helped herself to a slice of fruit from the tray.

"You followed my advice?" he exclaimed around a mouthful of food.

"Does this surprise you?"

He paused to finish chewing. "Yes, actually."

She leaned back in the chair and crossed one leg over the other. "Maybe it wouldn't be so shocking if you made a habit of giving people good advice."

I cringed and glanced at Nic, expecting the worst. But he just shrugged and washed down his food with a chug of coffee. "I'll factor that into my calculations."

I stared at him. Suddenly, I knew what was wrong—he was *happy.*

I'd been around Nic long enough to know that his moods usually ranged from disinterested to antagonistic, with disinterested being a good day. I'd never, ever seen him act genuinely joyful. Gloating over the death of his enemies, maybe, but never at peace.

What in the world happened last night?

Jael didn't give me a chance to interrogate him. "Send for Jayde, please." She gestured at Peng, who obliged. "We have something to discuss."

My stomach clenched when I remembered what was at stake. I abandoned my coffee mug on the end table.

Nic did the same and dragged his chair closer to mine.

"My team has been working nonstop to pull the guns from the field," Jael sighed, exhaustion stretching her voice. "So far, we've accounted for about twenty thousand."

I gripped my chest and muttered in tongues. That wasn't even half of the guns Jayde said General Jin had received.

Jael touched my knee. "We'll keep working—we have forty-eight hours. I have all my contacts spreading the message through their networks."

"But it won't be enough," Nic spoke for me. He folded his arms on his knees and leaned forward, his eyes watching me carefully.

"No," Jael admitted. "Beijing will burn."

"And you think we should let it fall," I said before I could stop myself. I recalled what she'd said about the operation being a suicide mission and wondered—briefly.

"No."

I looked up.

"I've consulted with my advisors, and they all agree: You're right." She pinched my knee, but it felt like she was grounding herself more than anything. "We have to warn everyone. You have to go on air and tell them the truth."

I stared at her as all my uncertainty evaporated. *We have to save this city.*

Nic muttered something under his breath that sounded vaguely like a prayer.

"If we use those guns, we'll lose too many of our own people, not to mention the catastrophic loss of civilian life," Jael said, confirming what I already knew. "If Asia shipped guns to our allies in other regions, we could be looking at a death toll in the billions."

"I can't be responsible for that," I declared. But this time, there was no fear in the statement, only conviction.

"No, you cannot," Jael agreed. "The good doctor here reminded me of something very important: Blue Fire is not a killer. You inspire people because you chose to save the world instead of yourself."

She glanced at Nic with a gesture close to a smile. He returned it.

Heavy footsteps sounded down the hall, and Jayde appeared in the doorway. Jael looked at him as she continued. "If you sacrifice Beijing, you'll ruin everything you ever stood for. And that is a sacrifice you cannot make."

Jayde folded his hands behind his back and said nothing.

"If people find out you sent your followers on a suicide mission, they'll lose faith in you—and I can't afford that. If we're going to keep our hard-won independence, I need the thunderbird to continue reigning after the war." Jael beamed at me, expression filled with nothing but pride.

I stared back. I'd never once considered that the thunderbird would be needed after the war. Blue Fire's job was to inspire people to fight for independence. Once we ended the United, the world wouldn't need me anymore—would it?

Jael didn't let me dwell on it. "You need to show the people that you care more about them than bringing down the government. You're going on air and telling them the truth. Tell them about the guns and warn them that Asia knows where they are. Give them a chance to save themselves."

"You're cancelling the operation," Jayde declared. There was no accusation in his voice—just a dejected, sullen sense of finality, like he was slamming the lid on a coffin.

"Not necessarily." Nic sat up straight. "Rebels are creative. When they find out that Philadelphia risked her life to save theirs, I think it will inspire them to do something equally insane."

I took a sharp breath through my nose as the hope returned to my heart. This is who I was—who the thunderbird was. This was who God called me to be.

I am Blue Fire, and this is my war.

"That is the hope," Jael agreed. The cunning sparkle returned to her eyes, but it was short-lived. "However, it's not so simple as recording a video and warning everyone. Unless we can also remove Asia, the people will still be in immediate danger. Asia has no doubt already put her army in place, ready to respond on operation day. As soon as she knows we've exposed her, she may retaliate and kill as many as possible—never mind the dozens of hostages she has in prison."

"Stanyard," I murmured. *Oh God, please protect him.*

Nic rubbed his mustache and frowned.

"We have enough evidence to expose her," Jael said, "but we need the Council to act immediately. If she gets wind of it, she will wipe her data and run."

"Then I'll tell the General," I declared. Adrenaline rushed through my system as everything snapped into place—my identity as a Nolan, the General's adoration of me, all the little miracles God had put in place to save the world. "If I tell the General, he'll act before she can. I'll say I found suspicious activity in my financial investments. He'll believe me—at least enough to investigate. I can call him—"

"That's not going to be easy."

I turned. Jayde pulled his phone out of his pocket. "Asia called an emergency council session that lasts until Friday. Not a single councilmember is allowed to leave the building until the crisis is over, the General included."

He stepped forward and handed the device to me. A news headline emblazoned on the screen confirmed his statement.

Nic read over my shoulder. "She made them sitting ducks."

Jayde nodded.

I pushed aside the gruesome thought. "Then I'll go to him."

Jael shook her head, rattling her earrings. "If it's an emergency session, they'll have the building on lockdown. They won't let anyone in."

"They'll let me in," I whispered. I remembered the General's benevolent offer and realized what I had to do.

"Come to the council chambers sometime, see for yourself. Tell them I sent you."

I closed my eyes and searched for the Holy Spirit. He answered, smothering the fear that burned in my lungs. This— this is why I was a Nolan.

The room had gone still. I looked up to find everyone staring at me.

I spoke slowly and clearly to force the words out around the anxiety in my throat. "I need to go to the council chambers. They will let me in; the General invited me."

No one argued, even though I could tell Nic desperately wanted to.

I kept talking, laying out the pieces of the plan as the Holy Spirit revealed them to me. "I'll expose her in front of the whole Council and warn the underground at the same time. It's the only way to prevent Asia from retaliating and give everyone time to run."

"Philadelphia," Nic prodded, the syllables sharp with grief, "what are you suggesting?"

The room spun. I gripped the arms of the chair and turned to Jael. "There's cameras in the council chambers, right? For when they broadcast sessions on TV?"

"Yes, of course."

"Can you commandeer them?"

She didn't answer. She stared at me, expression pained, as if she knew where this was going.

Nic grunted something I couldn't make out. He lurched out of his chair and began to pace.

I forged ahead. "If you can hijack the signal, we can use Data's program to broadcast it to the entire world. Make it mandatory viewing. We can warn everyone—it's the only way to reach all our allies at once."

Jael started drumming her foot again. I knew what that meant. I was right—I had to be. This was the only way.

Jayde moved beside me. "The resistance won't listen to Andromeda Nolan, though." His voice was barely above a whisper, as if he, too, knew how this ended.

No, they won't.

I pushed up my right sleeve and stared at the thunderbird tattoo on my shoulder—the mark I'd kept carefully hidden for the past week. "They'll listen to Philadelphia Smyrna."

Nic rammed his fist into the wall. He stopped, his back to me. His shoulders were heaving.

"I have to do this," I announced—for him, for me, for everyone. I looked at Jael.

Tears left two bright streaks down her dark face. "Yes. You do."

I closed my eyes and waited for the world to stop shaking.

For such a time as this.

"Philadelphia."

Jael waited until I met her gaze before continuing. "I won't be able to go with you. I'll have to stay behind and run the broadcast."

She was right—I needed her at the computer. This mission would fail if I didn't have someone to keep Data's program online and manage the algorithm.

Of course, that was only half the reason. If she came with me, she'd be incriminated—and then there would be no one to lead the war.

I forced a smile. "This is something I have to do alone."

"I beg to differ." Nic spun around. "I'm coming with you."

I shook my head. I couldn't lose him again—not when he'd already died once for me. "But Nic—"

"They'll probably recant my pardon anyway as soon as you make a scene. Might as well go out in style." The words were indifferent, but the look he was giving me was anything but.

"I'm also coming," Jayde announced.

I frowned at him. I wasn't sure I wanted him on this mission—I knew what he thought of cancelling the operation.

"You're not leaving the house without your bodyguard." He planted his feet apart and folded his arms behind his back, as if daring me to argue.

I didn't.

"Philadelphia," Jael pulled my attention back to her. "You know they won't be able to save you, right?" She laid her hand on my arm, her acrylic fingernails digging into my skin. "The General will arrest you. If they put you in jail, I'll do everything I can, but…"

She didn't need to finish the sentence. I knew what the word "if" meant.

"You don't have to save me," I replied, and let the tears fall. "Just save the world."

She stood up, and I followed. She pulled me into a hug. "That's my thunderbird," she whispered in my ear.

I soaked in the strength of her embrace. I took a long breath—*one, two, three*—then pulled away.

"You'll go tomorrow morning," she announced, wiping her eyes. "I need time to prepare Data's program. Do not leave until I send word."

I nodded and faced Jayde. "Find Peng," I said, drying my own tears. "There will be no food served in this house today. Not a single member of my household will eat until tomorrow."

"Yes, ma'am." He moved to obey.

I turned back to Jael. "Get ahold of any churches you can, ask them to join us."

She nodded.

"I know someone who may be able to help with that." Nic approached us. He laid a hand on my shoulder and looked at Jael. "Can you reach Warden Ivanova? I need to talk to Ryan."

31: PHILADELPHIA

"Hold still."

I sucked in my breath and obeyed, holding my arms perfectly straight as Narissa circled around me. I stood on a stool in my dressing room, facing the trio of giant mirrors that lined one wall. It was Wednesday morning, and Narissa had shown up before first light to outfit Blue Fire with one last dress.

The cut was similar to the gown I'd worn at the party, with a stiff collar and a flowing skirt. The asymmetrical hemline hit my knee on my left side and nearly touched the floor on my right. Unlike the other dresses Narissa had created, however, this one was sleeveless. The thunderbird tattoo on my shoulder stood out against my pale skin like a wound.

This dress was also strangely understated. The entire garment was made of cool, shimmery black silk. The skirt and bodice were covered with embroidery, but the thread was also black, making it almost invisible against the fabric. I studied the complex stitches and wondered what the design meant.

Narissa hadn't given me any details. She gave my hem one last tug, then grunted in satisfaction. "That'll have to do," she mumbled around the pins in her mouth.

She helped me down. "Thank you for working on such short notice," I said. "I'll pay you double."

"Oh, I've had this dress finished for a while. I've known operation day was coming for three months." She plucked the pins out of her mouth and stabbed them in a cushion. "But I'll take the money."

She arched a thin eyebrow. I smiled. I knew Narissa wasn't in it for the money, but Andromeda wouldn't need her family fortune, not after today. It might as well go to someone I cared about.

Of course, after today, Narissa might not be able to use the money, either.

She turned back to the dress bag she'd brought with her. She pulled a black velvet jacket off a hanger and helped me shrug into it. The soft fabric covered my tattoo and made the whole outfit look sophisticated and mature.

Narissa's cold fingers brushed my neck, and I felt something snap in place on the edge of my collar. "Leave the jacket on until you're ready to make a scene," she instructed. "When it's time, yank it off, and let your dress do the talking."

I nodded and struggled to come up with a proper goodbye. What would happen to Narissa after I "made a scene"? Would they punish the stylist who had turned me into a living thunderbird? Would they care?

Narissa must have read the anxiety on my face. She straightened my jacket. "Focus, Blue Fire," she admonished. "It's your time to burn."

The house was somber as we followed our morning routine. The staff tread softly and spoke in whispers, like they were conducting a wake. In a way, they were.

Peng found me while Nic and I were eating breakfast on the veranda. "I cancelled your afternoon appointment." He held a tablet in his arm like a waiter and typed on the screen.

"Very good," I said, once again grateful that I had him. I'd completely forgotten about my other engagements this week. "I asked my accountant to give you a bonus this morning—you should see it in your account already."

He bowed. "That's extremely generous, ma'am. Thank you. What time would you like dinner to be served?"

I frowned. Peng didn't know everything that was going on, but he was aware of my alternate identity. Surely, he realized I wouldn't be home for dinner. "That won't be necessary. And, Peng, if you need to leave…"

His lips twitched. "I need to winterize the east garden today. What time for dinner? 6:30?"

I smiled and tried not to cry; Narissa would commit murder if I smeared my makeup. "6:30 will be fine."

Cardiff and his slobbering dog were weirdly absent all morning, which was just as well; I wouldn't have known what to say to him. Nic and I went through the motions of breakfast without exchanging a word. I had a dozen things I wanted to say, but I didn't want to break the silence. I just wanted to sip my coffee, stare at the pool, and pretend for one last moment that everything was normal.

Jayde met us in the foyer when it was time to leave. "Jael sends a message," he announced as I approached. "She said everything is ready. She'll be watching the stream. Just go with the flow, and she'll flip the switch when it's time."

I nodded. For the first time in months, there would be no script. No one would be there to give direction or cut the feed if things went wrong. It was all on me, and I had one shot to save the world.

I am Blue Fire, and this is my war.

"Everything you need is on here. Text messages, bank statements, all the evidence we have." He held out a small tablet.

I took it and rubbed the dark screen, fully aware that the tiny hard drive contained data capable of destroying a nation. I slid it into the velvet pocketbook Narissa had given me to match my outfit.

I'd only packed two other things. The burnt powercell fragment—a sharp reminder of how many lives were at stake if I didn't pull this off—and the star of David pin Lev, one of my Jewish followers, had given me.

For such a time as this.

"Jael regrets she can't be here," Jayde continued, "but she wanted me to tell you that she's proud of you."

I smiled and forced myself not to attach any emotion to that statement, tucking it away in my heart for later.

"We need to go. The car's waiting." Jayde moved to open the door.

"Jayde," I stopped him, "you don't have to come. You've done your job."

"My job isn't over. I still work for the Nolans. Unless this is your way of firing me." He brushed an imaginary crumb off his sleeve. He wore his dress uniform, a pin with the United seal on his breast pocket. I noticed his omnipresent holster was missing.

"You're not carrying?" I asked, and was surprised at how nervous that made me feel. Not that it mattered; Jayde wouldn't be able to help me, gun or not.

He unbuttoned his jacket, revealing an underarm holster. He'd swapped his electric pistol for an old-fashioned handgun with a clip. "I don't trust Asia's guns," he explained, "even with a new powercell."

"They're not going to let you in the building with that," Nic warned.

Jayde shrugged and redid his buttons.

"Here. There's something I need to give you." I reached into my pocket and pulled out the clicker. I dropped it in Jayde's palm.

He stared at it for a moment. "Guess you don't need this anymore." He held the door open for me.

I gathered my trailing hemline and stepped outside. "I never did."

The main council chambers sat on the edge of Tiananmen Square—a somewhat ironic choice. Several priceless historical buildings had been demolished to make room for the structure; I suppose the meager sacrifice was China's gesture of goodwill towards the new world order.

The building had been constructed in the 2030s to commemorate the founding of the United, and at the time, the design had been avant garde. Now, it looked like someone had asked a badly programmed AI to design a beached spaceship. The building was little more than a giant concrete donut. The side curved upwards, shading the sidewalk in gloomy darkness, and the windows were spaced irregularly like a mouth of broken teeth. The whole place was undecorated except for the boring United emblem.

Police had the square gated off. Jayde presented my credentials, and they flagged us through. The whole street was ghostly quiet, devoid of the usual tourists. Jayde handed the car off to a valet, then led the way to the main entrance.

Half a dozen armed soldiers manned the security booth. "Thumbprint, please," one of them demanded of me.

I obliged, pressing my hand to the screen on the outside of the bulletproof window.

He glanced at his computer. "I'm sorry, Miss Nolan, but they're not allowing visitors today."

"I'm aware," I said politely, "but General Secretary Mong invited me."

It was the truth, but he didn't believe me. The guard glanced back at his partner.

The other soldier was frowning at Nic, who stood behind me. I tensed and wondered if I should have made Nic stay home; if someone recognized him, I'd never get in the building.

The second guard started to say something, but just then a staffer walked up, rattling off a request in Mandarin. She got halfway through her sentence before she spotted me.

"Miss Nolan!" She bowed. "Are you here to see the General?"

I smiled. "Yes, he invited me."

"Oh, he'll be delighted to see you. Come with me." The staffer turned to the guards and chirped something in Mandarin that probably translated to *"Let her in, you idiots."*

The guards obeyed, opening the side door and ushering us through. We bypassed the security scanners and hurried to follow the staffer down the curved hallway.

The interior of the building was just as austere as the outside. The corridor was cavernous and drafty, and our voices echoed like the place was haunted. Plaques and statues were scattered along the wall, leaving huge stretches of undecorated concrete in between. The only color in the whole place was the dark red carpet, which looked like a trail of dried blood running up the hallway.

"It's so great to meet you," the staffer gushed as she led us around the corner. "His Excellence has talked about nothing except your party."

"I'm honored," I said, and I was. "He wanted me to come visit him here, see how things are run. I hope I'm not interrupting?"

"Oh no. I'm sure they'll be going on break soon; he'd love to take lunch with you. Here, this way."

She dropped her volume to a whisper, and we all softened our footsteps. She approached a mahogany door and opened it silently. The chatter of agitated voices flooded the hall. We followed the staffer into the auditorium and stood in the shadows at the back of the room.

"Wait here," she hissed. "As soon as he's free, I'll bring him over."

I thanked her, and she disappeared. I stepped forward and studied the room. I had seen it on TV many times, but it was even more imposing in person. The place was built like a concert hall. The building was at least five stories tall, with several balconies and a domed ceiling painted with a map of the world. The floor sloped downwards, allowing everyone a clear view of the podium in the center of the room. The General Secretary and two other world leaders sat in places of honor on the rostrum, listening to some politician as he strutted across the open floor and ranted about the "violent insurrectionists." The proceedings were projected on screens that hung from the balconies—no doubt the same feed Jael was watching from her office.

I scanned the crowd. The main floor was lined with rows of mahogany desks and plush chairs. Most of the seats were filled, although a few politicians paced the balconies and open aisles, whispering into their devices. Each councilmember had their own desk, ordered alphabetically.

I read the names. *K...L...M... Mong.*

There she was, in a desk only two rows back from the podium. She sat with one leg crossed over the other, picking at her bloodred lipstick with a pointed fingernail. She seemed bored as she watched the proceedings, like she'd scripted the entire scene in her head and was just waiting for it to play out.

Next to her was an empty desk. The surface had been stripped of everything personal except for the metal nameplate bolted to the back of the chair.

NOLAN, THAMES

My breath caught in my throat. "Wait here," I ordered Jayde.

He nodded and pressed himself against the wall, unobtrusive.

I took a step forward. Nic caught my arm.

I looked back at him. He stared at me, expression almost angry. But I knew better.

"I have to do this," I insisted.

He didn't argue. He gave my shoulder a sharp squeeze, then let go, muttering one name under his breath.

"Jesus."

I whispered in tongues and felt the stirring in the Spirit, weak and fluttery under the scream of fear. I filtered the noise until the only thing I could hear was a suffocating, overwhelming sense of conviction.

I am Andromeda Nolan.

I squared my shoulders and shook out my skirt.

And this is how I will fight my war.

Then I walked down the aisle to Thames's desk.

A few politicians whispered and glanced in my direction, but the orator continued to hold the attention of the rest of the room. Asia didn't notice me until I slid into the seat next to her.

She jerked upright and slammed her heels on the floor. "Andromeda!" she hissed. "What are you doing here?"

I smoothed my skirt over my knees. "Isn't this my father's chair?" I spoke coolly, confidently—and just loud enough for everyone around us to hear.

The orator stopped and turned. The noise in the room died off to a shocked gurgle. The General Secretary looked up, and our eyes met.

He stared at me, looking a bit surprised, perhaps somewhat annoyed. I waited. It was fully within his power to throw me out of the courtroom, or worse.

One of the guards standing near the podium pulled his communicator from his belt and held his hand over the button.

The General grinned. "Andromeda! I see you decided to take me up on my offer. Come down here and say hello." He beckoned to me.

"Beg pardon, Your Excellency," the orator stuttered, "I was speaking…"

"You haven't said anything in twenty minutes. We could all use a break."

Several people snickered. The orator scurried back to his seat, thoroughly culled. The guard snapped his communicator back in its holder.

I got up and walked to the center of the room. The General rose and stepped down to meet me, grasping my hand with both of his before I could even offer a bow. "It's so good to see you."

"It's good to see you again as well," I returned with my prettiest smile. "Thank you for inviting me."

Asia stood. "Father, this is very inappropriate—"

He shushed her. "She's fine. I invited her. What do you think of the place, Andromeda?"

"It's gorgeous." I glanced at the screens on the balcony and saw that I was perfectly centered in the camera, my face visible to the world.

The Holy Spirit pressed on my heart. *It's time.*

"Thinking of taking your father's seat?" the General teased, his hands still holding mine. "That district is up for commission next summer." He winked. A few nearby advisors laughed.

I took a breath, but the air stopped in my throat. I spoke around the bubble. "Actually, I… I came to talk to you." I withdrew my hand from his grasp.

I heard Asia's heels clacking behind me. *Don't turn around.*

The General glanced at the crowd. "Is it private?"

"No." I slid back and straightened. "Everyone needs to hear this."

The guards around the podium came to attention. One reached for his holster.

"Andromeda!" Asia screeched, her voice warped like a corrupted recording. "This is unaccept—"

"I am speaking!" the General snapped. "Andromeda, this had better not be a joke." The threat was thick in his voice.

Whispers broke out across the crowd. I saw several people pointing at their phones and knew Jael had flipped the switch. Thanks to Data's program, I was now mandatory viewing on every registered device across the globe. The world was watching.

Be with me, Jesus!

I met the General's stare. "No, sir. It's about Operation Blue Fire."

Asia made a sound like she'd been strangled.

"What about it?" the General returned.

I knew I might only have seconds, so I spoke as fast as I could. "Someone is trying to frame you. They've used your credentials to authorize shipments of weapons to underground outposts all across the city. They're planning to let the rebels take control on operation day and blame you for it."

There were several shouted exclamations in different languages from around the room. The General arched an eyebrow. "Frame me?"

"That's ridiculous!" Asia mocked, her laughter bright and fake. "Andromeda, this is embarrassing."

"I have proof. Text messages, phone calls, money transfers—evidence that someone set up a fake company and used your signature to authorize it." I opened my pocketbook and held out the tablet. My hand shook so hard that I nearly dropped the device. *Oh God, please let him believe me!*

The General gestured. The soldier standing nearest to me grabbed the device and swiped on the screen.

Asia tried to read over his shoulder. "Father, if this is true, then we need to convene immediately and review the files—"

"Silence," he snarled. "Andromeda, I need you to be very clear. Where did you get this information?"

"My servers, sir." I braced myself and sacrificed the privilege I'd been hiding behind for months. "The Nolans own that company."

Someone cursed.

"It's true," the guard declared. He tapped the screen. "If these screenshots are real, then she's telling the truth."

The commotion in the room boiled over.

The General was the only one who remained calm. His stare was still fixed on me, as if he knew the worst was yet to come. "And why would the Nolans be involved?"

Asia yanked her phone out of her pocket and scrabbled at the screen. I knew that if she made even one call, this would all be wasted.

Now.

"It's her!" I yelled, pointing. "Asia and Thames were working together!"

The room iced over. Not even Asia moved, as if she were afraid that she'd seal her own fate if she breathed.

The General was the first to speak. "Min?" he exclaimed, and the heartbreak in his voice shattered time.

Asia lurched back to life like a cursed mannequin. "That's preposterous!" she slurred, her voice waffling between a deranged cackle and a violent shriek. "I don't know anything about this."

"She's been trying to overthrow you this whole time," I insisted. "First it was Red Rain—"

"Red Rain!" the General barked.

"I had nothing to do with that! This is insane. I'm calling my lawyer." Asia typed with both thumbs.

"Don't let her send any messages!" I screamed.

The guards obeyed me. One lunged forward and grabbed Asia's phone.

"This is an outrage! Don't touch me!" She tried to yank the device away and lost her grip, stumbling gracelessly on her tall heels. She struggled to compose herself and looked at the General with a grotesque smile. "Father! This is a disgrace. You'll let a *child* barge into *your* courtroom and accuse a councilwoman?"

"What if the girl is lying?" one of the advisors on the podium echoed.

"It's all true!" I exclaimed. "You can cross-reference everything. I can show you the factory—"

"You're pathetic," Asia cut me off. "I'll have you sued for slander. Now, give me my phone!"

I turned to the General. "Please, sir, don't let her make a call. If you do, dozens of people will die. She has hostages."

"Father!" Asia objected. "You're not going to allow this, are you?"

The guards didn't move. The General studied her, weighing her life with one cold stare. Then he glanced at me.

I bunched my skirt in both fists. This was all for nothing if he believed her over me. *Please, God! Intervene!*

The General straightened. "Lock down the building," he ordered, his voice commanding the room without a microphone. "Absolutely no one comes or goes without my permission. Shut down the livestream and cut off communications. I don't want anyone—"

I reached for him. "No, wait!" If he put the building in blackout, it would cut off Jael's broadcast. "There's more. Everyone who got those guns is in danger."

He stopped mid-motion. "What do you mean?"

"They're rigged with a faulty powercell. If you fire the guns, they will explode."

"*What?*" Asia gasped.

I dug in my pocketbook for the ruined powercell. "It's an intentional design flaw in the power core—we've tested it. It reacts at high voltage and causes the battery to melt, triggering an explosion." I held the fragment up, making sure it was visible on camera.

The General snatched it from my hand.

"She distributed at least a hundred thousand of these guns in Beijing and Washington," I explained, fighting to keep my voice steady as the adrenaline clogged my throat. "If the underground uses these guns tomorrow during operation day, you'll lose the city. She was trying to kill you, the Council, everyone."

"No, I wasn't!" Asia was trembling, barely able to stay upright. Hair flopped out of her bun as she gestured with both hands. "I didn't know about the powercells—"

"It's true!"

I whirled. Nic jogged down the aisle.

"You!" Asia took a drunken step forward. The guard behind her clasped her shoulder in warning.

Two more soldiers moved to block Nic's way. He skidded to a stop and lifted his hands in surrender. "I can vouch for everything," he explained. "I was working in the factory where they produced the powercells. At least a quarter million were shipped out."

A nearby advisor muttered an oath.

"What are *you* doing here?" the General demanded, clearly recognizing Nic. "Arrest him!"

The two guards grabbed Nic's arms. He didn't resist. "It's also true about Red Rain," he declared calmly, his eyes on the General. "She's been funding the project for over a decade. She was the one who gave me the base on Mars."

The sound that came from Asia's throat wasn't human. "Lies!"

"Min, if you take one step, I swear I will shoot you myself!" the General roared.

I took advantage of her terrified silence. "It's true, sir. She and Thames have been working together this whole time. Red Rain, Rott, Blue Fire—it was all her idea. The only reason Thames recorded those videos was to cover his tracks on Rott."

It was only after I finished the sentence that I realized the room had again grown deathly quiet.

The General narrowed his eyes. "How did you know Thames was responsible for the recordings?"

I hesitated. It wasn't too late; I could claim that I'd simply uncovered evidence on Thames's servers. It wouldn't even be a lie. I could escape with my money and my clean file and hope that everyone saw the stream and knew the guns were rigged.

But it wouldn't be enough. The underground didn't listen to Andromeda. They only followed Blue Fire.

And it was time for her to lead.

I looked at Nic. He nodded.

I dropped my pocketbook on the floor and straightened. A glance at the screen showed I was dead center in the frame.

"Andromeda…?" the General said haltingly.

"My name is Philadelphia Smyrna," I announced, my voice ricocheting around the dome. I slid my arms out of my jacket sleeves. "And I am Blue Fire."

Then I yanked my jacket off my shoulders.

Something under my collar snapped, and my dress came to life. With a crackle of electricity that I felt down my spine, the fabric lit up. Suddenly, all the embroidery glowed bright blue. Bolts of lightning jagged across the skirt, exploding in a shower of sparks near the hemline. In the camera, I could see that a thunderbird was stitched across my back, its wings fanned over my shoulders.

Several people screamed. Those standing closest to me drew back like I was a live snake. I ignored them all, spinning so that everyone could see the tattoo emblazoned on my shoulder.

"I am Blue Fire!" I shouted. "And I'm cancelling the operation!"

"Andromeda!" the General yelled again, and this time, it was a threat.

"Andromeda Nolan is dead!" I declared. I popped my blue contacts out and threw them on the floor. "Thames altered her file to protect me."

The General muttered an oath. Asia wailed. I whirled to face the camera so my face filled the screen. "This message is for everyone who follows Blue Fire. The operation is cancelled!"

"Stand down!" someone yelled.

I refused to look back. "You cannot use those guns! If you fire them, you will die, and you will destroy this city."

The commotion in the room escalated. "Don't shoot!" another voice ordered.

I yelled to be heard over the noise. "Think of all the people you'll kill! You will reduce this city to rubble and take thirty million innocent people out with you! That is not who we are!"

There were shouts and orders and motion everywhere, but no one touched me. No one tried to stop me. Perhaps because they, too, realized I was the only one who could prevent this.

"We are not like them." I glared at the screen, my eyes flashing with authority. "We do not fight with their weapons. I refuse to sacrifice an entire city to win the war. Please, hear me: Stand down. Destroy the weapons and run."

"Philadelphia!" Asia screeched like someone getting burned alive. "I will kill you!" She lurched, but the guard held her back.

"You have to run!" I shrieked. "She knows where you are! She's been tracking the guns. If you stay, the government will find you! Get out of the city!"

"Cut the stream!" the General ordered, and then everything happened at once.

Asia roared. She lifted her knee and slammed the guard in the shin with her deadly heel, knocking him back. Nic yelled my name and threw off his guards as several people rushed towards me. Asia grabbed the soldier's gun and whirled.

"Andromeda!" someone shouted, but it was too late.

Nic crashed into me just as Asia fired.

I landed on the floor. Nic screamed. I struggled to rise as my ears rang and the wind escaped my chest. The whole room spun, and all I could see was the blurred mural of the world twirling around me, like I was trapped in a globe rolling downhill.

"Watch out!"

The room slammed back into place, as if we'd crashed at the bottom. I saw Nic kneeling on the floor, blood oozing from his shoulder, and Asia leering over him with the gun, and knew we were not safe.

"Asia, don't!"

Her whole body twitched and stuttered. Her eyes were inhuman as she aimed the gun at me.

A gunshot exploded from above us. Asia lurched to a halt, wobbling on her stilettos. She didn't breathe, didn't scream, didn't move. No one reacted, as if the shot had stopped time. The only thing moving was the blood seeping through Asia's dress.

I scrambled up. Jayde stood on the balcony, his smoking gun in his hands.

He tossed the weapon aside. Our eyes met. *I told you I would shoot first.*

Time restarted. Guards on the balcony lunged for Jayde. Nic staggered to his feet. Politicians scattered like birds, shrieking. There were shouts and a call for an ambulance and the distinct sound of a body hitting the floor. Asia gagged.

I started to turn, but Nic grabbed me. He pulled me to himself with his good arm and pressed my face against his chest. "You've seen so much death," he hissed in my ear. "Let me save you from this one."

I relented. I covered my ears and closed my eyes as the room descended into chaos. I heard a siren blaring and the General barking orders. Doors slammed. Someone was crying.

And underneath it all were the visceral sounds of Asia dying violently.

Suddenly, the silence returned, thick and choking. Nic loosened his hold, and I lifted my head.

The room was in lockdown. Metal shutters covered all the windows while guards blocked the doors. Politicians clumped around the edge of the room, whispering in fearful clusters. Jayde still stood on the balcony, handcuffed between two soldiers, looking entirely unbothered by the situation.

I dared to turn around—just in time to see paramedics wheel a sheet-covered stretcher away.

I struggled to breathe, feeling, for the first time in months, like I could. *She's dead. Asia is dead!*

Nic muttered something under his breath and kept his hand on my shoulder.

The General knelt on the floor. He stared at the stain on the carpet for a moment, then took a deep breath and pushed himself to his feet. His gaze settled on me.

I stared back. He didn't seem angry. If anything, he was disappointed.

"I'm sorry I lied to you," I said, and in a way, I was.

He turned away. "Confiscate everyone's electronics," he ordered. "Absolutely no one leaves this building until approved by me."

Someone shouted an objection in Mandarin from the back of the room.

The General didn't even look in their direction. "If anyone resists, I will assume the worst."

I stiffened. The witch hunt had begun.

The General pointed at a guard. "Lock them up. No one speaks to them without my permission."

The guards on the balcony shoved Jayde towards the door. Two more moved towards us. Nic tightened his grip. I looked up into his scowling face and realized he was contemplating doing something very stupid.

"It's okay." I gently pried his hand off my shoulder. "I'll go."

He jerked out of his stupor. His eyes focused on me, and his expression broke.

I stepped away from him and faced the General. "Please, sir, he's injured."

He glanced at me, then at Nic. "Get this man taken care of, then bring him to my office."

The guards separated us. I followed one willingly to the door. As they ushered me out into the hall, I took one look back.

Nic still stood there, clutching his bleeding shoulder, body tense like he might bolt.

I gave him an encouraging smile, then stepped out into the hall.

It was only after the door shut behind me that I realized I may have missed my chance to say goodbye.

32: NIC

I spent the afternoon in a nearby hospital, getting my shoulder stitched back together. There was nothing I could do but lie extremely still while the regeneration machine did its work, so I decided to use the time wisely. I filled the hours praying silently and not-so-silently. It worked; when the procedure was done, I felt pretty good, all things considered.

I could only hope Philadelphia would still be alive by the time I got out of the hospital.

As soon as the doctor released me, they cuffed me and hauled me back to the council chambers. The building looked like a refugee camp. Police had the entire block cordoned off. Disgruntled politicians shivered in lines as they waited to be interrogated. Several were in handcuffs. Everyone looked like prisoners of war as soldiers screamed orders at them through megaphones.

They patted me down not once, not twice, but *three* times for weapons before letting me into the General Secretary's office. Why they hadn't checked me while I was half-naked in a hospital gown was beyond me. They finally deemed me clear and opened the door.

The General sat behind a behemoth desk. Three staffers were talking to him at once as they fired agitated updates. He silenced them all with a wave of his hand when he spotted me.

"Leave us," he barked in Mandarin.

The staff scattered. Only three guards remained. One of them pushed me inside, then shut and locked the door.

"Any electronics?" the General demanded, still in Mandarin.

"No sir, he's clear," the guard replied, clearly not realizing I could understand them.

"Good." The General flicked his own phone off, then tossed it on a thick mat on the corner of his desk—a dampening field, no doubt. The guards followed suit with their communicators.

The General leaned back in his chair and regarded me silently. I stood as far away from the desk as I could without stepping on a guard's toes and tried to figure out how to greet the man. Despite the fact that I'd dated his daughter for five years, I'd never actually met the General Secretary face-to-face, and I was none too thrilled about breaking that record.

Thankfully, he spared me the misery of proper etiquette. "I know who you are," he declared in English.

It was a pathetic threat; everyone in Beijing knew who I was. My fake trial had been a sensation, and I wasn't putting any effort into hiding my identity. "It's the mustache, isn't it?" I returned. I spoke in his native tongue, hoping that would buy me some points.

"I should have you hanged," he continued, taking me up on my offer and switching back to Mandarin.

This, too, was common knowledge. "Undoubtedly. But that seems like an awful lot of paperwork when you just pardoned me."

"Quite," he agreed. "In any case, I may have another use for you."

I took a whole step back, ramming into a guard's armored chest. "Ooh, I don't like the sound of that. Is going back to jail still an option?"

"We'll discuss it later," he deferred. "In the meantime, you and I both have a more pressing problem. Androme—ahh, Philadelphia."

I sighed. She was, as usual, my most pressing problem. "You're going to kill her, aren't you?"

He hesitated just long enough to be cruel. "I'm signing the execution order this evening."

How generous of you to give me a few hours to prepare myself. "She won't resist you," I said, then grimaced when I realized just how true that statement was.

His silence suggested he was aware of that fact.

"Just do *me* a mercy and make it quick," I pleaded.

He looked away, but not before I saw the truth spelled out in his eyes: He loved her, and he had no idea what to do with that information. I could see it written all over the pinched lines in his face.

I recognized that look, because I'd spent the better part of the last six months making the same expression in the mirror.

Suddenly, I knew why we were having this conversation. *Oh God, help me.*

I raised my voice ever so slightly. "You don't have to do this."

He glanced back at me with a frown.

I stepped towards the desk. "You don't have to kill her. You can save her."

"Don't patronize me," he groaned, even though I was quite sure the inverse was happening. "You know I can't."

"That's grammatically incorrect," I snapped, clenching my fists. "You own this planet. You *can* do whatever you want."

The guards shifted in my peripheral. *Patience*, the Holy Spirit warned me, and I forcibly loosened my grip. "You have the power," I repeated. "Let her live. Please."

He shook his head, eyes avoiding mine. "It's not possible. The Council will rule—"

"Then make it possible." It took every ounce of willpower to keep the anger out of my voice. "The Council will know that this is a suicidal idea. Operation day is tomorrow—if you kill her now, you'll make her a martyr. You'll seal your own fate."

"I will not show weakness towards this insurrection!" He was doing a terrible job of filtering his anger, which told me there was still hope.

"I'm not asking you to pardon her," I argued. "Just stay her execution, wait until the operation blows over. Then you can quietly send her off to prison. I know a good one in Russia."

He didn't get the joke. "That is not an option."

"Then why'd you call me in here? You don't want to do this. You don't want to kill her."

I was right, and that just made him more furious. "Do not mock me!"

"You want a way out. I'm giving it to you. Please, just consider—"

He slapped his hands on the desk and stood up in one livid motion. "I will not risk the stability of the entire nation for one life!" He gestured at the guards. "Get him out of here."

I eluded their grasp. "Why not? That's what she did for you."

Everyone in the room froze, and I winced.

"What did you say?" Mong snarled.

Tell him, the Holy Spirit coached.

I took a deep breath. "Do you want to know the real reason she came to Beijing?"

"What do you mean?" He stood back from the desk.

I looked him straight in the eye. "She was going to kill you."

He was silent.

"The rebellion found out 'Andromeda' had been invited to the state gala and knew that was their opportunity to get close to you. They rigged up a kill switch in her palm. If she had shaken your hand, it would have reacted to your DNA and sent you into cardiac arrest."

"That's ridiculous," he scoffed, and the flicker in his eyes told me that he didn't want to believe it.

"Run a medical scan on her hand. You'll find the wire remnants and subdermal scarring," I insisted.

He glanced at the guards. One of them snatched his communicator off the dampening pad and paged for a doctor.

I kept my eyes on Mong. "That's why she didn't shake your hand at the party. She wasn't being polite—she was saving your life."

He stared at the wall, and I knew he was replaying that moment in his mind, seeing all the red herrings he should have noticed before.

His gaze cleared, and he turned back to me. "Why?" he demanded.

There were a dozen answers to that question, none of which were relevant. "She spared you, and in exchange, she not only put herself at risk but also endangered the entire operation. She could have lost the war because she let you go. She was willing to risk a hundred more years of tyranny just to save *your* life."

I let the words hang between us as the Holy Spirit added His own commentary.

"The Lord is not slow in keeping His promise, as some understand slowness. Instead He is patient with you, not wanting anyone to perish, but everyone to come to repentance."

Suddenly, I saw the whole picture. I understood why God had picked Philadelphia, and it had nothing to do with Red Rain or Rott or the Nolans or Jael.

A few people might be willing to lose the war to save a city of thirty million innocent souls. But there were even fewer who would look the General Secretary of the United in the eye and prophesy life, freedom, and forgiveness.

Philadelphia Smyrna was one of those few.

I looked back up at Mong. "I guess you're lucky she's not more like you."

A knock on the door ended the conversation. "What?" Mong barked.

The door opened, and Cardiff waltzed in.

"Who let you in here?" Mong demanded, sounding as annoyed as I felt.

"I'm a Nolan," he chirped in his pretentious British accent. "Which, up until a few hours ago, actually meant something."

Mong folded his arms across his chest. "What do you want?"

"Unless I'm mistaken, that's *my sister* you've got in a holding cell."

She wasn't really his sister in any meaningful way, but I let him have it. Any votes Phil could get in her favor, the better.

"Yes," Mong hissed, "and that's where she'll stay until I say otherwise."

Cardiff propped his elbow in his hand and twirled his fingers, as if this conversation were beneath him. "Forgive me, but I'm not particularly in the mood to watch another family member die a gruesome death on live TV. Even if she is adopted."

Mong hesitated.

"I've come to offer you a solution," Cardiff declared. "Release her to me, and I'll get her off planet."

"Off planet how?" I demanded.

He spared me a sideways glance. "I literally own a space station."

Mong recovered from the shock. "What's in it for you?" he demanded.

"My sister doesn't die?" Cardiff returned, as if it was a stupid question, which it kind of was.

Mong huffed. "Since when have you cared about Androm— Philadelphia?"

I was tempted to ask the same question, but I wasn't about to argue with someone who was trying to save Philadelphia's life.

"Look," Cardiff sighed, "I'm aware I've made mistakes regarding my family. It's too late to apologize to my aunt and uncle, and it's too late to save my cousin. But it's not too late to do right by Philadelphia."

He attached a lot of emotion to that last sentence—a lot of anguished, humble, genuine emotion—and I somewhat hoped he was just putting on a show for Philadelphia's benefit.

Cardiff stepped forward and gripped the desk with both hands, getting eye level with the General. "Let me save her."

Mong glanced at me. I didn't love the idea of Philadelphia going off planet with her weird adoptive brother, but anything to keep her alive one more day. "You have the power," I reminded the General.

He inhaled through his nose. "What are you proposing?" he asked Cardiff.

Cardiff stepped back from the desk. "I have a transit ready to leave. We can be off the planet in three hours. The station we're going to is extremely remote. She'll be completely off the grid, unable to record any videos."

And unable to contact me, I realized, and almost changed my mind about the whole thing.

"No more Blue Fire, no more propaganda," Cardiff explained. "Best case scenario, her followers will think she's abandoned them, and they'll disband on their own. But even if they do concoct a story, at least you won't have created a martyr."

Jael would most certainly concoct a story, but Cardiff had a point. A public execution would galvanize the resistance; if the government left Phil's fate open to speculation, the media would have room to modify the narrative.

"In the meantime, you freeze her assets, mark her file, make it look like you're doing your due diligence." Cardiff gestured at the General's computer. "And after everything has blown over and you've taken care of this petty insurrection... we'll talk."

It was a good plan. I hated it, but it was a good plan. Cardiff would buy us time—time for Jael and me to figure out how to safely bring Philadelphia home.

Mong was silent. He exchanged a coded stare with one of his soldiers.

I put myself between them. "Please," I begged one last time. "Do it for her."

*

I ran to keep up as we followed a pair of guards through the gloomy halls of the basement to the holding cells. The General was surprisingly agile, especially considering he was at least twenty years older than me. At least he'd had the decency to let me out of the handcuffs.

Mong had made a few calls and then led us out the back way. Unsurprisingly, he had a hidden exit from his office to a private fallout shelter. We slipped through there to an empty stairwell, avoiding prying eyes. I could only assume the guards Mong had with him were undyingly loyal and could keep a secret, but frankly, I didn't care. As soon as Philadelphia was safely off planet, it wouldn't be my problem anymore.

Several armed guards and a man in scrubs waited outside of her cell. Mong waved his hand, and they unlocked the door.

I shoved past the others. "Philadelphia."

She sat calmly on the bench. "Nic!" She darted into the hall and hugged me.

I didn't let her savor it. "We don't have much time. You need to leave."

"What—" She stopped when she saw the General. She pulled back from me.

Mong gestured at the man in scrubs, who passed him a med scanner. Mong stepped forward and held out his hand.

Philadelphia swallowed and slowly extended her right hand, palm up.

Mong didn't touch it. He passed the med scanner over her fingers, squinting at the readout. Then he looked into her face.

They exchanged a wordless stare, and I knew they both understood.

Cardiff interrupted the moment. "My pilot's ready. Let's go."

Phil turned to me. "What's going on?"

"You're getting out of here," I explained. "Cardiff's getting you off the planet while the General looks the other way."

She whirled on him.

He folded his arms. "Stay offline," he warned, the threat uncensored. "If there's even the tiniest blip of activity on your file, I will retaliate."

She nodded. "Yessir. Thank you, sir."

He didn't respond.

Cardiff led the way down the hall. "We need to move!"

Philadelphia started to follow—then hesitated. She glanced back at the General.

I reached for her. "Phil…"

"Be kind to the rebels on operation day," she said. "If you punish them harshly like Asia did, you will lose control. The United will fall."

I could tell by the shift in her tone and the sheen in her eyes that she wasn't speaking her own words—and she was absolutely right.

"Leave," the General ordered. There was no emotion in his voice.

I grabbed her arm. She gathered her skirt and ran.

The soldiers led us down the hall and up a ramp to the parking lot. The police had cleared the area, their vans blocking the view from the road. A helicopter idled in the middle of the asphalt.

Cardiff whispered something to our escorts, then ran for the aircraft. "Come on!" he shouted over his shoulder. "We have ten minutes to be out of restricted airspace!"

Philadelphia pinched my arm. "You're coming with us, right?"

How I wished I was—and I realized, in that moment, it was within my power to say yes.

But there was something I had to take care of first.

"No. There's something I need to do here."

Panic flooded her expression. "But—"

"Phil. It's about Stanyard."

She sucked in her breath.

Cardiff climbed into the helicopter. The pilot cranked the engine, and the blades whirred to life.

I shouted to be heard. "Listen. I talked to Asia a few days ago, and something's wrong. I don't have any details. All I know is that they were transporting him and lost contact with the plane."

Her eyes watered as the wind from the chopper whipped her hair into her face. "Do you think he's…" She couldn't bring herself to say the word.

"No," I declared, and I still believed it. "Maybe he escaped, I don't know. But whatever it is, I need to find him."

"Let me go with you," she begged.

I started to object, but someone beat me to it. "Philadelphia!"

We turned. Dr. Smyrna leaned out of the aircraft.

I stiffened when I recognized something I should have seen all along: Cardiff had been prepared for this.

"Dad!" Phil shrieked.

"Hurry, please!" He beckoned with both hands. "We have to go! Your brother will meet us up there."

She started to pull away, but she still hadn't let go of my arm.

I gripped both of her shoulders and got down on her eye level. "Philadelphia. Listen to me. I need you to go with your father."

"But Stanyard—"

"I will find him. But you have to get off this planet while you still can. The General will kill you if you don't leave."

She started to cry. "But I can't leave you! Not again!"

"I know." She had no idea how much I hated this. "But you have to trust me. Let Jael and I handle this. As soon as I can, I'll come find you."

"But—"

"Philadelphia," I interrupted, and waited until she focused on me before continuing. "I promise I will come find you."

She resisted, her whole body withdrawing—and then she obeyed. "Okay." She swallowed a sob. "I trust you." She hugged me.

I hugged her back. "I promise," I repeated, although she wasn't the one who needed the reassurance.

She gripped my shirt. "I love you."

I froze as the entire universe ground to a halt.

"Philadelphia, please!" her father shouted.

She let go of me and ran for the helicopter. Cardiff offered her a hand, and she climbed in without a glance back.

Her father hesitated in the doorway and cast me a look that wasn't quite kind. But then he remembered his manners and mouthed a *"thank you."*

I didn't respond.

He dragged the cockpit door shut. The propellers kicked into high gear. I braced myself against the wind as the helicopter lifted from the pad. Philadelphia pressed her face against the window and waved one last time.

I stood on the asphalt and watched until they were out of sight. It was only after the helicopter disappeared behind a high rise that I wondered if I'd made a mistake by letting her go.

TO BE CONTINUED...

GET A FREE PREQUEL!

Sign up for my newsletter and download *Project 74* for free! Plus, as a subscriber, you'll be the first to know about new releases, get sneak peeks of upcoming books, and more!

Sign up at:
rachelnewhouse.com/subscribe

WANT EXCLUSIVE BONUS SCENES?

Become a Patron and get access to **exclusive bonus scenes** for this series! Plus, you can get digital ARCs, collector's edition hardbacks, and merch, or read my WIP as I write it!

Become a Patron at:
patreon.com/rachelnewhouse

DID YOU LOVE THIS BOOK?

Please consider leaving a review on Amazon or
Goodreads! It's one of the most important things you
can do to support an indie author. Thank you!

HI FROM RACHEL

Rachel Newhouse is an author, wife, secretary, and Sunday school teacher from Kansas City, Missouri. Her obsessions are sci-fi, dystopian, and kid lit. When she's not writing, she's cooking Asian food, growing chilis that are too spicy to eat, and watching wildly age-inappropriate shows like *My Little Pony* and *Gravity Falls* with her husband, Joe. She also really likes glitter. You've been warned.

Connect with Rachel:
bio.site/rachelnewhouse

www.ingramcontent.com/pod-product-compliance
Lightning Source LLC
Chambersburg PA
CBHW060907210726
48293CB00006B/1995